FLESH TONES

Also by M. J. Rose

Fiction
In Fidelity
Lip Service

Nonfiction
How to Publish and Promote Online
(with Angela Adair-Hoy)
Buzz Your Book
(with Doug Clegg)

FLESH TONES

A NOVEL

M. J. ROSE

Ballantine Books • New York

A Ballantine Book
Published by The Ballantine Publishing Group

Copyright © 2002 by Melisse Shapiro

www.ballantinebooks.com

Library of Congress Cataloging-in-Publication Data
Rose, M. J., 1953–
Flesh tones : a novel / M.J. Rose.— 1st ed.
p.   cm.
ISBN 0-345-45104-X (alk. paper)
1. Trials (Murder)—Fiction.   2. New York (N.Y.)—Fiction.   I. Title.
PS3568.O76386 F57 2002
813'.54—dc21   2002063111

Text Design by Kris Tobiassen

Manufactured in the United States of America

First Edition: July 2002

10   9   8   7   6   5   4   3   2   1

... have patience with everything unresolved in your heart and try to love the *questions themselves* as if they were locked rooms or books written in a very foreign language. Don't search for the answers, which could not be given to you now, because you would not be able to live them. And the point is, to live everything. *Live* the questions now. Perhaps then, someday far in the future, you will gradually, without even noticing it, live your way into the answer.

—Rainer Maria Rilke, *Letters to a Young Poet*

Acknowledgments

Writing is singular but getting published is plural.

Heartfelt thanks go to Loretta Barrett, friend and agent, her associates Nick Mullendore and Alison Brooks, and to my wonderful editor, Linda Marrow, and the team at Ballantine including Gilly Hailpern, Kim Hovey, Christine Cabello, Kuo-yu Liang, and Louis Mendez.

But it is not only the people whose names I know that I want to thank, but also the production department, the Ballantine sales reps, fiction buyers, booksellers, and librarians who have helped get this book into the hands of every reader.

Many gallery owners, artists, and scholars painstakingly answered my questions and I'd like to thank them all, especially The Forum Gallery in New York City and the Watson Library at the Metropolitan Museum of Art.

This book owes much to the advice and insight of Dr. Mara Gleckel and the support of: Doug Clegg, Angela Hoy, Carol Fitzgerald, Bob Tischenkel, Michael Bergmann, and Cheryl Barton. And although any mistakes remain my own, I want to thank my legal advisor Chuck Clayman.

My life as a reader and a writer has been enriched by Karen Templer and her creation Readerville.com. If space allowed I'd name all the 'Villians.

Which brings me to the end of these acknowledgments, where I close on a special note, with appreciation, to Katharine Weber.

PART I

It hardly matters now; once experience has become part of the past, can it matter how it got there, irretrievable yet persistent?

—Mark Doty, *Still Life with Oysters and Lemon*

O N E

New York City Criminal Court Building, Room 1317
Friday, December 4, 1992, 9:30 A.M.

Worried the jury will misinterpret my seeming calm for contempt or worse, my lawyer, Benjamin Marks, tries to make me understand that I need to show grief or exhibit sadness. If I can't, if I don't, he's not sure he can put me on the stand when the time comes. And if the jury doesn't hear me testify, Benjamin is not certain they will acquit me.

He says it exactly that way—*not certain they will acquit*—instead of just saying they might find me guilty.

But the female members of the jury will understand why I am numb. They will recognize me as just another woman who has loved a man too much. There are so many of us—not proud that we put a man first, of the sacrifices we made or of the prices we paid—but we know that if we had to do it over we would not do it any differently.

Of course I should have known better, but I got lost in the man named Slade Gabriel. And, although I might appear calm now, I'm not. I'm paralyzed.

Since Gabriel died, I've lost all feeling. Only take shallow breaths. I can't concentrate. And I can't cry.

Although aware of Judge Bailey welcoming the jury in his orator's voice, the bailiff, an elderly black man with a limp standing at attention and the clerk typist's fingers silently lifting and landing—I'm unable to link any of this ordered activity to me or my life.

Why aren't Gabriel's paintings hanging in this musty courtroom shedding their luminous light instead of the dirty tarp stretched across the wall hiding the mural of justice that Judge Bailey has just explained to the jury was damaged by a leak? Gabriel's paintings would explain everything.

"It is not the law in need of reparation in this room—simply the painted representation of her holding her scales," the judge says to the jury—the blur of faces that I cannot focus on. Not now. *Not yet.*

Instead I study the stretch of fabric. Edges unraveling, gaping like a badly hung drapery, the canvas, which smells of mildew, casts a dull pall, unrelieved by the weak winter light coming through the windows. Outside, the wind blows and bare branches tap, tap, tap against the panes, rattling the glass.

Judge Bailey finishes his introductory remarks, takes off his gold rimmed spectacles, wipes them with a clean white handkerchief, replaces them on the bridge of his beaklike nose, and nods to the assistant district attorney. "Miss Zavidow," he says slowly, savoring the ceremony. "Would you care to make your opening statement?"

From the moment the assistant district attorney rises, she focuses all her attention on the jury: "Ladies and gentlemen, Slade Gabriel is unable to come forward and speak to you of the circumstances surrounding his death, unable to point his finger at his lover, Genny Haviland, and say she did it, she murdered me. And so on his behalf, I point my finger at Genny Haviland and say she did it; she committed this gross and unholy crime."

Linda Zavidow partially turns away from the jury box—each man and woman following her movements with their eyes. Lifting her arm, she energetically points across the courtroom toward the defendant's table, at me.

Rubbing the palms of my hands up and down the sleeve of my

black cashmere sweater, I try to relieve the itching that has started up again and, at the same time, try not to open any fresh scabs.

What a clever choice the D.A.'s office made when they assigned Linda Zavidow to prosecute my case. A man up there might seem like a bully; a less attractive or older woman might appear envious of me. But Linda Zavidow, like me, is in her late thirties. With her soft green eyes, chin-length shining blond hair, and a wide wedding band on her finger she can get away with saying almost anything. Ultimately it will come down to her against me, won't it? And compared to Linda Zavidow I am dark, brooding, untamed; and certainly capable of—how did she just refer to it?—this gross and unholy crime.

"Over the next week or so," Linda continues, "my job as the prosecuting attorney will be to show you how deeply, how obsessively, Genny Haviland loved Slade Gabriel, and how that love turned into an equally great hate—so great it motivated her to kill him. I will fill in the background, set the scene, and present the evidence: a jigsaw puzzle of information for you to piece together.

"It won't be easy for you. You'll hear many hours of testimony from witnesses who will each swear to be telling the truth. Your job is to question each answer you hear. What seems plausible? What doesn't? Which witnesses are telling the truth? Which aren't? What does each have to gain? Or to lose?

"These questions will be most crucial when it comes to the defense's argument. Mr. Marks will have you believe Genny Haviland's story is reliable. But I contend it has been completely fabricated; not the truth at all, but a lie concocted to save her life."

Linda looks at me. As per Benjamin's instructions, I meet her eyes so she has no choice but to be the one to look away when she turns back to the jury.

She wants them to believe it's only the answers that matter, but from making films I know it's the questions that shape a story and move it in either one direction or another. By now, Linda's already talked to every witness and discovered which questions to ask and which to discard in order to elicit the right answers.

But what about all the other questions?

What about my questions? What does it mean that for the last four months I have been unable to say good-bye to Gabriel? Unable to mourn him? Why is it that although my future is in jeopardy, I am only able to think about the past with him? Gabriel once cautioned me that by trying to dissect what bound us, each to the other, I would trivialize it and make it suspect. He said our connection would defy time, that even if we tried, we would never be able to completely let go of each other.

During the years we spent apart, I had gotten used to missing him but that was simply missing someone who wasn't physically with me—he was still on this planet, just keeping some other place warm. Now he is not even a body buried somewhere, but ashes emptied out of a plane window, caught in the wind, blown far away.

"Although I have described this crime to you during jury selection," Linda Zavidow continues, "I would like to repeat it to you now as designated jurors with all the responsibility that implies.

"The Grand Jury of the County of New York by this indictment accuses the defendant of the crime of murder in the second degree, committed as follows: The defendant acting alone, in the County of New York, on September 18, 1992, knowingly caused the death of Slade Gabriel by drugging him with a narcotic and then suffocating him to death.

"This is a case of cold-blooded murder—" Linda says and then stops as if she's too shook up by her own words to continue.

Beside me, Benjamin Marks shakes his head, disapproving the assistant D.A.'s theatrics while behind me, my father breathes deeply. I, always in tune with my father even when we're angry with each other (as he is with me now), can almost believe his breath is being expelled from my mouth. It's killing him that he has not, *cannot*, protect me from this. But to do that, he would have had to be a different father and a different man.

"As a woman who has been in love," Linda's voice softens, "my heart goes out to Genny Haviland. What a fantasy Slade Gabriel must have seemed when she first met him twenty years ago! A successful artist. An attractive, charming, sensual man who was part of her parents' world. How could she not have idolized him? So imagine, if you will, how traumatized Genny must have been when this man proved not to be a fantasy at all, but a narcissistic, egotistical artist who didn't always treat the people who loved him well. Throughout their relationship he was cruel to Genny. Irresponsible. Ultimately impregnating her and then insisting—no demanding—she abort their child despite her own wishes and beliefs.

"But since when, ladies and gentlemen, is being selfish just cause for murder?"

TWO

On May 16, 1972, the Lycée Français, a bilingual private school on 72nd Street off Fifth Avenue, closed, as it always did on Friday afternoons, at one o'clock. I, as usual, headed downtown on Madison Avenue toward my parents' art gallery on 57th Street.

What was I thinking about that day? Of my graduation two weeks away? Of going to Sarah Lawrence College in the fall? Of Peter Gardner, the boy I'd been seeing for the last month or so? Or about staying by myself that summer, working at the gallery instead of going with my parents to the South of France where my maternal grandfather, Jacques Edouard, lived? (My father had actually opened his gallery with stock from Grandpapa. "My dowry," my mother jokes, reminding my father too often of how he got started.)

There was nothing unusual about meeting my father that afternoon: for years I'd spent my free time on Fridays with him—part of my art education, he said. We'd always start out at Haviland's and then either go to a museum or do the rounds of exhibits at the galleries my father thought were important for me to be acquainted with: the Forum, Hirschl & Adler, André Emmerich, and Leo Castelli.

But that Friday, my father was detained and not there to meet me. What rendezvous kept him away? Did it matter? Even if he had been there, could he have protected me? Or prevented what happened?

After saying hello to the receptionist, Dan Falcon, who was on his way out to do an errand, I went into Mimi Reingold's office. In addition to managing the gallery, Mimi was a painter who showed in the East Village. For me she was the highlight of working at the gallery, the big sister I'd never had.

On weekends, hanging out with my high school friends at the Bethesda Fountain in Central Park, I'd see Mimi and point her out proudly. She was one of the original bell-bottomed, tie-dyed, long-haired, braless children of Aquarius.

She had a boyfriend, a musician with a guitar, who sat on the edge of the fountain, eyes glazed over, strumming and singing Simon and Garfunkel or James Taylor: *"Oh, I've seen fire and I've seen rain . . . But I always thought that I'd see you, baby, one more time again . . ."*

Sometimes Mimi bought grass from the pushers who worked the crowd and shared it with us upon the easterly hillock we private school kids had commandeered.

My mother didn't worry about me being in the park, but my father was convinced it was a dangerous place and constantly warned me to be careful there. But as it turned out, his gallery that Friday in May proved a far more perilous place to be.

Housed in the Fuller Building, along with several other blue-chip art galleries, Haviland's has the prime location—second floor, corner. From inside you can peer down through large floor-to-ceiling windows and see both Madison Avenue and 57th Street.

At about three that afternoon, while standing in front of one of those windows, I noticed a man slouched against the bus shelter, passionately sketching in a notebook. Maybe it was his intensity, or the fluidity of his movements as he drew, or how isolated he seemed despite the midday crush of traffic, but I was mesmerized. Suddenly a yellow cab jumped the curb and careened out of control, zigzagging right, then left, heading straight for the man's back. Pounding on the glass, I shouted down to him to be careful, to get out of the way, but I was two stories up; my voice couldn't penetrate the thick glass.

Oh please, I whispered futilely, please—and then just before it would have been too late, the man leapt out of the way and flattened himself against the building. The cab hit the bus shelter and came to a dead stop. Broken glass flew, a garbage can rolled out into the street, pedestrians stopped and traffic started to back up. Craning my neck, I looked to see if the man was all right but the crowd had swallowed him up.

Shaking, I went back to the front desk and put my hands—which ached from pounding so hard against the window—flat on the cool slab of granite that sat atop two steel sawhorses.

What if he hadn't gotten out of the way?

Directly opposite the desk where I sat was a James Rosenquist cartoonlike acrylic consisting of two large panels, each of an identical chair and lamp. Understanding art better than many of the artists who create it, my father had explained to me that Rosenquist specifically used simple colors and recognizable forms to create an art devoid of cryptic underlayers. The diptych was calming after the incident on the street; there was no chaos in the flat colors and one-dimensional shapes.

And then something moved. Over by the front door. On the other side of the frosted glass a shadow hovered: oblique, mysterious. The door opened.

My breath caught. It was the man from the street—the man who'd almost been hit by the cab. Tall. Taller. Lean. Aloof. He wore black, paint-spattered jeans. The top few buttons of his white shirt were open, revealing copper skin. His face was chiseled and imperious, softened only by the black hair that fell in waves across his forehead and down his neck. His hands were large but graceful; easily holding an oversize manila envelope and sketchbook.

He examined the Rosenquist, turned, loped across the room and stopped in front of me.

"Can I help you?" I asked.

"Is Haviland here?" His gravelly voice scraped against my skin. Inspecting me, his eyes—black, blazing—roamed shamelessly while he rubbed his unshaven chin as if trying to figure something out. Everything about this man was oddly familiar to me, like a dream you're sure you've dreamt before.

He was still waiting for my answer.

"No, I'm sorry, Mr. Haviland is out."

"Can you give him this?"

He handed me the envelope, a ring glinted on his finger; an oval of gold embossed with an angel, its gold flashing in my eye for a moment.

I took the envelope and then remembered I wasn't supposed to accept unsolicited work from people off the street.

"What's in this?" I asked.

"Photographs."

"Of your work?"

"Yeah."

I was disappointed. He was just another anxious artist without a gallery; I'd wanted this man to be someone who didn't need my father. Extending the envelope back to him, I explained the gallery's policy.

His smile turned into a laugh. But rather than make me feel left out, it drew me in like a warm wave. "This work is hardly unsolicited. Haviland's been after my ass for years." And then as an afterthought, he added, "I've been with Marlborough."

He'd named the gallery that had handled Mark Rothko for many years and was now being sued by Rothko's children for its scandalous manipulation of their inheritance. Since the case hit the papers, several of the gallery's artists had left.

"Haviland wanted some photos to give the *Times* for a piece about my joining him."

"You're joining this gallery?"

"Yeah. Think I'll be happy here?" Another smile.

The phone rang, but I forgot it was my job to answer it until the fourth ring. By the time I'd transferred the call to Mimi, he'd gone off into another room to examine other Rosenquists.

Curious, I opened the envelope and found six photographs. My fingers stuck to the edges and left oily impressions.

I recognized those paintings and knew the artist's name attached to them. More than once my father had discussed Slade Gabriel with my mother, describing him as fearless, as one of the new generation's explorers taking giant steps away from abstract expressionism into the uncharted future.

The smell of the emulsion was sharp, the paper thick, glossy. Gabriel's paintings were brave, ruthless, without boundaries; color fields raped by color fields. The compositions were fragmented. Violent. Powerful. Passionate. My father had said Gabriel was—and from the photographs I could tell it was true—against all convention, which in 1972 was not yet conventional. I knew why my father wanted Gabriel to join the gallery. He'd always been most thrilled by art that breaks the rules—hadn't he broken rules all his life? Hadn't he taught me to?

Unable to extract anything more from the photographs I used my sleeve and wiped the surface clean, removing any evidence that I'd been prying. Then I shuffled them back into the envelope and waited, my stomach clenching and unclenching until Gabriel came out of the last exhibition room and headed toward the front doors. I watched him push on the steel U-shaped handle. In a minute he would be gone. I had to stop him, say something, not just let him get away.

"Wait," I blurted out.

He turned.

I'd known only that I had to stop him, but hadn't figured out what to say once I had. "Be careful, please."

It was all I could think of. How stupid I must have sounded.

"Say that again," he said.

"What?"

"Repeat what you said."

"Why?"

"Damn it, just do it."

I repeated the words.

"It's the same voice," he said astonished.

"As what?"

"I was downstairs in front of the building sketching, when I thought I heard a voice say 'be careful,' and that's when I looked up and saw this goddamn cab heading right toward me. The voice—it was your voice, wasn't it? But how the hell . . . ?"

His words drifted off as his eyes met mine, acknowledged me, absorbed me, and then stroked the whole length of my body.

Finally, full of me, he pulled open the door and left.

THREE

New York City Criminal Court Building, Room 1317
Friday, December 4, 1992, 10:05 A.M.

There are so many sets of eyes examining me at any given moment: peering, squinting, scowling, searching, that no matter where I look— at the bench, the jury box, the spectators, my parents right behind me—I'm exposed. Concerned about showing too much, or, more likely, not enough, I stare down at my hands—palms still itching—flat on the wooden table.

Benjamin slides a number two pencil and a pad of yellow legal paper in front of me. "What's this for?" I whisper.

"So you can make notes of anything you think we should discuss later," he says.

Questions I print on the top of the first page and involuntarily glance up to find several jurors intently watching my every move. Should I respond? How? I accidentally meet the gaze of the young man in the second row with a beauty mark high on his left cheekbone. He stares back at me brazenly, as if he has a right to examine me, as if I am some curio on display. Does he? Am I? It's immaterial. Of everyone here, I have no power to object but must abide by the rules of the court which dictate that I sit at this table until the evidence has been presented, the witnesses have been heard, and the judgment is pronounced.

Casting my eyes back to the top sheet of yellow paper, I travel the lines and curves of the letters back and forth until I'm lost in the abstract strokes and shapes.

"Mr. Marks, do you wish to make an opening statement?" the judge asks.

Benjamin nods and, unfolding his six-foot-three-inch frame, stands up. A city kid who got into college on a basketball scholarship, he has no airs about him; he's an ordinary guy in an ordinary suit.

"Thank you, Your Honor," Benjamin says respectfully, just as Linda had a half hour ago. He faces the jury and begins my defense.

"Ladies and gentlemen, let me tell you right off this isn't a straightforward murder trial as Miss Zavidow wants you to believe. In a straightforward murder trial, the police know exactly what was done and how it was done and the question for the jury is whether the suspect is or isn't guilty."

Unlike Linda, Benjamin doesn't lean in close to the jury; he doesn't try to make friends with them and he speaks simply with few dramatics.

"The injustice here, in this patched-up mess of a courtroom, is that Genny Haviland is not only being accused of a crime she didn't commit, but of a crime *no one* committed.

"Now, Miss Zavidow has told you what she intends to prove and I'm real glad she used that word, because *prove* is the operative word here. Miss Zavidow must prove—not suggest, not intimate, not repeat over and over until it starts to sound like the truth but *prove*—her accusation beyond a reasonable doubt.

"It's no secret; the lab reports and fancy experts will prove that on September 18, 1992, Slade Gabriel died, but that's all they'll prove. Nothing else. Because ladies and gentlemen, while there most certainly was a death, there was no murder."

Benjamin shakes his head and hunches up his shoulders and the fabric of his jacket rises and then falls back into place. Continuing to shake his head, his light brown hair falls over his eyes and he brushes it away without effort—as if brushing the hair away is, for him, as easy a task as proving I didn't kill Gabriel will be.

"We are here in this courtroom because of some circumstantial evidence, ladies and gentlemen, and nothing the assistant district attorney says to you, no witness she brings in, no evidence she introduces will do more than circumstantially suggest my client is guilty."

Benjamin turns and smiles at me. His eyes are sparkling blue but hooded with droopy lids that make him appear slightly tired all the time. How should I respond to him? Every one of my expressions is being registered by the jury who are forming opinions of me based on what they see before them.

Pensively, Benjamin strokes his mustache and then continues, "We're all accustomed to watching trials at the movies and on television. We're so used to seeing law as entertainment it's easy to get lulled into thinking that what goes on here is entertainment, too. But it's not.

"Only in the movies and on TV does every crime have a perpetrator and a victim, are heroes always good and villains always bad. Not here. So please, do me a favor, don't judge this trial against the ones that make you bite your nails or eat right through a bag of popcorn.

"That's the first thing I ask of you, the second—and this is probably the only time Linda Zavidow and I will agree—is please listen. With all of your heart and your intellect. Don't second-guess any of us and don't make up your mind until you've heard every single word and Judge Bailey tells you to go and deliberate. Because once you've rendered your verdict, ladies and gentlemen, Genny Haviland won't be able to change the channel."

Benjamin frowns and his thick eyebrows meet above his nose. "Genny Haviland. What do you know about her? Well, she's the creator and executive producer of a PBS show I'm sure you've watched—

especially if you have kids—called *Into the Paintings*, where children actually walk into the flat plane of a painting and explore the three-dimensional world they find there. Each episode is an adventure and an education. My seven-year-old and I never miss a show.

"What else? Well, Genny loves movies, she has a video library of over five hundred films, she's a voracious reader, and she likes to cook Italian food.

"She doesn't have any kids. She was married and divorced. No alimony by the way, she didn't want it. She's close to her family and her best friend has been her best friend since sixth grade.

"Genny Haviland just isn't that different from any one of us. Except she fell in love, the assistant district attorney says. Well, haven't you, each of you, at least once in your life, fallen in love? That's all Genny did, fell in love with Slade Gabriel and loved him so much that when he got sick and asked her to help him commit suicide, she didn't think of herself, but agreed. Wouldn't you do the same for your husband, your wife, your mother, your child?

"If helping the man she loved to die is a crime, Genny Haviland is guilty, but that's not what she's on trial for here. She is on trial for murder in the second degree, which she is no more capable of committing than any one of you is."

Benjamin sits down beside me and takes my hand. Is he doing this for the jury to encourage them to think of me as flesh and blood? Or is he doing it to reassure me?

The bailiff approaches the bench and slips the judge a note. He reads it, folds it in half, folds it in half again, glances at the clock at the back of the courtroom and calls a five-minute recess.

Benjamin and his associate, Sam, confer at the other end of the defendant's table. Linda Zavidow huddles with her two assistants. I look down at the pad of yellow paper in front of me and wonder if Gabriel was the only one of us who died last September.

FOUR

The court having been reconvened, Judge Bailey invites Linda to call her first witness. Linda asks Mimi Reingold to take the stand.

I haven't seen her for at least ten years. Now a successful conceptual artist, her personal style has become more pronounced. Her hair has gone from blond to platinum and she's dressed all in black. As she walks up the center aisle, she glances over at me and then takes the stand. After being sworn in, she sits down and Linda asks her first question.

"Good morning, Miss Reingold, for the record would you tell us your occupation?"

"I'm an artist."

"Self-employed?"

"Right."

"Can you tell me if you ever worked for the Haviland Gallery?"

"Yeah, from 1971 to 1979."

"And did you have occasion to know Genny Haviland?"

"Yeah. She was my boss's daughter and worked for me the summer before she went to college."

"Which summer was that?"

"The summer of 1972." Mimi nods her head as if she's keeping time to some far-off music.

"Did you have occasion to know Slade Gabriel?"

"Yeah."

"Could you tell us how you met him?"

"He joined the gallery that summer."

"Miss Reingold, could you describe Genny's relationship to Mr. Gabriel that same summer?"

"Yeah, they were lovers."

"Did Genny Haviland confide in you about her relationship with Mr. Gabriel?" Linda Zavidow asked.

"Sometimes."

"Were you concerned for her?"

"Concerned?"

"Because she was so much younger than he was?"

"Maybe in years she was, but at seventeen she had a stronger sense of who she was than half of the people Gabriel's age. It's different when you grow up in New York City and go to private school and your parents own a gallery like Haviland's. Genny had been having dinner with artists like de Kooning and Motherwell and Frankenthaler since she was five. And besides it was the early '70s. Drugs, sex, rock and roll. Anything goes. I wasn't into making judgments."

"Were you ever in the room when Genny and Slade Gabriel were together?"

"Yeah."

"How did they act with each other, Miss Reingold?"

"Gabriel was a private man, didn't show much emotion, but a couple of times I saw him stare at her, like he was making love to her with his eyes."

"And how did Genny respond?"

Linda's questions and Mimi's responses sent me reeling backward to that summer.

* * *

My parents sailed for Europe on the QE2 on a Monday night in the second week of June and I spent the night in their large Central Park West apartment alone with Peter, my boyfriend. I woke up the next morning disappointed.

Later, when I got to the gallery, Mimi raised her eyebrows. "What's wrong?" she asked.

"Did you ever go out with anyone just because he was there?"

"Shit yeah, whatever gets you through the night. What did Peter do?"

"Nothing. He's just . . . I don't know . . . he never lives up to my great expectations I guess."

"You read too much. You should listen to more music . . . y'know, *you can't always get what you want . . . but if you try sometimes . . . you get what you need.*"

She was singing, moving her whole body, her blond hair swaying to the beat she heard in her head. All I knew was that Peter didn't satisfy some longing I couldn't articulate.

Part of my job was to help Mimi sort through all the slides of Gabriel's work for the catalog accompanying his first show at the Haviland Gallery. Color catalogs on heavy stock with a monograph written by a top critic, scholar, or museum director offered descriptions and explanations of the work—work that too often collectors don't understand—and also served to elevate the artist's status.

My father was a master at making major artists out of minor ones because he knew how to manipulate the market. He brought important critics and collectors to the artist's studio for personal previews, arranging beforehand for the artist to present the visitor with a small gift—a color sketch or a drawing.

Very few dealers gave art away. Was my father's generosity bribery or a smart marketing device? A competitor once said the only thing my father loves about art is his Midas touch with it. But that was unfair. Just watch my father inspect a painting. Explore a museum. Talk to an artist. My father is seduced by art. How else could he have learned so well how to seduce others with it?

Before a show, my father romanced clients with private viewings, endeavoring to sell some of the work before the opening. Don't underestimate the power of those dots under the paintings that have been pre-sold, he explained. As more and more people discovered the glitz of the art biz, collecting became a popular hobby and to many uneducated collectors, who cared more about what the art did for their image than the actual image of the art, those dots were crucial reassurance.

Always present at my father's gallery on an opening night were curators of major museums, editors of prestigious art journals, of mainstream newspapers, of cutting-edge magazines like Warhol's *Interview*, as well as actors hired by my father, who'd memorized scripts to ensure the collectors were feted, complimented on their taste, and treated like celebrities.

Weeks later, over a fabulous lunch, my father would drop hints to one of these collectors about donating his new purchase to a museum—elevating the collector's status as well as garnering him a sizable tax write off, but more important immeasurably increasing the value of the artist's work which would in the end benefit the gallery as much as anyone else.

Whether it took six months or a year, with my father as his dealer, Slade Gabriel, a fledgling second-tier artist, was on his way to becoming a museum-quality celebrity.

By the middle of June, Mimi and I had finished sorting through the slides my father had taken of Gabriel's work. We'd categorized them, labeled them, and made the first cut, narrowing the selection down to sixty. Now, along with Gabriel, we were going to cut the sixty down to thirty and when my father returned, he'd choose the final fifteen or twenty that would make it into the catalog.

Mimi and I were in the conference room when Dan showed

Gabriel in. He wore paint-spattered jeans, a dark shirt, had a cigarette hanging between his lips, and was a half hour late.

"So where's Haviland?" he asked Mimi.

"In France."

Gabriel hesitated by the door.

"Why don't you come in and sit down?" she asked.

"How can we review the slides without Haviland? Isn't he putting my show together? This needs to be done right." Certainly not polite, he wasn't even civil but I was ready to defend him if Mimi had said anything—he had his career to take care of.

But she didn't—she just stared him down. "Yeah, he's putting the show together, but I do the catalogs."

"You?"

"Yeah. I did Rosenquist's catalog. Tuttle's. Mitchell's. But, hey, if that's not cool I can call Mr. Haviland in Europe and see how he wants to proceed."

Gabriel rubbed his unshaven chin and glanced over at me with red, ragged eyes. "No, let's get the torture over with now." He looked back at Mimi and gave her a half smile that was inclusive and intimate and just charming enough to work as well as an apology.

My cheeks were hot.

I turned away—afraid Gabriel would see I was jealous. That would make him laugh and make me feel even younger and more my parents' child.

Pulling out a chair, he slumped down, stretched out his long legs and inhaled on his cigarette while Mimi explained what we were looking for.

Then she turned off the light. Ten seconds of black. She switched on the slide projector. A shaft of light saturated the room in the sea green glow of a watery grotto.

Each advancing slide recolored our skin, our clothes, the walls.

Cobalt and olive. Rose and emerald.

The phone rang and I answered it: a client for Mimi.

"I'll take it inside," Mimi said to me. "See if Mr. Gabriel wants anything, like an ashtray. I'll be back as soon as I can."

"Do you want some coffee or a soda?" I asked him.

"No," he said.

I felt weightless as I got up, retrieved an ashtray, brought it back and put it down in front of him. My center of gravity seemed to have shifted; I was dizzy. In the gray green haze, even more clouded because of Gabriel's smoke, he brooded over his own painting.

He could have been a rough sketch drawn by Michelangelo, a study of a strong man enslaved by pain.

As he stubbed out his cigarette, the light shone on the beat-up gold ring on the small finger of his right hand: an ancient oval intaglio of an angel, fat belly, chubby legs, wings capping his shoulders. On certain men, rings can be flashy, vulgar, effete, but not on Gabriel. The antique fit his elongated fingers.

When he noticed me looking at him, his mood seemed to lighten. "Saved any more men lately?" he asked.

"No, have you almost been hit by any more cabs?"

"You know in China when you save a man's life you become responsible for him."

"Lucky for me, we're not in China."

"But if we were, could you handle the responsibility?"

"I can't imagine you wanting anyone else to be responsible for you."

"Don't you think it would be liberating to give yourself up to someone? To surrender your free will?" he teased.

"No, and I don't believe you do either."

"You're wrong . . . under certain circumstances . . . it could be extremely interesting."

Some other conversation ran deep beneath this one, a primitive communication; we were meeting, testing, sniffing, making an alliance.

"What's your name?" he asked. He lit a new cigarette.

"Genny."

Gabriel didn't ask and I didn't offer my last name. Did I assume he knew I was Haviland's daughter or had I intentionally omitted it, wanting to hide my connection to his new dealer?

"Genny," he repeated as if he was tasting the word, and his lips curled in a smile. "My savior." His voice was so low I could barely hear it. Without taking his eyes from me, he brought his cigarette to his lips and took a drag. Then he leaned forward, close to me. When he spoke again, I felt his breath on my cheeks.

"Will you go on saving me?" he asked.

"What do you need to be saved from?"

Before he answered he drew back, suddenly cautious of being too close. "Genny, you're not an artist are you?" he asked.

"No."

"Thank God."

"Why?"

"Because artists are like those fish, what are they called—piranhas—we eat our own kind." He laughed and I floated on the sound.

Then he raised his right hand and traced the outline of my lips in the air with his finger.

I sucked in my breath.

Certain moments in your life become instantly etched in your memory. Sitting at that long glass table with a man I didn't yet know, I'd lurched to a stop and was starting to spin in the opposite direction. I was aware of my breasts, my arms, my legs, my eyes; sensed my fingertips resting on the table; felt the expression on my face. I not only saw Gabriel, but was actually conscious of my eyes upon him. The air conditioner system was humming, the room was cold, but I dripped sweat.

Was it Slade Gabriel I wanted? The artist who stood apart willing—

even perhaps wanting—to suffer for his work. Or would I have felt the same stirrings for any man who could bring me into my father's world, and whom I could want in ways, at seventeen, I was too old any longer to want in my father?

Mimi came back and the next half hour was spent going through the rest of the slides. While we analyzed the transparencies of his abstractions I remained aware of Gabriel next to me. I listened to him breathing, watched him lean forward, absorbed in the process of making each selection.

"Not that one—the color is off," he said.

Mimi advanced the projector.

Another slide came up, then another. "No, that's lousy." He reached over, pulled out the errant slide, and crumpled it in his fist.

For a few seconds a blast of white light emanated from the projector glaring in our faces. Then Mimi pushed the remote control device advancing the carousel to the next slide.

"No, give me that." Gabriel took the switcher from her and reversed the carousel until he found the empty slot and the white light filled the screen and the room again and then he just stared at it.

Finally he stood up and walked, his arms by his sides, his palms against his thighs, right into the brightness. It intensified the blue of his jeans and shirt and cast a blue shine on his hair. About three feet from the screen he stopped, absorbing the light and being absorbed by it.

Mimi glanced at me with raised eyebrows and I shrugged as if I thought he was nuts. But I didn't—I was mesmerized by the intensity, by his ability to see something neither of us could.

After a couple of minutes, Gabriel returned to the table, scribbled some words in his sketchbook and then, without explanation, handed the switcher back to Mimi.

What had he been searching for? What had he been experiencing?

Gabriel's communion with the light enthralled me. Made me feel the same kind of wonder I'd sometimes felt as a child, sitting beside my nanny, Marie, watching a priest say the mass in church.

The next slide up was typical of Gabriel's work: a large, ten-by-five-foot fragmented pastiche of gentle shapes savagely ripped apart to leave ragged edges. I could see the influence of the bad boys of the '50s who blew up the canvas size and made paint the object of the painting, but Gabriel's work moved past that concept, past Pop, and was embracing minimalism.

I'd heard my father claim Gabriel, at thirty-seven, was at the beginning of his career spiraling. At Marlborough his paintings sold for three thousand dollars each; my father intended to get ten thousand dollars by the end of the year.

Every painting was entitled *Garden#__*. No poetics to hint at the painter's psyche, nothing representational to guide you through his work. Gabriel's gardens were splashed with colors, drawn out, juxtaposed, more violent than beautiful. If there were flowers they were blown up, if there was earth, it bled; this was his reaction to the war in Vietnam, to the boys who were dying, but to me, at seventeen, as sophisticated as I was, I didn't understand the depth of brutality in the paintings. I must have grimaced at some of the slides because when Mimi left the room for a second time to meet a client who had stopped by, Gabriel asked me why I didn't like his work.

"I suppose it makes me angry."

Gabriel didn't coddle me the way other artists did because I was their dealer's daughter. "That's good. That's what it's supposed to do. Isn't that what you want from a painting?"

"There is a Picasso of two people, lovers—" My skin flushed. "Whatever is between those two people, the feeling it evokes, gives me something to aspire to. That's what I want from a painting."

"A Picasso from his Blue period?"

"Yes."

"But you can't compare everything you see to that Picasso," he said.

"Why not?" I asked.

"It's too damn limiting. Too romantic. You're not a romantic, are you? For Christ's sake, for my sake, most of all for your sake, Genny, you've got to get over that."

FIVE

How could I, at seventeen, have been so sure of myself with a man twenty years older than me, and why hadn't he been aware of just how young I was?

Well, hadn't my parents always treated me like a smaller version of an adult? They never put beautiful things away when I was a toddler, because at the same time I was learning to walk they were teaching me the value of objets d'art. When they took me out to dinner it wasn't to childproof places but to fine French restaurants; my parents expected me to behave, and I did. I spent as much time with their friends as with mine, as much time at museums as playgrounds. Even my birthdays were different from other children's. I never had a party with a clown or magician, and my gifts rarely came from a toy store.

On the morning of my thirteenth birthday, my mother joined my father and me for breakfast. (Usually my father and I had breakfast alone each morning then he took me to school on his way to the gallery.) Beside my place were flowers in a small crystal vase, lilacs and roses, as well as several cards from France: one from Marie, my nanny, another from my grandfather.

My father was already dressed in a gray pinstripe suit and a white shirt with a starched collar and the initials JRH—for Jonathan Russell Haviland—embroidered on his cuff. His cologne and his coffee scented the air.

Most mornings my mother slept late, breakfasted in bed, bathed in scented water, put on her makeup in her pale pink bedroom, dressed in her walk-in closet, and finally, at about eleven o'clock, left for the gallery. That morning, however, she was already dressed in a lavender suit with one strand of gray pearls around her neck and one diamond band on her left-hand ring finger. Not too much jewelry, not too much makeup; my mother has always believed less is more, as long as the less is of the finest quality.

"Genny, eat your breakfast." My father was trying to be responsible, but his eyes were sparkling, he was as excited about my birthday as I was.

"I'm not hungry."

"You must eat, Genevieve." My mother never called me Genny. When my school friends called and asked to speak to Genny she would tell them no one by that name lived there. I would get furious with her. "But, Genevieve," she would say in her sweetly accented voice. "You have a lovely name, shortening makes it vulgar." I'd once asked her why she didn't give me a normal name like everyone else and she said she'd never, for a moment, thought her daughter would want to be like everyone else.

I liked her answer. Liked all of her answers, especially because she never answered with another question as my father often did.

After I had gulped down as much as I could of my breakfast, the three of us left for the gallery. As I settled down between my parents in our chauffeured car, my father took my hand and squeezed it.

I squeezed his back as tight as I could—it was our secret signal.

One night he'd come into my bedroom to wake me up from a nightmare. He sat in the dark, on the edge of my bed, trying to calm me down.

"I couldn't tell you I was scared," I sobbed, "because there were too many people watching. And you didn't know."

"Whenever you get scared, Genny, just squeeze my hand. You

don't have to say a word. I'll know and squeeze back so you'll know I'm here. Always. Protecting you." Then he'd bent down and I'd put my arms around his neck, filling my lungs with his soothing smell.

And he let me hold on for as long as I wanted to.

"*Voilà*," my mother said as we arrived at 57th and Madison. I threw open the door and ran ahead, urging them to hurry. They were taking so long and I wanted to know what surprise they had for me for my birthday. And why was it in the gallery?

Upstairs, I followed my parents into the large back room where most of the paintings were stored. That morning, dozens of them were on display, leaning up against the walls, the tables, the windows. Almost their whole stock was on view: a Gottlieb, two de Koonings, a Jasper Johns, a Pollock, two Joan Mitchells, a Giacometti drawing, and more. It was all there—not only the work of artists they handled, but paintings and drawings from my grandfather's gallery that he'd given them on consignment.

"Take whichever one you like, Genny, and Happy Birthday," my father said.

"*Joyeux anniversaire, mon chou.*"

I twirled around. The room was ablaze with colors, suffused with moods. Then, slowly and deliberately I walked up and down the room and back and forth, contemplating each canvas and drawing carefully. What a funny sight it must have been: a thirteen-year-old girl in her blue school uniform, kneesocks, and brown loafers, inspecting literally millions of dollars' worth of artwork.

I passed a big cobalt blue square, a tan canvas filled with oblong ovals of magenta paint feathering out at the edges, a painting with thin aqua and cherry ribbons of color flanking an empty white middle ground. Then in the corner, almost tucked away, less than three feet tall, washed with subterranean blues and greens, was a painting of an emaciated man standing, looking down longingly at a sleeping, supine woman.

"This one," I said at once.

My mother clapped her hands. *"Bon choix!"* she said as if I'd passed some kind of test.

My father kissed me on the cheek, his lips brushing my skin close to my hairline. "Happy birthday, Genny." His breath near my ear gave me shivers.

My parents exchanged glances. They were proud of my first effort at collecting. Shouldn't one of them have stopped to wonder if it hadn't been a strange choice for a child of thirteen to pick a Picasso of a man hungering for his lover?

It was this attitude, the way they spoiled me and accepted me into their world so early, their lack of normal parental concern, my mother's distance and my father's accessibility that shaped me. Maybe if they'd been traditional parents, I'd have a different kind of life now: a sensible life, an undamaged one.

That evening my father hung the painting in my bedroom and as I lay in bed, I studied the tall, thin dark man longing for his lover and imagined a man longing like that for me, and then I imagined myself longing like that for a man.

The next day I sat down at my desk and wrote my imaginary lover a letter telling him who I was, where he could find me, and that I would wait for him until he came. Putting it in an unaddressed envelope, I sealed it, then tore it up into bits and threw it—like confetti—out of my eighteenth-floor window. The flecks drifted down and littered the pavement. I didn't mind the people walking by, trampling my ripped up communiqué, because I imagined that soon one of them would know what was beneath his feet and come find me.

At night, in bed, it was never my hand between my thighs—it was his hand I imagined, moving me ahead faster and faster: my phantom lover making me come.

Too imaginative, too lonely, too sexually aware, too impression-able, too worldly, too innocent; I was waiting for a man even when I was still—by other people's accounts—a child.

In cartoons, the Road Runner runs right through stone, wood, or brick walls leaving behind a clearly delineated outline of his body. That was what I had in my head, a distinct negative space, an outline that remained empty until Slade Gabriel showed up and fit right in.

SIX

Two weeks after going over his slides, Gabriel called Mimi to tell her he'd located some of the early paintings Mr. Haviland had wanted to include in the show but needed some help sorting through them. She offered to send her assistant, Dan Falcon, but Gabriel requested me.

"But your paintings are pretty big. Dan will be much more help than Genny and—"

But Gabriel cut her off.

After getting out of the taxi on Greene Street, I wiped my sweating palms on my jeans, took a deep breath, and walked inside the five-story factory building where I rang the buzzer beside the name Gabriel.

"Yes?"

"It's Genny—from the Haviland Gallery."

"I'll be there in a minute."

When he came downstairs he opened the door and I followed him outside, down the steps, into the street, and over to a parked, beat-up old station wagon.

"We're taking a drive? I thought the paintings were here?"

"No. Do you mind?"

I shook my head.

The car smelled of oil paint and cigarette smoke and, as I breathed it into my lungs, I memorized it. Why did I, even then, think that I had to hold on so tightly to the times we were together?

Gabriel drove fast, speeding through yellow lights, racing red ones. Once he'd left the city he increased his speed even more and the scenery became a green blur.

"Am I scaring you?" he asked.

"No," I lied.

"You can't be as calm as you seem," he said taking the next curve more quickly. "I'd like to know what's going on inside your head."

"Just ask. I'll tell you."

He turned, taking his eyes off the road, and stared at me for a beat too long.

"No, not while you're driving. Be careful!" I shouted.

"Aha! I can make you afraid." He laughed.

The wide highway gave way to a narrower road which wound through the woods. While he drove, I studied Gabriel's hands moving on the steering wheel. Thick veins stood out in relief, light blue paint rimmed two fingernails, flecks of red stained another; paint even permeated the pores of his skin. I wanted to rub my face against the back of his hands, shut my eyes, and breathe in his scent.

Heat coursed through my body, settling deep in my stomach, between my legs. Afraid he could feel the warmth I was generating, I rubbed my hands against my jeans, creating another kind of friction. But he didn't notice; it had started to rain and now Gabriel was earnestly focused on the slippery twists in the road.

He pulled into a gravel driveway and we hurried out of the car and ran up a stone path to the front door of an English Tudor house that was opened by a man in his eighties. He had a white beard and thick white hair and smiled as he reached up and put both his arms around Gabriel. "Slade, I can't tell you how good it is to see you." Then he stretched an arthritic hand out to me; the skin was rough, callused. "I'm Ryan Callahand."

"I'm Genny." Would he notice if I'd left off my last name? What if he asked me what it was?

"Come in, both of you. Come in. I made coffee, had my housekeeper buy some cookies. Let me get them."

"No, you take Genny inside and sit down. I'll get everything," Gabriel said and left. Clearly he knew his way around.

Callahand and I stood in the foyer for a moment while he leaned on his gnarled wood cane and appraised me. "You an artist, too?"

"No, I'm here to help. I work at the gallery."

He grinned. "Is that so? Here to help? How?"

"I actually don't know. Mr. Gabriel asked Mimi, she's the woman who runs the gallery while my—boss is away, if I could come with him."

Callahand appeared concerned. "A young thing like you; you watch out for Slade." He gestured toward the interior of the house and I started to follow him when he turned back. "You're so pretty, you probably should watch out for me, too," he said, winking, taking the edge off the warning.

The living room was crammed with comfortable couches, armchairs, footstools, at least ten vases overflowing with flowers and stacks of gardening books in piles beside every seat, but it was what hung on the walls that made me stand still, mouth agape, staring. There, crowded together, too close to one another, were a dozen paintings of flowers exploding off their canvases, bigger and truer than real flowers, half-representational, half-abstract, each exquisitely rendered.

"Gabriel painted these, didn't he?"

"When he was fifteen. Still a boy. I was the head gardener at the Botanical Gardens in those days, and he came by every afternoon after school to paint and draw. Slade practically grew up there, you see, his mother worked for me and I . . ."

Callahand stopped for a moment. Now, because I am guilty of doing it too, I realize he was only stopping to remember and relive another time with Gabriel. But that afternoon I wasn't concentrating on his words, I was riveted to those amazing flowers, trying to understand the difference between them and the more abstract ones Mimi and I had been working with for the last few weeks.

"During the war, Gabriel's father was a pilot who flew planes off warships, one of a thousand young boys who took off from the decks of aircraft carriers and never came back. Slade didn't know him except as a story about a man in a plane and a burst of flame. So, I tried to fill in a little, encouraging Alice, that was Gabriel's mother, to bring him with her when she came to work.

"He loved the gardens. I never saw a baby study anything the way Gabriel studied those flowers."

"How old was he when he started drawing?" I asked.

"Must have been about four. I remember a rainy day when he was inside helping me pot some plants. He liked working with the shovel and the dirt. We'd finished and I was making up labels when I got interrupted and walked off. Gabriel picked up my pencil and started drawing them.

"His talent burst out of him fully developed. No slow starts, no false moves. This little boy knew how to draw. There are things you can't explain in this world. How Slade could draw like that was one of them. After that he never stopped, would sit and draw for hours without making a peep."

"I figured you'd be in here." Gabriel put down the tray of coffee things. Reverently he poured Callahand a cup and then turned to me. "Do you want some, Genny?"

Each time he said my name I shivered; no one had ever said it like that before—like it held out some kind of hope. "Yes."

As we drank the coffee Gabriel never even glanced at the paintings on the wall, but I couldn't take my eyes off them.

"What did you feel like when you were painting these?" I asked.

"That was years ago."

"But you must have been very happy when you were doing them, don't you remember that?"

"I thought you understood about being such a romantic," he teased, but I heard it as a warning; I'd trespassed on a well-guarded place.

As Callahand put down his cup it rattled in the saucer. "Do you remember, Gabriel, how long you'd stay out in the gardens painting those flowers? I'd stop sometimes and watch you work; you wouldn't even know I was there."

"Let's not do this," Gabriel said.

"It's not a bad thing to look back every once in a while," Callahand said. "You can learn from the past."

"Not about my painting."

Callahand seemed ready to argue but changed his mind. "Slade, why don't you show Genny around?"

I followed Gabriel out of the living room into a glassed-in sunporch. Peering out through the steady rain, I saw the gardens as a blur of green, rose, and lavender.

"Would it be so bad to look back at your paintings?" I asked.

"What's the point?"

"Maybe it would help you understand," I said.

"What do you know about what I don't understand?" He gave me one of those half smiles.

If I'd already gone too far, there was no reason not to finish what I'd started. "I watched you examining your paintings. Even though you're unhappy with them you have this certainty about what you are doing—"

He was leaning against the door—watching me with the same intensity he'd used to inspect the slides of his paintings in the gallery.

"Go on," he challenged.

"It's not just passion. Lots of artists have that. You don't even notice the struggle, do you? It's immaterial. Everything is, except the paintings."

"You make it sound so idealistic, Genny. It's not. It's an addiction and a curse."

But that wasn't all it was. I'd seen his work and I knew. I had my father's eyes.

"There was a bottle of wine in the kitchen. Want some?"

I nodded and he left. Without him in it, the room grew larger. I noticed its colors, its furnishings. The air was damp. Something stirred, beginning; a part of me was waking up. When Gabriel returned with two glasses and the bottle of red wine, he told me Callahand had fallen asleep.

Gabriel led me upstairs to a small half-round room painted a deep forest green, with a curved wall of windows facing a pine grove. Those trees and Callahand's collection of owls—carved out of wood, cast in bronze, crafted from stones and twigs and perched on the windowsills and nestled on branchlike shelves—made the room seem like a tree house in the middle of a forest.

We sat side by side on a couch that was covered in something soft and worn. He poured the wine into the goblets and handed me one. It tasted dark and warm, like the rain.

Without putting down his glass, Gabriel leaned over and kissed me, at first softly and then with slightly more pressure. One world shut down around us and another opened up for the first time.

Oh.

This was what Picasso's lover had felt.

Gabriel's lips, mine. My tongue, his. Our mouths having met now danced on and on, together in a wet darkness.

After watching and waiting for such a long time had I finally found my long-imagined lover?

Pulling apart for a moment, I looked at his face. He, too, seemed amazed. "What is it?" I asked.

"I'm not lonely with you," he whispered into my mouth, cupped my face with his large hands, and kissed me more.

I shut my eyes.

I shut them now, thinking of what it was like that day in Callahand's house in a strange half-round room, the melodious sound of the rain outside, Gabriel's scent enveloping me. On that afternoon, I crossed over and learned what it is like to leave your mind and become your want.

Soon I was unbuttoning my blouse, stripping for him, thrusting out my small breasts and watching his reaction. He gently pushed me down and lay on top of me rubbing his cheek against my skin, scratching me with his beard. He took a single finger and lightly traced my nipple, puckering the skin.

At some point, the rain stopped and the clouds broke apart and a pale light illuminated the room, washing over us. We made love in that light, Gabriel often pulling back to gaze at me. I memorized how his dark hair fell against my pale chest, how he smelled, how his tongue moved in such small circles on my skin, how he moaned when I finally, brazenly reached down, unzipped his pants, and released him from his tight jeans.

After two hours in a trance, lips swollen, groggy from the love-making and the wine, Gabriel and I walked outside to the garden, down the stone path to a pond where ducks swam on the glassy surface.

"I'm married," he said to me.

I heard it, nodded, and shrugged my shoulders. He thought I was sophisticated to take the news so nonchalantly when it was only that I was far too young to understand what his revelation meant or to be upset by it.

"We're separated. My wife and my daughter are living out on Long Island. A trial separation. We're giving each other some space. We never belonged together, but I was too busy to see that and now there's Lizzie . . . anyway, I'm not sure how it will work out."

"None of that matters."

And it didn't. In fact, it made sense to me then. It explained why I'd had such a strong sense of having only a finite amount of time with him, why I'd been memorizing every moment.

That night Gabriel and Callahand cooked dinner: a big pot of pasta with tomato sauce, a salad from Callahand's garden, and a hard crusty loaf of French bread. And of course more wine.

"Why don't the two of you stay tonight?" Callahand said over coffee.

It had started to rain again and the crackling thunder reverberated through the house. My parents were far away in Europe and all I had to do was call Bertha, our housekeeper, and tell her I was staying at a friend's.

Touching, licking, smelling, feeling, and grabbing each other, Gabriel and I hardly slept.

"I should have waited for you," he said in an anguished voice sometime during the night.

"But you didn't know I existed."

"No, but I always believed there was a perfect fit, a right response . . . someone who'd know how to take away the pain."

When he finally fell asleep about dawn I remained awake, breathless, gazing at his face against the pillow, memorizing it, for what? For this? For the times when I would have nothing but those memories of his face. Of his black hair falling forward. His long neck. His big hands. His fingers stained with paint. At last, I fell asleep, my face inches from his hands.

I woke, soaked in sweat. I was shaking from a recurring nightmare I'd had since childhood, only this time Gabriel had been my victim instead of my parents or my old nanny, Marie. In the dream, Gabriel and I had been in my father's study, sitting on the couch, close together but not touching. The bright light in the room hurt my eyes and I tried to dim the lamps, then to shut them off. But the light remained constant. Frustrated, I took a silver letter opener off my father's desk and pierced all the lightbulbs in the room. The glass burst and slivers fell on the floor. Still, the light remained harsh, steady, strong. Gabriel said the light was on for good. That was impossible, I said, there had to be a way to lessen it. No, he argued, it was irrevocable. That's when I turned on him with the letter opener. . . .

Leaning on my elbow, I watched Gabriel sleep on his back, his head nestled on the pillow, his right arm extended, his hand curled around the mattress edge, his left arm flung across this chest. His body was taut, covered with fine black hair. The sheets, twisted, redolent of the combined smells of our sex and sweat, were pushed away from his body except for a corner lightly draped over his torso. Underneath, I could see he was hard.

Through the mullioned window, the sun warmed Gabriel's skin and I inched closer and closer to him, until it warmed me, too. Still asleep, Gabriel rolled onto his side, reached out and found my hip. Beneath his fingers my flesh prickled.

Against my thigh, I felt his pulse throbbing. Counting the heartbeats, I altered my breathing until I was in sync with him and when his fingers slipped down my hip and came to rest on the inside of my leg, I shivered.

This was Slade Gabriel, an artist my father was going to make into a star.

My father.

What would my father do if he found me there? His seventeen-year-old daughter, naked in bed beside Gabriel. But I knew he'd never blame me. He'd pick up the crimson blanket from the floor, protectively wrap me up in it, and send me out of the room. It would be all Gabriel's fault.

Yes, Gabriel was creative, certainly he was beautiful, and his shoulders were wide and his back was broad enough so that when he held me, I disappeared. He'd protect me, too. Now it wouldn't only be my father. There would be two men to protect me.

But from what?

Each other?

After breakfast we drove to the beach, taking along food for a picnic, an upright beach chair for Callahand, and blankets for us. Helping the older man down to the shore, Gabriel slowed his own quick pace and walked cautiously.

"Stop worrying!" said Callahand. "I'm not that bad, just some rusty joints."

But Gabriel wasn't comforted; Callahand's infirmities were making him anxious. We laid out the blankets and sank down on them, but Gabriel wouldn't relax and soon he took off for a walk down the beach. Tired from not having slept much, lulled by the sound of the waves, I fell asleep. When I woke up Callahand was sleeping and Gabriel was still gone.

Gabriel's sketchbook was on the blanket, a pencil stuck between two pages. It was the same sketchbook he'd been drawing in when I saw him from Haviland's window, the same one he'd brought to the gallery when he worked with Mimi on the slides. Spiral-bound, cardboard-covered, the sketchbook's corners were frayed and bent back and its cover was smeared with paint.

I got up, stretched, walked down to the water and watched the rough waves curl up and roll ashore wetting my feet. Still early in the season, the water was cold and when I returned to the blanket, I dug my toes into the hot sand to warm them.

Curious, I flipped open Gabriel's sketchbook. Inside were tightly drawn diagrams, notes, sketches, scrawled words, signs, splotches of coffee, and cigarette ashes rubbed into the paper. I tried reading his words upside down so if he came back it wouldn't appear that I was prying but rather that the wind had blown the book open. But upside down his scrawl was illegible.

After checking for Gabriel up and down the beach, I turned the book around, inspected a detailed drawing of a single leaf, and devoured the block of words beneath it.

Light green to deeper green to dusty red browns. Use one leaf, enlarge it until it loses recognition. Take it from spring to fall. Disintegrate it.

I turned the page.

What colors and shapes read as hopeless? Gray every color down. Depict the loss age brings. The loss of strength. Of independence. Bleaching bones. The parchment of old skin.

There on the beach, listening to the waves crash, smelling the sea, I kept reading, trying to find Gabriel's secrets so I could use them to make myself indispensable to him.

A shadow fell on me. Gabriel's long body dripped water like rain. "What are you doing?"

"The wind blew the book open and the drawings were so beautiful," I bluffed, "I couldn't resist."

He took the book out of my hands, closed it, shoved it deep in a canvas bag, then knelt down beside me and laughing, asked me if I was a spy for the gallery.

He smelled of the sun and tasted of salt water. I forgot Callahand sleeping beside us, forgot the people walking up and down the beach. Gabriel was touching me, his hands around my waist, his feet rubbing my calves, his lips on my neck.

Pulling back, he leaned on his elbow. "You'd make a wonderful painting, lying in the sand like that."

"Will you paint me?"

"No, I'm searching for something in my paintings and I've already found you. Now, all I have to do is figure out what to do with you."

"Fuck me," I whispered, giving myself chills.

Had I ever been that brash? Before Gabriel, sex had been silent musings, half-awake dreams, a girl-child's fantasies. Even with Peter, sex had only been a way of getting on with growing up. I was not a virgin when I met Gabriel, but I was still innocent. With him, I emerged and I seethed.

Taking my hand, Gabriel pulled me up and together we walked toward the shore. I held back but he put the flat of his hands on my back and pushed me forward into the freezing water.

After we'd swum out thirty or forty yards, Gabriel pulled me to him and rolled my bathing suit down from my chest, past my waist, and my hips, and the water was a different kind of cold on the skin that had been covered by the suit.

A current rushed between my thighs or was it Gabriel's hand fluttering there like a small fish? Thinking we were too far away to be seen, I lay back and floated, half my body above the waterline: my breasts, my stomach, my pubis exposed. Was Gabriel licking the water off my breasts or was it the waves?

Grabbing me by the waist, Gabriel pulled me to a standing position and held me tight against him. With one hand on my waist he pushed up, trying to enter me but having trouble in the water until the slick I'd worked up anointed him. With my legs around his waist, my arms around his neck, he bounced me on his cock while the sun beat down on us and the waves broke against us.

Walking back to the blankets I suddenly worried. "Do you think anyone saw us?" I asked him.

"Probably," he said grinning. "Do you think it turned them on?"

I'd discovered a secret.

While we ate French bread and runny cheese warmed by the sun and ripe red grapes, Gabriel and Callahand talked politics. I listened and watched Gabriel's mouth move, how he chewed bread, how he ripped hunks off the loaf with a violent grace.

"It is an undeclared illegal war, the beginning of more war. What will keep us from doing this on and on? From putting our soldiers into any country we please and fighting God-knows-how-many-more senseless battles?" Gabriel asked Callahand.

"We were so proud of what we were doing in World War II," Callahand mused.

"A noble war?" Gabriel said sardonically.

"You don't think war can be noble?"

"Murder, blood, guts hanging out of open wounds, the stench of bodies. Mitch coming back from 'Nam in a body bag. His parents holding onto each other as if that was all that was keeping them standing. He was twenty-one years old, Ryan, what's noble about that?"

"The ideal."

"The ideal should be peace."

Gabriel wrapped his big hand around the wine bottle and poured with a ferocity that sent some of the red liquid sloshing on the beach blanket, bleeding through the white fabric, spreading farther and farther.

"Look at that . . ." He pointed to the stain. Callahand and I both did, but neither of us saw what he did.

"Peace is an impossible concept, Slade, in a world where there are a hundred different religions and a hundred different races. We'll never achieve the kind of peace you're looking for."

"You're saying there can never be peace, so we should throw up our hands and forget about it?"

"No, I'm saying you have to find some place where you can have your own small peace, and get pleasure out of that."

"My Zen master."

"Don't be flip," Callahand cautioned.

"I'm trying for something else."

"You're trying to stop a war. I know, but I think you might be getting lost in the process. Find your own peace, Slade."

Gabriel stroked my arm while Callahand talked. Could I be Gabriel's peace?

"And what about you?" Gabriel turned to me. "You haven't said a word. What do you think?"

"Nixon is an asshole. The war is unconstitutional."

"Do you want to come to Washington with us when we march?" Gabriel asked.

I'd been against the war, had marched in New York and been part of the moratorium with most of my high-school friends, but now all I could think of was that Gabriel had included me in plans that stretched further than the weekend.

That night Callahand insisted we stay again; I wondered if he was lonely. Now I think he must have been worried about Gabriel.

After we barbecued steaks on the outdoor grill, we sat on the deck and finished the wine.

"I haven't been in the city in a long time," Callahand said.

"Come back with us," Gabriel offered.

"Maybe in a few weeks. I'd like to go to a musical. To a museum. Do you ever go to the Modern anymore?"

"Why? To stand next to people who ogle rather than understand, who barely glance at a canvas by Morris Louis or Ellsworth Kelly or Helen Frankenthaler and say things like, my daughter could draw better than that?"

"But classical drawing isn't the aim of those paintings," I said with conviction.

"Sure, but how many people understand that, Genny?"

"People can learn to look at a de Kooning and see the destruction of a bomb or the terror of a concentration camp. You can be taught to understand how the Kennedy and King assassinations influenced Warhol," I insisted.

"Right. In some lofty art school. But who's going to explain it to the plumber or the garbageman or the housewife from New Jersey? And do you think those people care we're pouring our fears onto the canvas?"

"You have to find some peace, Slade," Callahand said for the third time that day. He sighed. "I'm going to retire for the evening. Good-night, children." He started to rise but it was slow going and Gabriel got up and helped him out of the room.

"Just stiff is all," Callahand said as he put his hand on the banister and dragged his bad leg up after him. "Stay down here, Slade, I can manage."

Gabriel was silent until Callahand had disappeared upstairs.

"He was the strongest son of a bitch I knew." He nodded his head sadly back and forth. Not knowing how to offer solace, I remained quiet.

"It's not going to happen to me," Gabriel said as he shook a joint out of his pack of cigarettes and lit it. After inhaling a long drag, he passed it to me. I took a toke and passed it back.

We stretched out on the back lawn of Callahand's house, gazing up at the sky, the sweet smell of grass permeating the air, the sound of crickets resounding and growing louder.

"It's swirling like a van Gogh," Gabriel said and started humming "Starry, Starry Night." Then he stopped and said, "There can never be another van Gogh."

"There will be other artists."

"No, something is dying," he said.

"What?"

"I look at what we are creating, what I am creating, and it all has to be translated. That's wrong. We've grown cynical. We've lost our humanity. Painters like me are becoming obsolete; painting's becoming obsolete."

He leaned over and gave me a different kind of kiss than the others; a desperate kiss.

"So good," he mumbled.

"What?"

"When I kiss you . . . it's like making a discovery. I need discoveries."

"Is that what's wrong with your marriage?"

"Don't ask so many questions. You question everything. There are mysteries out there—thank God—like the light. The light is a mystery. You can try to figure it out, try to understand why it exists and miss it entirely."

Gabriel's next kiss lasted a long time and while he made his desperate connection, I spiraled upwards, a multitude of sensations inside my mouth, inside my body.

And then: "Genny . . ."

"Why do you say my name that way?"

He said it twice more, the same way, his words moving inside me like an uncoiling electric wire. "Genny," he said, way down low in his throat, the sounds traveling over rocks to get to me. "When I say your name I see a flower opening."

But that wasn't how it sounded. That night, when Gabriel said my name, it was as if he were watching a flower die.

"Why are you so sad?" I asked.

"Shh . . . you want to know too much. It's all been decided, you . . . me . . . ages ago. The questions don't matter. This is all that matters, touching you . . . here . . . here . . ."

Gabriel was using me like a drug and I encouraged it. The more solace and silence he found in my body, the less likely he'd be to leave me.

We were driving back to New York City that Sunday afternoon when Gabriel said, "I'll drop you. Where do you live?"

I couldn't tell him the truth. It was too late for that. I'd begun with a lie of omission by leaving out my last name and I was going to have to keep the lie going. So I told him I shared a tiny apartment with two roommates—making it sound unappealing enough so that he wouldn't want to come upstairs—and gave him an address around the corner from my parent's Central Park West apartment where my friend Tory lived. I knew her parents would buzz me up.

To Gabriel in the car, everything would appear normal.

I got out in front of Tory's building, went inside, and then watched from the vestibule until Gabriel drove off. Once I was sure he couldn't see me in his rearview mirror I walked back out and around the corner to my building.

Upstairs, I turned on all the lights and walked through every room. Would anything be different now that I was different? In the living room a Jasper Johns target hangs over the fireplace. A Frankenthaler commands one wall. A Sandro Chia on another. In the dining room is a huge Warhol. A Rosenquist. My friends called the apartment a minimuseum.

My friends. I called Tory first.

"Oh my God! Genny, where were you?"

I started to tell her about Gabriel, how he'd had Mimi send me down to his studio, where we'd gone, but I cut the story short—talking about him was diluting the impact of what had happened—I didn't want to share him.

"Is this the painter you told me about? The one who's, like, thirty-something?" Tory asked.

"Uh-huh."

"What will your parents say?"

"I'm not going to tell them."

"But what if they find out that you're seeing one of their artists, a guy who's practically their age?"

I changed the subject and while I listened to Tory talk about her weekend, I absentmindedly went through my pocketbook and found a wine label, a cork, and a book of matches from the diner where Gabriel and I had stopped to have lunch.

As soon as I hung up, on separate small sheets of notepaper, I wrote a description of each day we'd spent together.

Fri. Drive to Conn. With Gabriel. Callahand. Flower paint-ings. Rain. Kisses in a room like castle turret. Not lonely. *. *.

Sat. Beach. Water. Read notebook. Swimming. *. *.

Sun. Sleep till one. *. *. More beach. Find starfish. Drive back. Lunch. Fake address.

I'd always remember what each word and star meant. I was keeping a record, filling up a green Lord & Taylor shoe box with slips of paper and assorted paraphernalia. Making a box of days to have when Gabriel was gone.

SEVEN

When Gabriel showed up at the gallery that Monday morning to drop off the paintings he'd borrowed from Callahand, he barely acknowledged me. I refused to let him know it bothered me and found work to do at the desk. Or at least made it seem like I was doing work. But I wasn't. I was frozen. Staring at papers, reading nothing. Listening to every word Gabriel said to Mimi.

After he left, Mimi asked me what was wrong.

"Nothing."

"Yeah right. Let's try again: What's the matter?"

And so I told her about the weekend and that I must have been stupid thinking it had meant anything to him other than a good lay, a diversion.

"Oh Gen, he's just a typical chauvinist. Forget him."

I wanted to.

I tried to.

And I very nearly had until the next afternoon when he called.

"Haviland Gallery," I answered the phone.

"Genny?"

"Yes?" Could he hear my heart beating in my voice?

"Listen, I'm sorry about this, but I can't see you again," Gabriel said.

I thought he must have found out I was Haviland's daughter and had freaked out over it. My stomach cramped.

"You're creating havoc with my discipline," he continued. "I have half a dozen canvases to finish for the show. I am supposed to be painting . . . and all the hell I want to do is get in bed with you."

I knew I had to say something to downplay what was happening between us, so he could feel comfortable about seeing me again.

"So let's go to bed. Once you get off, you'll be able to paint, no problem."

"That's not what I'm saying. You're in my head. I'm married. I have a kid. I'm only separated; I can't make any promises. I might not even be here in two weeks. Can you handle that?"

I couldn't handle it. I'd only known him for a few days and I'd already changed. What would happen if I spent more time with him?

"Sure, I can handle it," I lied. Wasn't it worth it if I could have another day with him?

"My place on Greene Street, remember? Hurry," he said, hanging up.

In 1972, SoHo was a foreign part of the city to most New Yorkers, an unknown area of abandoned factories only recently discovered by artists who needed big open spaces to accommodate their enormous canvases. The Village had been the artists' lair in the '50s, but since then rising rent had driven them farther downtown, south of Houston Street. It wasn't chic but it was much cheaper.

Today hip clothing stores, trendy restaurants, and hundreds of galleries line the streets, but then there were only two old Italian restaurants, the Spring Street Natural Restaurant and Bar, and two struggling galleries. The other storefronts housed plastic molding or piece-goods businesses. But upstairs in those old factories, an artist could find a mammoth loft, full of light and fine architectural detail, for only a couple of hundred dollars a month.

Gabriel's studio was on the fifth floor. It was not his home. That was the house in Amagansett, Long Island, where his wife and daughter were spending the summer. But he obviously lived here, too, at least some of the time. On the coat hooks near the door was a jean jacket with yellow paint smeared on the back and a black winter over-coat with a splatter of bloodred paint dripping down the arm. Beneath the hooks was a pair of black lizard cowboy boots and a pair of snow boots covered with a layer of dust.

The furnishings were spare, one corner partitioned off with a pale beige and black lacquer shoji screen, in another was a wood table and four chairs with splashes of green and purple paint on the chair legs.

Against a wall, facing the center of the studio, was an overstuffed couch covered with so many drips of paint it looked like Jackson Pollock had used it as a canvas.

Where there weren't windows, there were paintings soaking up the space and the sparseness, making the large loft feel small.

"Can I see?" I asked but he led me behind the screen onto an unmade bed.

"Not now."

He stroked my cheek with a paint-stained hand. I breathed in turpentine and linseed oil, raw scents compared to my father's cologne.

"I'm your responsibility, remember?" His voice was so low I had to strain to hear him. "You saved me from the cab . . . now save me from the paintings."

"Why do you have to be saved?"

"Because I can't give up this stupid quest even though it's so fucking painful."

"Has it always been so painful?"

"You really want to talk about this?"

"Yes."

He seemed grateful. "I don't usually talk about it. No, it hasn't always been this bad."

"Can't you go back to how it was before?"

"That's gone off to Vietnam. With Mitch."

I'd wondered about Mitch since he'd mentioned him to Callahand on the beach. "Who's Mitch?"

"A kid who took one of my painting classes at the League. A fucking genius working at some bakery in the Bronx until I hired him to stretch and prime my canvases so he could have some real time to paint."

"And then he was drafted?"

"And killed. . . . Shit, Genny, just come here."

I crawled into his arms and lay on his lap. He leaned down and ground his mouth into mine so hard our teeth hit.

In the middle of the night, I woke and saw him working naked, in front of a canvas, a cigarette dangling from his lips, a brush in one hand.

"Can't you sleep?" I asked.

He came over to the bed and stood above me staring down at me.

"Get up. I want to paint you."

I got out of bed and walked, naked, to the middle of the room while Gabriel pulled out a box of acrylics and prepared a palette. I assumed he wanted me to model for him.

"Stand still." His husky voice rumbled.

The brush was like a soft wet tongue as he led it down my thigh. Around my ankle. Up my calf. Between my legs. Across my stomach. At first, the paint felt clammy but it quickly dried, tightening on my skin. I was an object, his creation. I didn't look at what he was doing. I studied his face. This was not the painful process he had described hours earlier. He was painting me not the way he painted his abstracted gardens, but the way the younger Gabriel had painted those exuberant flowers hanging in Callahand's living room. It excited me.

He laid the brush down and brought me in front of the mirror.

I was steaming hot, sexually aroused beyond anything I had ever known. Gabriel had studied my naked body for three hours, had brushed paint on me so softly he could have been whispering against my skin. And in the mirror I saw what he made. My stomach and legs were green leaves, stems holding up the flowers. Above my belly button and up my long torso and breasts I was multicolored lavender, purple, pink petals falling softly over one another. My shoulders were sloping silken petals falling down. My neck was a stamen reaching up. Only my face was untouched. The brown hair waved out from its center part falling down my back and framing my face. I seemed even thinner than I was, lost amidst the glory of the flower.

From behind, he pulled me to him and standing up in the middle of the studio he made love to me, gently at first, not wanting to ruin his handiwork. I was streaking him with colors, leaving blue, purple, lavender smudges everywhere. Stroking him, my fingers left rose colored swirls on his flesh, my ankles across his back left violet smears. Sitting on him, I splashed green on him. While he sent spasms shattering inside me, I rained blue drops of sweat on his chest and palm prints of salmon on his neck. I came watching his eyes shut and his lips curl in pleasure.

Gabriel always smiled when he came. In the end it made every act of sex no matter how base into an act of love. It's the most gentle memory I have of him. An animal, ferocious, ranting, grabbing, crazy, but softly smiling at last, in orgasm.

We scrubbed each other off in the shower, the colors turning muddy swirling down the drain.

"Will you come back tonight?" he asked.

"Yes."

"Will you come back every night?"

"Until you stop wanting me to," I said.

"Do you think that will happen?" he teased.

"Of course."

Those were the lies I told to make myself seem tough, to reassure him I could handle the uncertainty of our being together, because I knew if he thought I was vulnerable, I'd lose him.

"And that's okay with you?" he asked.

"Nothing lasts, does it, Gabriel?" Steam from the hot shower clouded around us.

He laughed. "You read that. You don't believe a word of it."

I stared at him, water streaming down my face like tears. "Don't believe me, I don't care."

"You're a little bitch, aren't you?" he said.

"Am I?" Pushing him against the shower wall, I rubbed his body with mine.

I learned the power of my sexuality by keeping Gabriel satiated that summer. How high it made me to know how much he wanted me and to watch him give himself to me. Experiencing that intensity changed my life; I had found my addiction. For some people it's amassing money, attaining celebrity, creating, parenting, or piling achievements on top of one another; for me, it was passion.

I never stopped craving the high I experienced with Gabriel, and I never felt it with any other man. After Gabriel left me, I tried to deny it, but my cravings haunted me, leaving me unsatisfied and searching until, by a miracle, I found Gabriel again.

The days of the summer passed. When we were out, or making love, or walking down the street, or seeing Gabriel's friends, I worried about what he didn't know about me and felt guilty, too, because I was lying to the man I was falling in love with.

But I was good at lying.

I always have been.

I spoke to my parents once a week while they were in Europe that summer. My mother asked about Peter and I told her he was fine. It wasn't hard to lie. Besides, what good would it have done to tell my parents the truth: that their seventeen-year-old daughter had become a thirty-seven-year-old artist's lover and was spending the summer with him.

Gabriel did not know how young I really was. That was a deception I got caught up in one night toward the middle of July. We'd been seeing each other almost every night for two weeks.

At two o'clock in the morning, we were at a party at Dierdre Barrett's loft. A painter in her fifties, the critics claimed her color masses, studded with metallics, blazed new ground. She shunned the uptown art scene, instead selling her work out of her own loft. She was dedicated, radical, unmarried, high on her own success. Dierdre's paintings hung in museums all over the world. She was a mother figure for a group of younger artists who floated back and forth from the endless parties in her studio to the endless parties at Andy Warhol's fashionable Factory.

"Its anti-art. Art that makes fun of all the generations of art that came before it," Dierdre said while extravagantly waving a cigarette stuck in an ebony holder, letting the ashes fall to the carpet like bird droppings.

The air in the loft was full of sharp cigarette and sweet marijuana smoke. Half-empty wine and jelly jar glasses sat atop every surface. Gabriel, downing Scotches, was talking to two other painters and periodically locating me in the room with his wild, hungry eyes.

I knew I didn't have to worry about going to parties with Gabriel because the artists I met with him didn't show uptown and weren't invited to my parents' parties. Except for Dierdre, they were relatively undiscovered artists who at best had been included in downtown group shows in galleries that didn't even have signs outside the doors.

There were other young women at the parties, some who were about my age. No one cared. We were distractions, swimming in successful artists' wakes.

Mimi from the gallery was there that night. We sat together gossiping about the artists we knew.

Dierdre walked over to Gabriel and put her hand on his ass. He spun her around and kissed her ugly lips. The group around them laughed.

"You're too old for me, you goat!" she said.

"You wish," he said and kissed her again.

I must have been watching them because Mimi said: "You're not serious. You can't be worried about her, are you?"

"Not her, no."

Dierdre looked across the room at me.

"Genny, you've got to lighten up about this guy, y'know?"

The music playing was the Rolling Stones. *I can't get no satisfaction.* Guttural. Driving. Pulsing through the room, making even the smoke move to its rhythm. Gabriel found me with his eyes; he was ready to go.

I had been ready to go since I got there. I never wanted to share Gabriel, to watch him talk to other people, touch them, laugh with them. While this lasted, I desperately wanted to be alone with him.

The streets were deserted as we walked to Greene from West Broadway. Gabriel sang songs that had been playing at the party, first the Stones's song, then the Beatles's "Lucy in the Sky with Diamonds," then he sang a song that hadn't been playing, "Unforgettable," in an off-key, half-soused version that warbled all over the place.

"Sing with me Genny."

"I don't know the words," I said.

"Don't know the words?"

He stopped in the middle of the street. The moon was almost full and the night was lit with its bluish glow. There were no cars on the cobblestone street and the factories, some decrepit and badly in need of work, rose up around us creating a canyon.

"*Unforgettable, that's what you are . . .*" Gabriel's words echoed. "Come on girl, sing."

"I really don't know the words."

Incredulity washed his face. Then, "Genny, how old are you?"

"Twenty-three," I lied.

He was stunned. You could tell he had never thought about how old I was or how old he was, but he was thinking about it now.

"I'm going to be twenty-four in the fall," I offered.

"Shit, I'm robbing the cradle."

What if he knew he was robbing Jonathan Haviland's cradle and that I was only seventeen. His daughter was already eleven.

Twenty-three had sobered him up and when we got back to the loft he was still talking about the age difference.

"My wife and I are the same age. Went to the Art Students League together. We grew up during the same world war. Sing the same songs. She knows all of 'Unforgettable' . . . ."

"What difference does it make?"

"There is such . . . doesn't it . . . ?" Searching for the right words, he stumbled over the wrong ones. Gabriel was better at painting his feelings than expressing them. "Does it bother you? I mean, does my age bother you?" he asked.

I was sitting down on the floor looking up at him.

"Men my age are boys."

I heard how stupid that sounded, but Gabriel didn't because he didn't want to. He wanted reassurance. He sat down beside me, examined my unlined face, my long hair, my black leotard, my bell-bottom jeans, my black suede clogs. He gathered me up in his big arms, enclosed me, enveloped me, and hid me from the world in that place that smelled of tobacco and alcohol and turpentine and oil. He stroked my hair and then he held me at arm's length.

"Genny. Genny—Fuck! What is your last name? I don't even know your last name. Or what you want to do with the rest of your life. Or where you grew up. Tell me."

"Genny Edouard." I used my mother's maiden name. My middle name. Half a lie. "I was born here in New York." No lie. "I've saved up and am planning on going back to school this fall to get my degree."

"What else don't I know about you?" Gabriel asked.

"That I can't keep my hands off you," I answered, clutching his penis through his jeans. He was instantly hard and as we kissed I unzipped his pants and pulled him out. We were twisting around on the floor, halfway to disappearing into each other when he pulled away and muttered: "Got to set the alarm."

We were going fishing in the morning on his friend's boat.

"We have to leave at four so we can be out at the boat by six-thirty. That only leaves two hours for a nap."

"An hour and a half . . ." I said as I straddled him, covering his face with my long hair, making him forget the rest of his questions so I could forget my lies.

The next day we got to Montauk at six-thirty and were greeted dockside by his friend, Tony Segal, a record producer and art collector.

I was wearing sunglasses and one of Gabriel's big paint-stained sweatshirts over my clothes to keep off the chill. We were groggy and bleary-eyed but Tony was wide awake and when he shook my hand, he looked me over carefully. "I think we've met," he said.

We had. At an opening at my father's gallery. When I shivered I knew it was not because of the cold morning air.

"Well, maybe we can figure out where." I ignored the flip-flops my stomach was doing. Maybe he wouldn't remember, or remember only that he'd met me at the gallery. Luckily, as we got under way there was no more time to talk. Tony was busy getting the boat out of the harbor and Gabriel helped.

It was a damp, silent morning, shrouded by the gray mist. The farther out we went, the heavier the fog became until we lost all visibility. Overhead an occasional gull cried and around us we heard the steady sound of the boat breaking through the water, but there was nothing to see, no vista ahead of us or behind us.

By the time we reached the fishing grounds, three hours later, forty miles offshore, the sun had burned off the fog. Tony shut the engine and turned on a tape deck. The first chords of Beethoven's Fifth broke the silence.

The water was calm. For as far as I could see, there was nothing but the ocean.

While Tony worked on putting out the chum stick, Gabriel took great pains to teach me how to use a rod and reel. "Hold the line here on your finger. Let it drag. Watch for a movement. Feel for it. A tiny change, like this, and you've got a bite. Want to try?"

"What I really want to do is go swimming," I said.

Tony and Gabriel laughed.

"Not here, you don't."

"Why?"

"Just watch," Tony said.

As we drifted, the slick of oil and bits of butterfish from the chum stick spread behind us, churning in the waves before disappearing from sight.

After fifteen minutes, I saw a single fin slice through the ocean swells. Within a half hour we were surrounded by sharks.

Standing in between Gabriel and Tony, I peered over the side of the boat where a half-dozen sleek blue sharks gulped down the food, vanished under the boat, and circled back for more.

Bits of white desiccated flesh swirled in the water.

And then the waves picked up.

"Be careful, Genny," Gabriel warned. "That's not a good place to stand if—"

All at once Gabriel's rod tipped—he had a bite. Grabbing the pole from its holder, he sat down in the chair. The reel whistled as the line spun out fast.

"I think you've got a big one. Get ready for a fight," Tony said as he strapped Gabriel into his seat.

A half hour later Tony and I were both riveted to the battle Gabriel was fighting with his shark. Now it was *his* fish. He owned it. He'd won it already with his effort.

But the fish didn't want to be owned.

The veins stood out on Gabriel's forehead, his hands had turned white at the knuckles. Sweat ran down his face and every so often he growled or grunted.

"Pump with your legs," Tony ordered.

The sun was directly overhead and it was so hot not even the ocean spray cooled us down. The water dried as soon as it hit our skin.

"Keep the line smooth. Wind it, Gabe!" Tony yelled.

Gabriel swore.

The wind picked up again. Waves tipped the boat toward the water and then picked us up high. Grabbing onto the steel railing, I rode the swells thinking that nothing had ever felt as exciting.

Thwack. Thwack.

"What was that?" I asked as the boat leapt into the air.

"There's another big one under the boat," Tony said.

Suddenly water splashed into Gabriel's face stinging his eyes. He blinked. Again and again. Tony got ready to take over if he had to but Gabriel recovered.

I was looking down into the water—trying to catch sight of the monster, when I finally saw the flash of opalescent blue. Illuminated by the sunlight, the shark's back shimmered. "I can see it."

Tony followed my glance. "Yeah, it's a big one. Almost three hundred pounds."

Gabriel groaned.

I'd seen sharks in photographs, in movies, even mounted on walls, but it was different seeing one so close that even with the water separating us I could count his teeth when he opened his wide jaw.

The awe turned to fright and made me sick to my stomach.

"Shit. It's foul-hooked," reported Tony, who'd seen something else.

About five minutes later, the fish broke loose. And Gabriel? He laughed with admiration at the sea creature who had bested him.

About four-thirty that afternoon we started back to Montauk and not too far from shore, Tony suggested that we go swimming. At first, I hesitated. Seeing so many sharks in the same water just miles away had spooked me but Gabriel talked me down. "If it wasn't safe, I'd tell you," he said.

Later we went into town for dinner and had lobsters and corn and blueberry pie at a local place. We also had a lot of wine. Then back at the boat, Tony brought brandy in snifters up from below and we sat on the deck drinking and talking.

The setting sun glowed, gilding the clouds with colors that might have come from Gabriel's palette. I rested my head on his shoulder and watched the sky painting change, darken, and dull.

"So are you going to let me see your new paintings before the opening?" Tony asked Gabriel.

"If you're buying."

"If I remember correctly, I'm just about the only one who did buy from your last show."

"Don't remind me," Gabriel said lighting a cigarette.

"Why did you stay with Marlborough so long?"

"I tried to get out sooner but they caught me on a technicality."

"What technicality?" Tony asked.

"Some clause requiring me to give them four months' notice if I wanted to terminate. I didn't know. Never read the fine print."

"You're too much a painter for your own good," Tony said.

"I'm too many things for my own good."

"Don't make the same mistake this time. Haviland's a damn good dealer, Slade, but he's also a damn good businessman. Have a lawyer read the fine print—at least read it yourself."

Even though I was in full view of both these men I felt as if I were eavesdropping.

Tony lit a joint, inhaled, and passed it to me. I inhaled. Keeping the smoke deep in my lungs, I passed it on to Gabriel. Between the grass and the brandy, I was beginning to float on top of the water like the boat.

The sky grew dark enough for stars to be visible.

"Art dealers are all peddlers. Promoters, showmen. It's easy for me to recognize their moves. They're the same as the ones I use, just in a different area," Tony said.

"As long as they work for me, not against me," Gabriel said as he blew smoke out.

"Well, Haviland will work for you. The man's made an art out of making artists. Uses every promotional trick in the book. But who am I to talk?"

I wanted to tell them they were wrong, that my father didn't use tricks, that he loved the art he sold, that he cared about the artists he represented.

"Genny, how long have you been working at Haviland's?"

"About a year." Another lie.

"What do you think about the place?"

"The artists seem to be happy." It was true, my father kept his artists happy.

"Well, he's smart, his split is sixty-forty in the artist's favor when everyone else has gone fifty-fifty," Gabriel said.

"Guess he figures the more he makes the more he makes," Tony said.

As I listened to this conversation, I began wondering for the first time about my father's ethics. How many of the things he did were questionable? Illegal? If there was worse I wanted to find out about it, but Tony and Gabriel had stopped talking about the gallery.

I drank what was left of my brandy, watched the boats swaying on the water, and listened to the sails clanging against one another. Gabriel stroked my leg and I glimpsed Tony watching his friend's hand disappear beneath my long Indian print skirt.

Tony got up. "Can I offer you anything else before I turn in?" he asked me.

"No, thanks."

"You know where everything is, Gabriel. G'night," Tony said and went below.

It was quiet on the deck. The sea below gently rocked the boat and the sea of stars above offered enough light for me to see that half smile on Gabriel's lips as he moved closer to me.

"If I'd have caught that fish I would have made a necklace of shark teeth for you."

"Then I'm glad he got away."

He laughed, bent down, and kissed me.

His hair fell across my face and I breathed in his smell mixed with the less familiar ocean scents. Still kissing me, he unbuttoned my shirt, pushing it off my shoulders, exposing them to the air.

His mouth moved from my lips to my neck. Teeth bit gently, lips licked my skin wet. Warm breath blew against my flesh.

"Oh yes," I murmured.

He repeated the sequence.

I arched up pushing my body toward his mouth.

"Does it feel good?" he asked.

"Mmmm . . ."

"Tell me—tell me how it feels." It was so quiet that even Gabriel's low voice sounded too loud. "Tell me, Genny."

"Shhh . . . he can hear us," I whispered, suddenly aware that Tony's cabin was only a few feet away.

"Tell me how it feels."

Hadn't he heard me? Or didn't he care? Did Gabriel want Tony to hear us?

I could have insisted that we be silent or I could do what he wanted and take this opportunity to make myself irreplaceable and give Gabriel more than another woman might.

Then Gabriel was moving in me in rhythm to the boat's rocking and I *was* telling him how it felt—how perfect—how I didn't ever want to feel anything else.

Gabriel's eyes were shining as he watched me. Behind him were more stars than I had ever seen. I was feeling the breeze on my thighs, on my stomach, his hands gripping me one way and his legs gripping me another way but I did not stop talking. I did not stop telling Gabriel exactly how it felt even when there was so much sensation that I lost the reality of my body and couldn't hear the words or remember where I was.

"What is moving? Is that you or me or the sea?" I asked.

"It's all of us," Gabriel answered.

It was erotic, dangerous. And yet I had a sense of being safe, knowing absolutely that if I wanted to stop that would be fine with Gabriel, too. But I didn't. The power I was experiencing satisfying Gabriel was more intoxicating than the sensations he aroused. And becoming aware of that power was what finally brought me to orgasm.

Afterward, Gabriel carried me to bed in one of the cabins. "Are you all right?"

"I'm fine," I said—slightly shocked, but pleased with myself.

"Are you sure?"

"I'm fine, Gabriel."

He was frowning.

"What's wrong? Is it so hard to accept that I'm not afraid?" I asked.

"No, not that."

"Then what?"

"You're too much of what I want," he said, bending down and kissing me chastely on the lips. "And I suck people dry, Genny. Absorb what they have like a sponge. I need their energy to paint. I'm afraid I'm going to do it with you."

"A psychic vampire? Yeah, right. Someone must have been very angry with you to tell you that. It's not true."

"How can you know?"

"The same way I know what you want."

"But what if it's true, what if I'm just using you?" he asked.

"What if I want you to?"

"I can't be using you if it's what you want." He laughed.

"I know," I managed before I fell asleep.

EIGHT

New York City Criminal Court Building, Room 1302
Friday, December 4, 1992, 12:15 P.M.

We've recessed for lunch and Benjamin leads my parents and me to a small room that's been made available to us for the duration of the trial.

"There's Ham," my father says and breaks away to walk ahead and greet him. From his gait, I can tell his spirits have been momentarily lifted. I knew Ham was on Linda's witness list—but I didn't know he would be called this early on.

About the time I got my first directing job and forever dashed his hopes of my taking over the gallery, my father, prime for a protégé, met Ham, who was searching for a mentor. Their association lasted for several years. Then Ham, who had a more idealistic view of the art world, left to open a gallery in an abandoned garage on the edge of SoHo where he developed radical artists who believed in change and challenges.

Instead of seeing Ham as a reminder of his own limitations and rejecting him, the two remained close, my father treating him as a prodigal son who has done him proud.

Ham is a wonderful man—and we have been friends for years. For a short time, we had even tried dating but it hadn't worked out. I never quite saw him clearly. Not him or any other man. For years I viewed everyone through a haze of having loved Slade Gabriel.

Ham bent down and kissed me on the forehead.

"I didn't think you were taking the stand today?" I asked.

"I'm not. I just wanted to be here for you."

I don't know how to respond. It has never occurred to me that any of my friends would come to the trial.

"It's okay, Gen, you don't have to say anything."

For a moment I wonder if I have actually vocalized what I had been thinking. No. Ham has always been like that: the kind of friend who intuitively knows what to say, when to show up, and when to back off.

"Genny?" Benjamin calls from just inside the room. "We have only forty-five minutes and there are things we need to go over."

I'd rather sit on a bench in the hallway with Ham and be quiet because—unlike everyone else—he wouldn't ask anything of me. In all the years I've known him, he never has.

"Go ahead," Ham says. "And Genny?"

"Yes?"

"Deep breaths . . ."

I nod.

Inside on the table are sandwiches and coffee and sodas. I take the closest sandwich, not bothering to read what is written on the white wax paper. As everybody eats their food and sips their drinks, Benjamin questions me and I do my best to help him. Everyone pretends not to notice that I neither eat nor drink.

A few minutes before the recess ends, Benjamin leaves to make a phone call. As soon as the door shuts behind him, my father clears his throat, takes a sip of coffee and then, in a controlled voice, asks me why after all this time I never told him about my being with Gabriel when I was seventeen.

"What difference would it have made? That was between Gabriel and me."

"You made a fool out of me. You knew. Gabriel knew. Only your mother and I didn't know. You were seventeen, Genny. You had no right to hide something that important," he says.

"Aren't there things about your life"—I include my mother in my glance—"that neither of you have ever told me?"

Neither answers.

"No?" I ask sarcastically. "Well, what about my Picasso? It was mine. You gave it to me and it was the most precious thing I owned but you never even told me you were going to sell it. I had to find out when I came home on school break. I walked into my room, threw down my bag, looked up at the wall and it just wasn't there anymore."

I don't tell them how long I stared at the space on that wall where my Picasso had been and how hard I wept. They had stolen part of my soul and sold it at an auction house.

"Genevieve. . ." my mother starts to say something but I do not give her the chance.

"I moved my entire bedroom around so I wouldn't have to see the spot where the painting had been and that awful Warhol print you put in its place. And I waited, but neither of you apologized. All you ever said was that it was the smart time to sell."

"But, Genny you never owned that painting. It belonged to the gallery," my father says.

"You gave it to me for my birthday. At least that's what you told me. Until it wasn't convenient anymore."

All these years later, my anger was still close to the surface.

I glance down, noticing the uneaten sandwich, and push it away.

"You were nineteen years old. Picasso had died. I had to act at the most opportune time," he says, defending himself.

"That's not the point. You've always done exactly what you wanted to. Both of you. And now that you find I'm just like you, you're indig-nant. Don't you find that hypocritical?"

"Gabriel should have known better than to get involved with a seventeen-year-old girl. Damn him, didn't the bastard have any self-control? I was his dealer for God's sake . . . he could have had some respect for me."

"Oh but he did, as soon as he found out who I was he stopped see-ing me."

"Only to come back twenty years later and seduce you again? What for? Hadn't he done enough damage? What a fool you both made out of me." My father's voice is loud and in the small windowless room, it reverberates.

"A fool out of you?" I ask—my voice now raised to the level of his. "It had nothing to do with you."

"Genevieve, Jonathan," my mother says. "What's done is done. Isn't this bad enough, that we are sitting here? Do we have to make it worse?"

My father looked at me as the jury has been looking at me—as if trying to see through me.

I don't turn away from the jury when they stare—I'm becoming immune to their scrutiny, to strangers' eyes boring into my soul—so why should I turn away from my own father? He is no stranger. He has been looking at me my whole life. Even when his gaze should have made me flinch, it never did.

At night, after Marie said my prayers with me, turned off the light, and left—leaving my bedroom door partially open—I put myself to sleep by masturbating. I was ten, and looking back, I'm not sure I knew what I was doing—only that I had to do it in the dark and se-cretly. And that it felt good.

One night, after I came and caught my breath, I opened my eyes and in the shadows of my partially opened doorway, saw my father, silent and still like a statue. Had he been standing there long enough to see me thrash my legs and throw off the sheets in my frenzy?

I had my answer the following night, after my father came to say good-night. For the first time, when he left, he shut the door tightly behind him.

Back in the courtroom, Mimi Reingold returns to the witness stand and Linda resumes her cross-examination.

"Do you know why Slade Gabriel stopped seeing Genny at the end of the summer of '72?"

"No, I don't."

"But you do know the relationship ended?" Linda asks.

"Yeah," Mimi says and nods.

"Did Genny tell you?"

"She didn't have to. All you had to do was take one look at her." Twisting in her seat, she crosses one leg over the other and then re-crosses them. Her right foot rhythmically taps against the floor—there was always loud music playing at the gallery when Mimi worked there.

"She seemed what—distraught? Devastated?" Linda encourages Mimi.

Benjamin stands. "Calls for conjecture on the part of the witness."

"Sustained. Can you rephrase your question, Miss Zavidow?"

"Did Genny tell you how she felt about Mr. Gabriel once he stopped seeing her?" Linda asks.

"Yes, she said she hated him, that she'd hate him for the rest of her life."

"Thank you, Miss Reingold, I have no more questions Your Honor."

Judge Bailey takes off his glasses and wipes them with the now wrinkled handkerchief he's used twice before. "Mr. Marks, do you have any questions for the witness?"

"Yes, I do, Your Honor."

"Go ahead."

Benjamin asks his first question while he's still sitting beside me at the defendant's table, "Miss Reingold, let me make sure of this. When exactly did Genny tell you that she hated Slade Gabriel?"

"At the end of that summer," Mimi says.

"She was just a kid then, wasn't she? Just seventeen, am I right?" he asks.

"Yes."

"Do you think she really hated him or was she just talking out of anger, the way kids do?"

"I object, Your Honor," Linda stands. "Miss Reingold is not an expert on how kids talk."

"Sustained. Do you have another question, Mr. Marks?"

"Just one more. Miss Reingold, have you ever said you hated a man after he left you?"

A Sunday, late in August, the weekend before my parents were due home from Europe. Gabriel had gone to visit his friend Harry Toneky at his studio and had come home stoned and depressed.

He opened a bottle of wine as he described Harry's paintings—each a single dot, each dot a different color, each background the same color, and told me how they had talked about those dots and the progress minimal conceptual art was making.

Eventually he fell asleep by the foot of his easel and I decided to let him sleep it off and went home to Central Park West, bringing my dirty clothes with me.

The next morning, Bertha, our housekeeper, shook her head at me as she took my laundry out of my room. The gallery was always closed on Mondays and I was still in my robe, drinking coffee and reading in bed.

"What am I supposed to say to your parents when they come home?"

"About what?"

"About where you've been, about what you've been doing?"

"Where have I been? What have I been doing?" I teased her.

She shook her head again and lowered her voice with worry. "I don't know. I don't know."

"Then you don't have to be concerned with what to say, right?"

"Girl, I know you've been bad. I can smell it. You just better be careful, you hear?"

My friend Tory called, interrupting Bertha's lecture.

"What did you do this weekend?" she asked.

"Gabriel painted. I stayed in the loft and read."

"That's not very detailed."

"I can't remember any details," I lied.

"You are the expert at details, Genny. You savor details. How come when it comes to this guy, you clam up?"

"How is Peter?" I asked. She and Peter had started going out and, even though she knew it didn't matter to me, she was uncomfortable about it.

"Answer me, don't be such a jerk. I broke up with him. Why does it still bother you?" I asked.

"I don't know."

"So, what did you do this weekend?"

"We went to his parent's house," Tory said.

"Your mother let you? His parents must have been there."

"Of course they were there. I had to spend the night in the guest room. But about two o'clock in the morning he sneaked into my room. Genny, do you think he'll go out with other girls at school?"

"Does it matter?" I asked.

"How can you say that? Of course it matters."

"I'm not sure. If when he is with you he really wants to be with you, then what else can matter?"

"You don't believe that." Tory was incredulous.

"I do."

I was lying to myself, but I wanted to believe what I was saying because there was no question in my mind that once I went away to college Slade Gabriel would see other women. Wasn't he seeing me while he was still legally married to Nina?

I returned to the loft early that afternoon, finding Gabriel sitting in front of his easel, staring at a blank canvas. An empty bottle of wine lay on the floor by his foot.

"Why did you leave?" He sounded disappointed.

"Why were you so out of it?"

"More and more I realize it just doesn't matter whether or not one more painter paints one more painting." He threw the canvas to the floor and squirted violet paint on it right from the tube. Getting down on all fours he ground his cigarette into the paint and smeared the whole mess across the canvas with his hands.

"It's so fucking self-serving. Harvard graduates. Yale School of Art. Too old at thirty-seven to be new and too new to be old. Mark Rothko is dead. So is Pollock. They killed themselves. Gorky killed himself. The rest of us kill ourselves drinking, doing drugs."

His hands smeared with the violet paint, he got streaks of it in his hair, on his cheeks and on his lips.

I took a towel off the counter, wet it with turpentine, and started to wipe his hands clean. Grabbing me he held my hands up to his face, smelling my skin.

"You never smell of paint," he said and then the phone rang.

He listened to the voice on the other end of the phone. "I'll be there as soon as I can."

His daughter, Lizzie, had been riding her bike and was hit by a car. The doctors said that except for a few bruises and a concussion she was all right. Still her doctor wanted to keep her in the hospital in Southampton for observation.

"I'll probably stay overnight. But if you want to you can hang out here instead of going back to all those roommates of yours. Maybe you'll be here when I get back."

Gabriel called a few hours later. Yes, his daughter was fine. But he wanted to spend a few days with her. He'd be back by the weekend.

Actually, that made things easier for me. My parents were returning home the next night and I'd been dreading how I was going to manage without making them or Gabriel suspicious.

It was an uneventful homecoming and my mother and father were both back at the office by Wednesday afternoon.

On Friday I met Tory and we went downtown to the Village shopping for clogs on Eighth Street, eating pizza, and seeing *A Clockwork Orange*. It was almost seven when I walked in the front door, right into the middle of one of my parents' cocktail parties.

Circling the room, I kissed the people I knew, many of whom were like family to me and answered questions about my summer and plans for college. The room hummed: conversation focusing on the upcoming season.

I was still making the rounds and didn't hear the doorbell or see the front door open. I was unaware of who'd come in—people were always coming and going during those soirees—so I hardly paid attention when by father called me over.

"Genny, come say hello, the two of you must be old friends by now, working together shoulder to shoulder all summer long. Tell me Gabriel, did my daughter fill my shoes?"

Panic fluttered in my chest. My father stood beside Gabriel, whose dark eyes bore into me.

"Yes . . . of course . . . she did." He spoke more slowly than usual, trying not to let on that anything was wrong.

Proudly, my father put his arm around my shoulder. Gabriel was nodding stupidly. Was he noticing how much I looked like my father?

"Did you know she's starting college in a week? Genny's going to attend Sarah Lawrence. My little girl's growing up."

I would have been embarrassed if I hadn't been in a panic over what Gabriel was thinking. What was he going to do or say? What would happen next?

Gabriel just kept nodding like one of those plastic dashboard toys until my father ushered him off to introduce him to someone who'd just arrived. I escaped to my room, where I sat on the edge of my bed and shook. Wrapped up in my own arms I watched the door, waiting for Gabriel to break away and come to me.

At about nine o'clock I went back outside. By now the apartment was deserted, the party was over, and my parents had gone out with some of their friends to dinner. I gulped at leftover glasses of vodka and Scotch and smoked what was left of the cigarettes found in the ashtrays. Water had pooled under the glasses on the coffee table, the air was stale, cocktail napkins crumpled into tight balls littered the top of the piano, and the canapés had already dried up, their edges curling.

I went downstairs, hailed a cab, and gave the driver the address of Gabriel's studio.

His loft's door was unlocked. I opened it, but as I walked in, Gabriel stepped in the doorway and blocked me from entering. Angry and halfway to being drunk, he must have been waiting for me. "How the hell old are you?" he hissed.

"Seventeen."

He clenched his fists by his sides.

"Can I come in?"

"I'm moving back out to Amagansett."

"Because of me?"

"Despite you."

I couldn't understand. The noise of my blood was beating loudly in my ears. "To spite me?"

"*De*spite you. I decided this week . . . being with my daughter in that hospital room. I decided then. I would try. Not so much for me, but for them. Because we're a family."

"What about me?"

"You're seventeen!"

"But you didn't know that when you decided to go back to Nina."

"No. But it sure as shit makes it easier now."

"Does it?"

"Yes," he said.

"You fuck. You selfish fuck. I'm glad for you. So glad it's easier. I wouldn't want you to suffer over your decision."

"If I'd made the opposite decision, I wouldn't be able to be with you anyway," he said.

"Why not?"

"Stop asking questions, goddamn it!"

"Not until I know what I need to know."

"You'll never know everything you need to know."

"Why wouldn't you have been able to be with me?" I asked.

"Because you are my dealer's *goddamned* underaged daughter. I could go to jail!" he screamed.

"I wouldn't let them put you in jail."

He laughed derisively at me, at the little girl in his doorway. "You could stop them? You could stop your father?" He spit the words out.

"I was going to tell you," I said.

"When, after you got tired of the joke?"

"It wasn't a joke. I just couldn't ever figure . . . how to . . . when to . . ."

"Go home."

"I want to spend tonight with you."

"Go home." He had not said my name once.

"Fuck me. Please! One more time."

I moved closer to him and rubbed up against his body. I still might have a chance to change his mind, break his resolve. Taking his fingers in my hand I made him unbutton my blouse and cup my breast.

"No one will know, just one last night," I whispered in his ear, letting my tongue dart out and lick the soft flesh of his lobe, sucking it, scratching it with my teeth, memorizing its slightly waxy taste and the smell of paint, liquor, and sweat on his skin.

As I unbuckled his pants, he moaned and leaned back against the doorframe. I stroked him with the palm of my hand. Gabriel allowed this but made no move toward me.

Down on my knees, I took him in my mouth, sucking on him. Still he didn't touch me, just stood above me, his hands by his sides, his face twisted as if this were torture, but he let me continue.

And then just seconds before he was about to come he suddenly grabbed me by the hair and pulled me up and off him and shoved his engorged penis back in his jeans.

"Get out of here. Leave me alone."

When he saw I had no intention of moving, he put his hands on my shoulders and pushed me. As I stumbled out into the hall, I heard the door close behind me. I stayed there for a few minutes, listening to his footsteps retreating, to glass breaking, to cloth—canvas—ripping, and then I walked to the elevator.

Downstairs, in the empty street, running on uneven cobblestones, I twisted my ankle but kept running until I found a taxi down the block, and falling back against the plastic seat, mumbled my address to the driver and tasted hot tears dripping into my mouth.

I cried all through the night, hugging my box of days to my chest, rocking back and forth, certain I would think of a way to convince him it was all right to be with me again. We were supposed to be together. Hadn't Gabriel said that?

At six o'clock in the morning when the sun rose beyond the park, I heard noises and knew my father, following his morning routine, was retrieving the paper from the front door, making coffee, and going into his study.

When I was little, I used to creep into his study almost every morning and he'd let me sip his coffee and give me some of the paper so I could pretend I was reading, too. That morning I sat down on the thick rug by his feet, leaned against his legs, and he automatically stroked my hair.

"You know, Mimi has told me what a terrific job you did this summer. I'm so pleased Genny. Did you enjoy it?"

I wasn't hearing his words, nor their meaning, I was letting the carefully clipped clean sound wash over me and soothe me with its familiarity. I turned my cheek so instead of my hair, he stroked my skin.

Suddenly I envisioned Gabriel and me together in his loft, at the beach, on the boat. What would my father think of me if he knew about those nights? Could Gabriel be angry enough to tell my father about us and turn my father against me?

"What's wrong, Genny?" my father asked, his hand feeling the tear on my cheek.

"Wrong?"

"You're crying," he said.

"I . . . I . . . I'm scared . . . about going off to school." Another lie.

"It's not that far away darling, you can come home as often as you want. Naturally, you're scared. I know your mother believes you're too grown up to get homesick, but I was homesick in college. When it gets bad, just pick up the phone. Or get on the train. We'll be here." My father reached down and softly wiped away my tears with his fingertips.

I hated Gabriel for his obstinacy, for disappointing me with his moralizing about my age, for going back to his wife even though they didn't belong together. While my father held me, I held onto that hate. Alive, it grew, filling me like hot liquid, strengthening me; in a perverse way connecting me to Gabriel. And when the old loneliness came back, that loneliness I knew before I met Gabriel, I fought it with that hate, which by then had a texture: scratchy, sharp, and lethal. That hate sustained me and I vowed if he ever came back to me I would send him away, repeating it over and over like a mantra, trying to make myself believe it until finally, I did.

My life after that flowed in an expected course. I did well at college, dated, perhaps too much but never very seriously. After graduating with honors, I quickly found a job at a film company.

I transferred all my passion to my work and by 1982 was made an assistant producer at PBS, working on a series about Broadway legends. It was then that I met Nicholas Parrish, a fund-raiser for the network. Nicky was not an artist. He was sane and low-key. We were good friends for three years. We probably should have stayed friends but I rationalized that the easy camaraderie and affection I felt for Nicky was safer for me. We married in 1986 at the Pierre Hotel with more than two hundred guests in attendance.

If Nicky and I had had children we might have lasted longer, but as it turned out we didn't and were divorced in 1989, the same year my series *Into the Paintings* was picked up.

The show was successful. I achieved recognition in my field, even winning two Emmys. Through my work, I enlarged my circle of friends, tried to make some of them into lovers—like Hamilton Lane—whom I had met at one of my weekly dinners with my father. (My mother joined us when she wasn't in Paris where she was spending more and more time as my grandfather aged.)

Because of *Into the Paintings*, I kept abreast of what was going on in the art world, which meant I heard about the upward spiral of Gabriel's career whether I wanted to or not.

Occasionally my parents talked of him or I would see an article about him in a newspaper or art journal. I read reviews of his work in *Time* and personality pieces in mainstream magazines like *Vanity Fair*.

I knew when he finally divorced his first wife, when he moved to California (although he kept the studio in New York and the house in Amagansett), and when he remarried. Whenever I saw his name in print I dismissed the stab of longing I felt, rationalizing that I was only one of many women who couldn't forget their first love. I was in control. Not plagued, not obsessed.

I convinced myself. I'd built a life—not admitting I'd built it on top of a shattered one. I'd learned my lesson about the kind of passion Gabriel and I had shared. No different from any narcotic, it brought both euphoria and destruction. I preferred living midrange: no highs, no lows. And I swore that if he ever did come back to me, I'd keep my promise to myself and send him away.

PART II

Lost Face, never again to be seen by me,
Where shall I go now for comfort, what door try,
Trusting to find behind it comfort, as in the days
When you were behind some door—the door of the sitting room,
The door of the kitchen, a different door from this,
A door with a knob, a door that could be opened?

—Edna St. Vincent Millay

NINE

Outside the courthouse window, the flat gray sky threatens snow. The wind, caught between the buildings, howls. I see the tree branches bend so far back they should break, but they don't. Inside, at the rear of the courtroom, someone coughs up phlegm and clears his throat. The judge searches for the cougher and then, unable to find him, looks down at Linda Zavidow.

"Miss Zavidow, if you're ready, you may call your second witness."

Catching the light from the harsh overheads, Linda's wedding band gleams as she picks up a sheaf of papers. Her streaked shoulder-length hair swings forward and two men in the jury follow the movement with their eyes.

"The prosecution calls Detective Reggie King, Your Honor."

The bailiff opens the door, steps out in the hallway, and shouts the detective's name. Once, then again. The mechanical clock above the door ticks ahead thirty seconds, and then forty, and then the bailiff limps up the center aisle, and over to Linda.

"Your Honor, I need a few minutes to find out how long Detective King is going to be detained," Linda says after talking to the bailiff.

"The court will take a five-minute recess." Judge Bailey bangs his gavel and stands up, smoothing down his long black robes. He's not a tall man but the robes lend him stature. He is an impressive figure as he leaves the bench and disappears into his chambers. Beside me, Benjamin straightens out a pile of papers and impatiently curses under his breath.

The postponement bothers the jury, too. They fidget, stretch, stare out at the spectators and at me. The stops and starts don't matter to me. What do I have to be impatient for? In prison or out, a half-life of days and nights without Gabriel awaits me. I suppose I'm terrified, but I can't quite reach the feeling, can't find its edges, not since Gabriel died.

"A detective called the apartment for you, Genny. Detective King. He left a number and asked you to call him back, immediately. Why do the police need to talk to you so urgently?" This was the first thing my father said to me when he arrived at Gabriel's house in Amagansett, the seaside town on the eastern tip of Long Island. There I had waited, without eating or sleeping for thirty hours—since Monday afternoon, September 18, 1992—unsure of what I was supposed to do now that it was over. Now that the plans had been played out, now that Slade Gabriel was dead.

My father tried to get me to talk while we were still inside the house, but I couldn't, not until we were in the car on the way back to Manhattan. He pushed the button raising the glass partition between us and the driver.

"Now tell me, Genny, what happened?"

He sat close to me, the fabric of his gray Italian suit crushed against my navy trousers. Why hadn't he taken my hand? If only I could subtract thirty years and be his little girl again, with possibilities ahead of us, no history behind us.

I had to tell him something, but did it have to be the truth? And which truth? How much of it should he hear? Was my father asking for a confession or an explanation? Conscious of separating the two, I told him enough to satisfy him without involving him.

I had no distance yet. Even as I spoke I could still smell that particular combination of tobacco and oil paint that clung to Gabriel's clothes, feel his large hands holding mine, see into his black fathomless eyes.

"Goddamn it Genny." My father's voice pulled me back to the present. "Are you actually saying he mattered to you so much that you helped him commit—"

"He didn't 'matter so much' to me—I loved him."

My father's manicured fingers clenched in his lap. "How can you sit there and so calmly tell me you loved someone who allowed you to put yourself at risk like this?"

"I'm not at risk."

"You didn't speak to that detective. I did."

"I'm not at risk," I repeated.

My father's face was so close to mine I felt his breath on my cheek when he exhaled a long sigh of . . . what? Sadness? Frustration? Pity? "Damn him!" he said and then pursed his lips together, making them disappear into one angry line.

Which Gabriel was he blasting? His daughter's lover, one of his oldest friends, or the rebellious artist whose death would now replenish the Haviland Gallery's coffers?

"Why did you ever get mixed up with him? Didn't I warn you? Why didn't you listen?"

"By the time you talked to me, it was already too late." I looked past him out of the window, surprised to see the blur of cars passing, the trees, the houses rising beyond the highway. I had forgotten there was anything beyond my words and my father's face, which had now settled into a mask, bitter and betrayed.

Even though we were sitting inches from each other, there was a great distance between us. My father had stepped back and removed himself from me once again and I didn't have the energy to make him understand that if nothing else, Gabriel's death might bring us back together.

What was upsetting him the most? His loss? My love? Was my father jealous or bereft?

After a long silence and without explanation, my father picked up the cellular phone and called Samuel Ryser's office but the lawyer wasn't in. "Tell him Jonathan Haviland called again. Tell him it's still imperative that I speak to him as soon as possible. Where is he?"

After snapping the receiver into place, he addressed me: "When we get home, there may be reporters waiting. I don't want you to talk to them. Walk straight from the car into the lobby. Once we're in the apartment, Bertha will answer the phone. No comments until I speak to Samuel and don't call the detective back or take his calls. There are specific laws about assisted suicide. It would be prudent if we knew as much about them as we could."

"I know about the laws. There won't be any problems," I said in a monotone.

"Don't be naive."

Up ahead a car slowed down and my father's driver leaned on the horn, swerved to the left, and sped up to pass the offending car.

"It should be raining. Daddy, why isn't it raining?"

He didn't know what I was talking about, didn't know I was thinking about my beginning with Gabriel, twenty years before, when it had rained at Callahand's house, but he understood the confusion and loss in my voice and despite his anger, his eyes softened and he pulled me toward him. I slackened against his chest, smelling his fine cotton shirt and something else—leathery, evergreen, and familiar.

"No questions, Genny, not now," he whispered into my hair.

And finally I was six or seven again and my father and I were playing the game: how long could I study a painting, or a drawing, a piece of sculpture, or a landscape out a window and not ask a single question. Through this game I discovered how to share his silence and how to regulate the rise and fall of my chest until we breathed in perfect synchronicity.

My father and I are too alike. It has caused problems and set up dangerous alliances. In control, cool to our passions, aloof to our obsessions, my mother left us to each other while she traveled between her two worlds without regret. We yearned and brooded, but gradually learned to give each other solace—so much so that it has crippled us.

The two of us differed from her even physically. Both my father and I are tall; my mother is petite. Her soft blond curls fluff up and frame her face, but my hair, like my father's, is the color of roasted chestnuts and falls in heavy waves to my shoulders. With our brown eyes, my father and I look at each other and see ourselves. When I look at my mother, into her light blue eyes, I see only her . . . the foreigner among us.

The rush hour traffic on the Long Island Expressway that warm September night prevented us from getting home until almost seven-thirty. There were no reporters to greet us yet. Bertha, who was still with my parents, had dinner ready and even though my father and I both tried, neither of us ate much.

Afterward, my father brought out a bottle of cognac and as we sat together in the living room sipping the amber liqueur, the anger between us slipped away for a while.

We'd stoked that anger for many years. I'd infuriated him first by refusing to work at the gallery and instead pursuing a career in film; later by divorcing Nicky Parrish, whom my father had liked. Finally, more recently, I'd incensed him by taking Gabriel as a lover. But my father was no innocent either. He'd infuriated me, too: as a businessman with his greed, his ethics, and his unreasonable demands, and as a father by promising more than he was willing or able to give.

We talked that night to keep each other company, but too often, in the middle of a sentence, Gabriel swooped past, sending me reeling. Each time the fresh shock and numbing certainty of his death settled on me, our conversation came to a halt.

Then my father would introduce a new subject and hearing him, I'd wonder how long I'd been lost. How many minutes had passed while I'd been in the tunnel Gabriel's death had created?

The phone rang often. After taking the call, my father reported to me who it had been and repeated each condolence. It was, after all, something to fill those long hours of waiting, until we would sleep, until we would wake, until we would bury Gabriel and say good-bye to him.

Artists, dealers, museum directors, the art press and, of course, collectors continued to call until well past eleven. By then the brandy had done as much as it could to take the edge off the day. That blurring was as close to relief as I would get. Not drunk but listing, I allowed my father to lead me into the bedroom he shared with my mother when she was home. He was going to sleep in his den.

After giving me one of my mother's Pratesi robes and a nightgown, he left me to undress and I went into the bathroom.

It took time, there were buttons, zippers, pulling, folding. How many days had I been wearing these same navy pants and white shirt? Why was so much effort required to do the simplest things? I hit my elbow on the towel rack, heard a crack, and felt a shot of pain. Sitting on the cold marble floor, I rubbed my elbow. Knees up, my head pressed against my flesh, I coughed up dry sobs and behind my eyes, saw Gabriel's body again: long, lean, muscled, stretched out on the bed, his black eyes open, burning into me.

Coming out of the bathroom, I glimpsed myself in my mother's dressing-table mirror; her elegant lace nightgown too small for me, the sleeves exposing my wrists, the hem revealing my ankles, the fabric pulling across my breasts. Moving closer to the dresser, I picked up my mother's antique cloisonné brush and brushed my hair the way I remembered she brushed hers. Yes, I could imitate the smooth strokes but not the secret smile that played on her lips as if some idea was keeping her perpetually amused.

I'd always wanted to be more like my distant, beautiful mother, to get closer to her, close enough so that we could be interchangeable.

Startled by a knock on the door, I dropped the brush and it crashed on the dresser top.

"Are you all right?" my father asked as he came in.

He looked at me in the mirror and I looked back at him, two people, in their own way for their own reasons, crazy with grief, both desperate to buffer the sadness. The distance between us disappeared as my father put his hand on my shoulder.

"You should try and get some sleep," he said.

"I can't."

"You have to make an effort." Moving away, over to the bed, he pulled back the covers for me. "Come, get in."

Like a child or an invalid, I followed his instructions and climbed into the bed, laying my head down on the pillow as my father pulled the crisply ironed sheet up around my chin. The bedding smelled faintly of my mother's perfume—a French perfume called Jicky—a light clean smell of orange blossoms and limes.

"Close your eyes," he said, shutting off the bedside lamp.

"It won't matter, I can't sleep for longer than a few minutes at a time. Last night I only slept for an hour. I don't think I slept at all the night before."

"Then I'll get you something," he said and left, shutting the door behind him and leaving me completely in the dark.

As a child I'd hide in that darkness often waiting for my mother to come in so I could spy on her. My favorite hiding place was in her closet standing among her clothes, rubbing her silks and cashmeres on my skin. I'd listen to her talking on her phone and peer out watching her hand making small circles on the bedspread as she inspected herself in the mirror while she spoke.

Once when she opened her closet to hang up her clothes, she caught me there.

"Genevieve, what are you doing?"

"Playing hide and seek," I lied.

"With whom are you playing?" she asked quizzically. I was odd to her, a creature she didn't quite understand.

"With you," I said, making her laugh.

"It is good you're not afraid of the dark. I'm proud of you."

"I'm not afraid of anything." I wanted her to be even more proud.

Why did my mother's private world obsess me? Was it so I could find a place for myself in it? Or was it so I could have what she had?

While I waited for my father to come back, my hands began to itch again—they'd been itching like that since I'd run from Gabriel's loft on Monday morning. Under the covers I pressed my palms together hoping the pressure would bring some relief but soon I was scratching again, faster and faster, giving in, making them bleed, causing fresh pain.

Then the door opened and a shaft of light from the hallway fell across the bed. Thrusting my hands under the back of my legs, the fine Italian linen wicked up the blood.

"Here, take these." My father held out two small white pills that seemed to glow an iridescent milky-blue.

My palms were burning now. "I can't."

"Why on earth not?"

"Those are the same sleeping pills I gave Gabriel—" I started shaking.

My father sat down beside me on the edge of the bed and for the second time that day, held me against his chest. Willing myself to stop seeing those pills in my own hand the day before, I concentrated on the smell of my father's skin, on the repetitive motion of his hand smoothing down my hair. I inhaled on his inhale, exhaled on his exhale; we were in sync. My father. My lover. My father. Which one was this? Opening my eyes, I tried to figure it out but in the dark it was hard to tell. Gabriel? No, it was my father, holding me tightly against the night.

But he was not just my father holding me, he was a man and I'd been aware of that since I was a child.

My father had taken me to the Museum of Modern Art for the afternoon and before we visited the galleries we had lunch in the members' dining room at my father's regular table overlooking the sculpture garden.

My father always had wine with lunch and even though I was only twelve, he offered me sips throughout the meal. When we were almost finished, a man my father obviously knew came over and after he said hello he leered at me just a little.

"Genny, this is Mr. Goldstone." I didn't want to, but I shook his hand as was expected.

"I won't mention this to Maguy," the man said and winked at my father.

My father laughed. "I'd appreciate it, Max."

Once Mr. Goldstone walked away I asked my father what they'd meant and as he leaned close to me to let me in on the secret, I smelled his leathery evergreen scent. "He thinks you're my girlfriend," my father said proudly, not making a joke of it at all.

My father, as he always did, took my hand as we walked out. But that day there was something uncomfortable about feeling the moistness of his flesh and the rigidity of his bones. He had touched me all over my body all my life, but that was the first time I pulled away.

Upstairs we spent half an hour in front of a Magritte painting. My father was teaching me about surrealism, but I was learning about something quite different.

I woke up in the dark, an unfamiliar nightgown twisted up around my waist, my legs spread, sheets crushed in my clenched fist, my hair sticking to the back of my neck, and my naked skin slicked with sweat. I was gasping for breath, peering into the darkness with no clue to its depth. That lightlessness was a presence pressing me into the bed as forcefully as Gabriel did when he laid his body on top of mine. But inside, where he should have been, it was hollow.

Usually, I slept naked with only a comforter covering me, so whose bed was this? Whose nightgown? Noises beyond the room suggested Gabriel painting in the studio—except—wasn't there something wrong with Gabriel? Or was that my dream? Fighting to traverse the space from sleep to wakefulness I came up on the far side of my nightmare only to realize it was not a nightmare. The fear hit first and then the cold. I knew where I was and why.

This was my parents' apartment, their bedroom, their bed. For a while I lay there, trying but failing to avoid the rush of consciousness. Then I got up, pulled my mother's pale green robe around me and left the bedroom in search of my father, who I knew would be, as he always was early in the morning, drinking coffee and working in his study.

"It's only six o'clock. Couldn't you sleep any longer?"

"I shouldn't have slept at all," I said guiltily.

"I know, it seems indecent that your body keeps functioning, doesn't it? You want there to be some momentous break in the continuum to mark the occasion, but it doesn't happen like that. Nothing ever does. Drama is always surrounded by the mundane."

About to reach across my father's desk for his coffee I saw the *New York Times*, open to the obituary page. I read and reread the same line of type, over and over, unable to make any sense of it. Finally giving up on the words, I stared at the photograph of my lover standing in front of one of his paintings until the photograph turned into an insane pattern of black and white dots. Only the five-word caption beneath the dots remained in focus: SLADE GABRIEL, DEAD AT 57.

Now, taking my father's cup, I drank from it; hot liquid filled my mouth, burned my tongue. When I glanced up my father's eyes were on me, liquid brown like the coffee.

"I spoke to your mother. She's on the first flight out of Paris and should be home by three or three-thirty this afternoon. We agreed to close the gallery for the funeral and then the rest of the week."

"The funeral? When is the funeral?"

Listening to my father describe the arrangements, part of me detached and splintered off. Always able to simultaneously observe and act, record and respond, I'm expert at pretending to be paying complete attention while I'm really busy storing away facts for later.

As I listened to my father, I also was aware of how cautiously he navigated around the phrases that might have been difficult for me to hear. But I did hear them, and when I did, my body swayed as if I were losing my balance and all that might bolster me was his presence.

About eight o'clock, Bertha knocked on the door and told us breakfast would be ready in fifteen minutes. We both went off to dress and then met back in the dining room where we sat down at the far end of the long table in the same places we had taken the night before; only now the morning light from the living-room windows flooded the room and there were no shadows.

We had eaten, slept, now we ate again. Time was passing and each moment was taking me further away from what had happened toward what would happen.

Bertha brought breakfast. Unlike the night before, when we sat in semidarkness and pushed the food around our plates, we both began to eat. I was almost ashamed by my hunger. However, as soon as I tasted the eggs cooked in sweet butter, I gagged. Dropping the fork, I pushed away the plate.

"Genny?"

"I can't eat. I can't. How can I? For a minute I think everything's all right, then I remember . . . then I remember that it's Gabriel—that he's dead—that I—"

My outburst brought Bertha out of the kitchen. In her sixties now, she had an unlined face, but her age showed in her eyes. This morning she looked even older.

As she moved to pick up my plate the armful of silver bracelets she always wore jangled. "Can't you get yourself to eat something?" Her Jamaican accent, like her bangles, made music.

I shook my head.

"Are you sure, child? Not even some toast?"

I shook my head. "No, but I'd like some coffee."

"I'll bring it right out."

While Bertha was in the kitchen the phone rang and, returning with the coffee, she told my father who it was. While he took the call in his study, I sipped the coffee. For the second time that morning, I gulped it down while it was too hot and burnt my tongue.

Across the living room, through the large windows, gray clouds rolled in. I imagined Gabriel dipping his brush into a glistening glob of white paint, mixing in some green, dragging in a drop of black and creating that color.

"An astute decision, Fred." I could hear my father on the phone. "Yes, we both are aware of how this kind of thing drives up prices."

In the pause that followed I filled in Fred's gushing voice thanking my father for cutting him in so soon.

When my father returned I couldn't pretend I hadn't heard the conversation. "Closing the gallery in Gabriel's honor?"

Was I shocked my father had lied? No. It was, after all, my father who'd taught me about deception. We'd protected ourselves from my mother with untruths.

"It's all right that I'm going away for a while isn't it?" my mother would ask my father.

"Of course, Maguy, do what you have to do."

"You don't need me to go with you to school do you? You're not afraid are you? Not Genevieve?" my mother would ask.

"No, Mama, I'm not afraid."

"When I grow up, Daddy, can I marry you?" I asked.

"Of course, darling."

All lies.

"My conversation may have sounded mercenary, Genny, but remember I'm a businessman," he said, sitting down at the table.

"I know that. I'm a businessman's daughter."

"What exactly does that mean?"

The air in the apartment was still. Nothing moved. Somewhere in the street a car alarm sounded. On. Off. On. Off. And I opened my hands out as if to say—you know what it means, you and I and Gabriel all knew what it meant—and unaware, exposed my hands to my father.

Staring down at my bloody palms, he grabbed my wrists so he could inspect them more closely. I twisted to pull them away, but he was stronger.

"*What on earth?* Genny, what the hell is wrong with your hands?"

"I haven't been able to stop scratching them. It started right after I gave Gabriel the pills."

"Do they hurt? Are you in pain?"

"No, it looks worse than it is."

"I'm going to call Doctor Nealander."

"Absolutely not. I'm fine. Let go of me."

My father insisted on bandaging my hands.

In the master bath, I sat on the wide edge of the marble tub watching him take supplies out of the medicine chest and line them up on the sink ledge: cotton balls, Q-Tips, hydrogen peroxide, a tube of antibiotic cream, and gauze pads. Kneeling on the marble floor in his fine Italian suit, my father used a wet cotton ball to gently swab the dried blood. When he revealed a network of thin scratches, some fresh, some with hard crusts starting to form, he couldn't hold back an astonished breath.

After soaking another cotton ball in peroxide, he pressed it against the palm of my right hand, then repeated the action with my left, letting the liquid slowly seep into the sores. Next, using a Q-Tip, he spread a light layer of antibiotic cream on my skin, so gently I felt only the slightest pressure but it was enough to start the itching again.

"Please, stop, I can't stand it," I pleaded, trying again to pull my hands back, but my father held tight, ignored me, and continued until he'd covered both my palms with the cream.

The entire bathroom was mirrored. As he lay gauze pads on each of my palms and taped their edges to my skin, I watched multiple impressions of us—a sixty-seven-year-old man at a thirty-eight-year-old woman's knees, her hands open to him, his ministering to her pain.

Somewhere behind us, the phone rang again but my father remained on his knees in front of me, holding my bandaged hands by my wrists. He was putting so much pressure on them, they began to ache. My father hadn't said a single word during the whole procedure and then, finally, reluctantly, he broke his silence with a low rush of words that caught in his throat, "My God, Genny, what have you done?" he asked.

Before I could say anything, Bertha came to the bathroom door. "Mr. Haviland, Santos is on the house phone saying there are policemen here; he says he couldn't stop them and they're on their way up." Usually Bertha took her time with words, half talking half singing them, but these came out in one long rush, fast and strung together.

While she stood in the doorway, waiting for his instructions, the doorbell chimed. Frightened, she clasped her hands in front of her breasts, sending her bracelets clanging. "Oh Mr. Haviland, that must be them, the police. What should I do?"

"Go back to whatever you were doing before. I'll take care of it, Bertha," my father said as he rose, taking time to close the cap on the ointment and put the bandages and things away.

"Genny, I don't want you to come out. I still haven't talked to Samuel." He left before I could explain that I already knew what to say when and if the police questioned me. Gabriel had prepared me.

My father's footsteps echoed as he made his way down the hall.

Following ten feet behind him, I watched him cross the foyer, open the front door, and ask the policemen if he could help them.

The door blocked my view but I heard a man with a Brooklyn accent introduce himself as Detective King and his partner as Detective Corello. King asked if I was there and if they could talk to me. My father told him I was resting. The detective said it was important. My father said he understood but it would be more convenient if they could return when I was feeling better.

Detective King reassured my father I wasn't under suspicion, that there was no need for any concern, that this was just a routine questioning but the sooner he could do it the better it would be for everyone.

His politeness was cloying.

I emerged from the shadow of the hallway into the foyer. "I think I'd like to get this over with now," I said to the three of them. Annoyed I'd disobeyed him, my father glared.

"Thank you Miss Haviland," said the Brooklyn detective still standing outside in the hallway. "I'm Detective King. This is my partner Detective Corello." He gestured to a younger man, who smiled at me.

"Why don't you come inside?" my father said, controlling his voice.

They followed my father into the living room, Detective Corello surveying the paintings on the wall while Detective King kept his eyes on me. I sat in a corner of the champagne velvet couch and returned his glance. King was about fifty, built like an athlete with broad shoulders and a thick neck, stern and formidable, nothing like his younger partner who was better dressed and had kind, surprisingly sympathetic eyes. I turned back to King and looked him in the eye to show him I wasn't afraid.

"We'd like to ask you some questions," Corello started.

"Why don't you both sit down?" My father gestured to two Ruhlmann chairs flanking the couch. King looked unhappily at the upholstered chair, said his back was bad, and would my father mind if he pulled up one of the straight-backed chairs against the wall?

While King pulled over the chair, Detective Corello settled back in one of the Ruhlmanns, opened his notebook, clicked his pen, and turned to me.

"We're sorry to have to inform you that Slade Gabriel died Monday morning in the loft the two of you shared," Corello said.

"Yes, I know . . ." I visualized the light-filled loft, the whitewashed walls, the paint-spattered couch, the stacks of canvases, and the bed where Gabriel's body . . . I clasped my hands together and felt the pain. That helped. I needed to concentrate on what was being said. I had to stay centered.

"Can you tell us where you were on Monday morning? "

"I really do not feel comfortable having this go on without there being a lawyer present," my father interrupted.

"That's Miss Haviland's decision. Miss Haviland, would you like to have a lawyer present?" Corello asked.

"No." I turned to my father. "I'd like to get this over with." Turning to the younger detective, I answered his question. "I left the loft about ten o'clock."

"Where were you headed?"

"To my father's gallery to drop off some papers for Gabriel and then out to Amagansett to meet with a carpenter."

Corello's pen moved across his pad. "Did you happen to see anyone in the vestibule of the loft when you left?"

"I don't remember."

"Take a minute, see it in your mind, the inside of the building. Outside on the street, was anyone hanging around?"

Corello's questions seemed pulled from the standard script of a B-grade suspense film. I wanted to tell him, but instead I answered him.

"I can't remember."

King pulled his bottom lip in, pressing down on the wet flesh with his teeth while Corello continued: "Was anyone angry at Mr. Gabriel? Had he received any strange phone calls or mail? Had he been arguing with anyone?"

"I don't understand. Are you looking for a suspect? Do you think Gabriel was killed?"

The detective leaned forward in his chair and spoke softly, just to me. "Miss Haviland, what do you think caused Mr. Gabriel's death?"

I reminded myself that I knew how to answer questions like these. I could handle this, could disassociate, manipulate, charm, even lie if I had to. Trying not to think about the guns these men carried, not to think of how easy it was for them to arrest people, not to dwell on the system they operated in, whose rules I didn't know, I said: "The pills, the plastic bag, Gabriel explained it all in the note he sent, didn't you read the note?"

"What note?" King leaned even farther forward in his chair.

"The note. Gabriel's lawyer—Richard Shipper—he has the note. Have you talked to him?"

"Yes, we have in fact talked to Mr. Shipper. He didn't mention a note."

"He should have it by now."

"Did you see the note, Miss Haviland?"

I shook my head.

"Then why do you think one exists?" King asked.

"Any more questions and I want our lawyer here," my father interrupted.

But King persisted. "Please tell us about the note." His eyes had narrowed on me and I knew, because of the way he stared and the way he'd ignored my father's request, that something had shifted. I felt the energy surging from him.

"Miss Haviland, tell me why you think Mr. Gabriel's lawyer has the note."

My father put his hands on my shoulders, pulling me back toward him, away from the policemen.

"No Genny, I don't want you to say another word."

Detective Corello ignored my father. "Genny, what's the matter with your hands?"

I followed his glance down to the bandaged hands in my lap. "I scratched them."

"Both of them?" His voice was understanding. "That must be damned uncomfortable."

"It doesn't matter. The note matters. You won't stop looking for it, will you?" I was talking loudly and to me my voice sounded just right—nervous and tight.

"Genny, I mean it, I don't want you to say anything further. Do you hear me?" My father's hands gripped my shoulders. Corello closed his notebook and put it away.

My father stood and the policemen followed. The three men crossed the room. My father opened the front door. Corello stepped through, but then stopped and turned back to me. I tried to hold myself erect, to stop from swinging out into space, untethered and unsecured. It mattered how I appeared now. It would have bearing on what they thought. It would affect what would happen next.

"Genny, the answer is no, we won't stop looking for the note." Corello's voice was soft with sympathy.

Detective King made a disgusted noise with his tongue against the back of his mouth and impatiently walked past his partner and out the door.

TEN

New York City Criminal Court Building, Room 1317
Friday, December 4, 1992, 2:35 P.M.

Sergeant Reggie King's face is expressionless as he takes the oath and then sits down. For him, this is all so routine. Linda puts him through the preliminaries and then: "Can you describe what you found in the victim's loft, Detective."

"The deceased—" Detective King starts.

"Slade Gabriel?"

"Yes, Slade Gabriel was in his bed. He was wearing a cotton kimono-type robe. He was naked underneath and had a plastic bag tied around his head."

"Was the plastic bag the only evidence you found?"

"No, there were two empty vials of Seconal on the nightstand beside the bed."

"Was there a glass on the nightstand?" Linda asks.

"No, but we found a glass and a couple of mugs in the kitchen sink. They had been rinsed out already by the cleaning lady before she went into the bedroom area and discovered the deceased."

"Okay, Detective King, let's backtrack. Would you describe the plastic bag on the victim's—"

"Objection," Benjamin shouted.

"You know better than that, Miss Zavidow," the judge admonished her. "The clerk will strike that from the record. Proceed, Counselor, with caution."

"Detective King, would you describe the plastic bag you found covering the deceased's head?"

"It was an ordinary bag, the kind you put lettuce in, or to freeze food, and it was tied with a piece of ordinary twine."

"At this point, Your Honor, the people would like to offer into evidence exhibits A through C," Linda says as she returns to her table and picks up several evidence bags. Inside one are two vials of Seconal, inside another the twine, and in the last, the plastic bag.

Despite Benjamin's warning that I would have to see these things, I am unprepared for the sight of them—as evidence—passing from hand to hand. My stomach clenches.

Through the window, one of the bare winter trees bends in another strong gust of wind and a single dried out leaf that was tenuously hanging on blows off, disappearing from sight.

Linda holds up each item as the detective describes it.

"Those are two plastic vials of Seconal. The prescription and dosage instructions are typed on each label."

"And for whom was all this Seconal prescribed? Whose name is on the labels?"

"Genny Haviland."

Unaware I've been biting the inside of my mouth, I'm surprised by the taste of my own blood and gag.

Benjamin glances over to see if I'm all right. So do one or two members of the jury, but Linda draws their attention back to the plastic bag containing the piece of twine.

"Detective King, could you describe the way the twine was knotted around Mr. Gabriel's neck."

My teeth start to chatter. I'm freezing cold and something is happening to my perceptions, as if the volume of the voices in the room has been turned up and the action has been slowed down. My timing is off. Have minutes passed or seconds?

"It was more like a bow, the kind of thing a woman would—"

"Objection!" Benjamin rises beside me. "The witness is drawing a conclusion."

"Sustained."

"Detective, were there fingerprints on all these pieces of evidence? Let's list them, one by one. The pill vials?"

"Yes."

"Whose fingerprints?"

"It has been stipulated that only the defendant's fingerprints were on the vials."

"Genny Haviland's?"

"Yes."

"Were there fingerprints on the glass or the cups in the sink?"

"No, they had been washed."

"Were there fingerprints on the plastic bag covering Mr. Gabriel's head?"

"Yes, Genny Haviland's fingerprints were on the bag."

"Did you find anything else, Detective?"

"Yes, we found a strand of Genny Haviland's hair twisted in the knot of the twine."

Several members of the jury react with disgust.

"It's all right," Benjamin whispers to me. "Of course your fingerprints would be on the pill vials, the bag, your hair twisted in the twine—you helped him, didn't you? Don't worry."

And then he sees I'm not worried, that he's not reassuring me, only himself. I'm simply an observer here, just watching, waiting for this trial to build to its conclusion, hoping that when the end comes it will bring with it some kind of closure and perhaps allow me, finally, to feel loss, horror, and perhaps the full impact of what has happened.

"Okay." Linda picks up a piece of paper from the table and reads it. "Let's backtrack, Detective. What circumstances brought you to Slade Gabriel's loft that Tuesday morning?"

"About ten A.M. we received a phone call from Miss Stephanie Wallace. She was overwrought and hysterical having just discovered her employer's body. Detective Corello and I drove over to the residence, questioned Miss Wallace, examined the scene, and called the coroner."

"When did you first have reason to speak to the defendant?"

"The next day, Wednesday, September 20, around nine-thirty or ten in the morning."

"Can you describe that meeting for us?"

"The meeting took place at Miss Haviland's parents' apartment on Central Park West where she was temporarily staying."

"What was the purpose of that meeting?"

"To inform her of Mr. Gabriel's death."

"How did she respond?"

"She'd already been told by Miss Wallace sometime the day before."

"Have you had much experience with bereaved lovers and friends, Detective?"

"Unfortunately, yes."

"Based on your experience what was Miss Haviland's reaction—"

"Objection. Your Honor, please!"

"Sustained." The judge once again takes his glasses off and rubs them with his handkerchief. "Please, Miss Zavidow, you know better than that."

Linda doesn't react to the reprimand, just comes back with her next question. "Detective King, please describe the rest of your meeting with the defendant."

"We asked Miss Haviland if she knew of anyone who might have wanted to harm Mr. Gabriel. She seemed surprised we suspected he'd been killed. Upon questioning her further, Miss Haviland told us she believed Mr. Gabriel had committed suicide. Even asked us if we had found the note.

"Neither Detective Corello nor I had said anything about the scene of the crime, no information had as yet been released, but Miss Haviland knew he'd taken pills, knew about the plastic bag. Either she had set up the murder to imitate a suicide and was lying—"

Benjamin interrupts the testimony. "Your Honor, I object. Once again, the detective's drawing a conclusion."

"Sustained."

"Have you found a note, Detective King?" Linda asks.

"No, there is no suicide note."

"What other reasons led you to believe Mr. Gabriel's death was not self-induced?"

"He didn't touch the pill vials. And Miss Haviland had plenty of reasons to want him—"

"Your Honor, I object," Benjamin interrupts.

"Sustained."

"Detective King, after that meeting Wednesday morning, when was the next time you had occasion to see Miss Haviland?"

"At the funeral the next day," he answers.

"You mean Slade Gabriel's funeral, Detective?"

ELEVEN

The service was scheduled to start at ten o'clock in the morning on Thursday at Frank E. Campbell's on 81st Street and Madison Avenue, but at nine-fifty we were still in the car on the corner of 80th Street, stuck in a double line of twenty-five other black limousines all inching their way up the block. Slade Gabriel's funeral had generated as big a traffic jam as any one of those record-breaking auctions at Sotheby's or Christie's in the late '80s, before the crash.

It had taken only seventy-two hours for the pundits to declare Gabriel's death symbolic of New York City's demise as the center of the art world. No great New York City artist had died since Andy Warhol almost ten years before and Gabriel's death was simply the right death at the right time, coinciding with gallery closings, disappointing auctions where reserves weren't met, and a fall season of openings that so far had generated little enthusiasm.

When our car finally pulled up in front of the red brick building the crowd surged forward. These were the celebrity hunters who gathered wherever more than four black limos lined up. And while some might have recognized Gabriel's name, I doubted any of them knew what he did. Gabriel had never had one of those culturally explosive retrospectives the city's museums were famous for.

With a gloved hand, a uniformed doorman opened the white

doors and my father, my mother, and I walked into the colonial style foyer.

People came up to embrace me. I think someone squeezed my shoulder and someone else grasped my hand. My father put his arm around my back, bolstering me up and my mother whispered in my ear, "You are all right, Genevieve, aren't you?"

"Yes," I lied. It was the first time since she'd returned home that she'd asked, there among the crowd of acquaintances and strangers, where I couldn't really tell her anyway. Of course I wasn't all right. I was merely conscious of activity going on around me, of seeing through a veil of fog, unable to connect to any of it.

"Genevieve," my mother said taking me by the elbow, "come, let's take these seats."

Sitting down in the pew, in the chapel—not a church but as close as I had come to one in many years—I thought suddenly of my nanny, Marie. Unlike my mother who has always worn a size six, Marie was a buxom woman with wide hips and a full stomach. I remember her holding me, smelling her buttery scent, reaching out to touch the black onyx cross she always wore, and hearing her fervent prayers.

By the time Gabriel's funeral service began, twenty minutes late, all the seats had been taken and many people were forced to stand, jammed into a space that couldn't accommodate them. Despite the air conditioning, a heat had started to build. Still cold—I had been cold for days—I would have welcomed heat but not this suffocating heat, full of human scents and smells. Seated around us and lined up in the outside aisles were faces I recognized, but no one I cared to see. Whether you knew Gabriel or not, if you mattered—as an artist, collector, critic, or dealer—you were in that room sweating into your Armani suit, taking a tissue out of your Chanel bag, or—if you'd come up from downtown—clasping your hands behind your black jeans and casting your eyes downward toward your Doc Martens.

The service was short. No priest or minister or rabbi spoke. Art was the only religion practiced and the eulogy was delivered by my father.

"I've never met a man who was more passionate about his art, treated it with more reverence, or sacrificed more for its purity. Who never compromised or lowered his standards. Which is why," my father said, directing his words to me, "Slade Gabriel will never die. He breathes in every color he ever laid down on canvas. All we have to do is look at one of his paintings and he is summoned up before us, bursting forth with energy. Many of you here probably heard Gabriel ranting at one time or another about how he thought art was dying, about how, in the '90s, it had nowhere left to go, that art had outlived itself. I think he was wrong, that his paintings prove he was wrong. Isn't every one of them a reaffirmation of life—and isn't that in itself a reaffirmation of art?"

Straightening up as if finished, he caught himself, remembered something and continued: "But paintings are not all we have left of Slade Gabriel, there is his lovely daughter, Lizzie, and her daughter, his granddaughter, Sophie. Indeed Slade Gabriel has left us a legacy and with it his immortality is ensured for decades to come."

In the first row, Lizzie bowed her head and her shoulders shook. Her mother, Gabriel's ex-wife, pulled her daughter close and Lizzie leaned on her shoulder. Beside me, my mother's hands rested in her lap. I must have seemed brave, not crying, not in need of comfort. Still sleepwalking, the distance between me and everything happening around me hadn't diminished. I couldn't connect to the funeral. It was a public spectacle—not a place for me to say good-bye to Gabriel, even if I had known how.

My father returned to his seat beside me and his arm encircled my shoulder. From where we sat, I could see the closed curved top of the coffin gleaming in the chapel's subdued light. I waited to be overcome with emotion, for feeling to fill up the void. Gabriel is in that box, I said to myself, but still no tears came.

As people around us filed out, I followed my parents into the aisle, but then instead of turning right, toward the exit, I turned left, into the oncoming crowd, and walked back toward the casket.

So overbearing was the scent of the flowers, I was immediately nauseated. I swallowed, wet my lips, and put my hands out. The wood was smooth like silk. My bandaged hands made me clumsy as I tried to find a grip. I wanted so badly to lift the lid, to see him one last time and to tell him . . .

"Let's go, Genny," my father said as he took my arm to lead me away.

I struggled against my father. It was pointless, but I persisted.

"I have to see him."

"You can't darling, his family doesn't want the coffin opened."

"I don't care, I have to tell him . . . how sorry . . ."

Forcefully, my father pulled me away, away from the coffin and the flowers, toward the aisle where Detective King stood, watching us.

My father ushered me past him and several other people who'd stopped to stare at me, through the foyer and into the street where my mother was waiting. Hit with the obscene sunshine, I shielded my eyes and saw Lizzie, carrying her baby in her arms, flanked by her husband and her mother.

Lizzie stepped toward me. "I know—" her lips twisted, "—that you killed him—"

My mother stepped between us and blocked Lizzie from me, and my father—his arm still around my back—conducted me several yards down the street where our car was waiting in line. But even after I couldn't see her anymore, I could still hear her, "—you killed my father."

The detective heard her, everyone else there did, too, but when my parents and I got into the car none of us talked about it. In fact, none of us spoke at all until Jerry, my father's driver, had maneuvered us out of the traffic and turned west on 83rd Street.

"Samuel has put me in touch with a good lawyer, Genny. His name is Benjamin Marks and we have an appointment with him tomorrow morning." My father's hands unclenched. "Goddamn it, I just can't believe you're embroiled in this. Didn't Gabriel realize he was putting you in jeopardy?"

"*Shh,* Jonathan, it won't do any good now," my mother tried to soothe him.

We turned onto Fifth Avenue and passed the Metropolitan Museum of Art, where I'd spent time with Gabriel, and with my father long before that. The museum's curator of Twentieth-Century Art had been at the funeral home and had stopped and spoken to my father before the ceremony. They'd huddled for several minutes. It wouldn't have surprised me to find they'd been plotting a retrospective.

"Why does Genevieve need to see a lawyer?" my mother asked.

"Samuel wants her to be prepared if the police press charges."

Driving down Fifth Avenue, the park was on our right and though the temperature was still warm, the leaves were beginning to turn; bright yellows and strong reds, colors Gabriel hadn't used in his palette since the seventies. I pressed my palms together until I felt the pain. I didn't want to think of Gabriel, not now, not in the car, not until I was by myself.

"Why not wait until it is necessary to see a lawyer? Why upset Genevieve any more than she is already upset?"

"Avoiding it won't make it go away, Maguy."

"Surely a few days more won't matter, just to give Genevieve some time."

They continued talking about me as if I weren't there until I interrupted to tell them I wanted to go home, not home with them, but downtown, to the loft.

My father insisted that my mother go with me, to make sure I'd be all right. I agreed only after she promised not to stay, not even to walk inside with me. I didn't want anyone to displace the air any more than it already had been disturbed. I wanted what was left of Gabriel's breath to myself.

Just before we dropped off my father, he announced he was going to arrange to have the movers come for Gabriel's paintings.

"No, not yet," I said.

"They're too valuable to keep in the loft. They should be in the gallery."

"Please, not yet." I put my hand out and stroked his wrist. My mother turned away. It's not hard to get what you want from a man when you know his secrets. It didn't matter that this was my father. He was a man who wanted to take something from me.

"Genny, it's not safe for them to remain in the loft."

"Gabriel always kept them there. It was safe before."

"But it's not now."

"Just for a few weeks?" My father's skin was softer than most men's, the texture finer.

"Two weeks, that's all," he said just before he got out.

Watching him walk toward the building, I saw that his step was quick and his posture straight. In the last few days, some of the depression and anxiety he had been carrying for the past six or seven months had lifted. Now that Gabriel was dead, my father's business problems were over.

As the car continued downtown, I imagined my father ensconced in his study making lists of Gabriel's canvases, figuring out which two or three to sell now to titillate the market while he hoarded the rest for Gabriel's posthumous show.

"Perhaps you would like to come with me when I go back to Paris?" my mother asked.

"Why would I want to leave here?"

"To get away from the memories for a while."

Letting my head fall back against the car seat, I closed my eyes on an image of red hair spread like a lick of flame across a pillow. I tried to form a question and then lost it as the car stopped in front of the Greene Street loft. Despite her promise, my mother insisted on seeing that I got upstairs all right.

We entered the vestibule and took the elevator up to the fifth floor. Although the police were finished with the crime scene, the front door was still sealed with yellow plastic police tape. Slashing at it with the edge of my key, my bandaged hands became entangled in the sticky ribbons. Helping me, my mother peeled the tape off and pulled it away.

I put my key in the lock, opened the steel door, and was assaulted by the familiar scent of oil paints and turpentine and then the strange smell of something musty and foul.

"Stephanie must have forgotten to take out the garbage," I said, stepping inside. As bad as the smell was, the disarray was worse. Nothing was in its right place; the four chairs usually around the dining table were pulled out haphazardly. One had fallen over and lay on its side. The couch had been moved backward and left at an angle, its cushions and pillows strewn on the floor.

Far more disturbing were how all the paintings—at least thirty— had been pulled out of the slots where Gabriel stored them. They were stacked back to front or front to front and leaning against the wall or just piled recklessly on top of one another—all in danger of being scratched or scraped.

"Animals!" my mother hissed as she picked up a painting by its outer edges, slid it back into its protective compartment and then moved on to the next one, unaware that I, too, was leaning, like those paintings, against the wall, unable to move.

In the middle of the loft, stood Gabriel's easel. Empty. His last painting, missing.

"A painting's gone," I finally said.

"Are you sure?"

"There was a canvas on the easel. It's not there. It was his last painting."

To me it was his last painting and that was enough reason to panic, but my mother had to also be thinking about the money. While he was alive a good-sized Gabriel went for two hundred thousand dollars. After he died, the price at least doubled.

A missing painting was a fortune lost.

And so we started pulling out the paintings my mother had put away. It took us almost a half hour to go through all the canvases, but we finally found that last painting.

Unlike the completely abstract gardens of the '70s and '80s, Gabriel's newer works were more clearly articulated and the bright brash colors of the older style had been replaced by a darker, more enigmatic palette. These were night paintings shot through with light.

He had told me he wanted to create an iconography of light.

Don't focus—let your eyes roam around the canvas. Fill your eyes with the composition. Can you make it out? It's a night garden of blues, purples, and greens; tangled, confused, and lonely. Now look harder—it would be desolate but for those figures—yes they are figures—naked and intertwined, illuminated by a single shaft of light. Follow it . . . upwards . . . do you see? Yes. There. The suggestion of fibrillating wings, stilled just now before ascending and heading home.

Of all his gardens only this one was populated, and more than once, when he had been working on it, he'd cursed at the elusive flesh tones.

Unaccustomed to painting people, he'd finally asked me to sit for him.

Naked, I watched him alternate between studying my skin and the colors he was mixing on his palette and then on the canvas until he got it right.

When he finished he turned to me and, with the same smile I'd seen on his lips only when we made love, told me to come and look.

Gabriel had done more than get the flesh tones right—the man's skin radiated vitality, the woman's shone with sensuality. She was silk, he was rope. You wanted to reach out and touch them. You understood why they were touching each other.

While I continued to look—lost in the composition—Gabriel stood behind me and pressed the whole length of his clothed body against my naked one. He kissed the back of my neck and traced the line of my spine with his tongue. His fingers grazed, stroking up and down my arms, around my waist, between my thighs—streaking paint all over my body.

Reaching behind me I tugged at the zipper on his jeans and the buttons on his shirt. Then the two of us, naked, intertwined, wrapped up in each other—mirroring the figures he had painted—made love in front of his last garden.

"Gabriel once told me that we all have an Eden in us. What keeps us outside of it are our worries, fears: our preoccupation with mortality . . . you find it when you find yourself. Following someone else's path won't get you there."

"That certainly sounds like Gabriel," my mother said sarcastically.

"What does that mean?" I turned on her.

"I'm sorry, Genevieve, but you are glorifying his selfishness instead of seeing how much damage it caused."

"Why do you think he was selfish? Because he wouldn't give in to someone else's values?"

"Oh please. He was arrogant and smug."

"No, he was passionate and dedicated."

"We see it differently, Genevieve."

For the first time I heard disgust in her voice. Directed at me or Gabriel—I couldn't be sure. "I can't believe what you are saying. You revere artists. You understand them. You care about what they create."

"It's what he destroyed that makes me hate him," she said.

There's pity in her eyes and it's directed toward me. I'm torn between loving her and defending Gabriel.

"You think I was his victim, don't you?"

"Aren't you?" my mother asked.

I returned to putting away the paintings. And then so did she. We worked in silence until finished.

"It's so dusty in here still. Let me call Bertha and have her come down to do a more thorough cleanup," she said once we were done.

"No, I don't want anyone else here. I'll do it later. Tomorrow. Next week. What difference does it make?"

Taking off her black St. Laurent suit jacket, she hung it over a chair and started in the kitchen, putting away the dishes left in the rack, scrubbing the counter top and throwing away the spoiled food she found in the refrigerator. I stood a moment watching her, mesmerized by her movements, absorbed by her the way I had been when I was a child. Why was she so fascinating to me: a mystery I was still trying to solve?

Filling a bucket with water so hot the steam dampened her hair and tightened the curls around her face, she sprinkled the wooden floors with the water and then swept them clean. I'd never seen her do housework before. Perhaps she never had, but she'd certainly seen Bertha do it and if my mother knew nothing else, she knew how to pretend. Hadn't she done it for years as a wife and mother? She had all the actions down, but I knew, beneath the surface, without the light on, she was someone quite different.

Finished with the studio, she went into the bedroom area behind the screen, and like her shadow, I followed, watching as she swept up a pile of lint and dust and dirt. Suddenly she stopped—sniffed the air—put down the broom, approached the bed, and began to strip it.

"Leave that," I said.

"No, it's soiled," she said, continuing to pull at the sheet.

"I don't want you to touch our bed," I yelled and pushed her away.

"Listen to me," she said, rubbing her arms where I'd been too hard. "The sheets, they are dirty from when Gabriel died. Soiled. Can't you smell?"

The bad smell was Gabriel's?

I stepped away, sat down on the floor of our partitioned bedroom and looked up at my mother—the way a child does—watching the muscles tense in her thin arms as she struggled to pull the sheeting off, wrapped it into a bundle, lifted it up, and took it outside to the hall.

When she returned she opened all the windows and let the wind in to blow away the stench. And then my mother, so much smaller than I, wearing that good black wool suit, sheer black hose, and high-heeled black shoes, sat down next to me on the floor.

"Are you certain you will be all right here by yourself? You won't become depressed?"

This time I wouldn't lie to protect her from the feelings she was afraid for me to have. "I don't know, but you can go."

"First, let me help you make the bed," she said.

"No, I'll do it later."

"I could go to the grocery across the street and get you some food."

"No, I'll go."

"Isn't there something you need?" she asked almost desperately, but I had never learned how to ask her for what I needed.

We left the loft together, my mother carrying the soiled bundle of bedclothes. Downstairs, I lifted the silver garbage can cover and she dropped in both the sheets and comforter.

When we kissed good-bye, my mother's cheek was soft and slightly hollow and the feel of it made me sad.

In the Korean market on the corner, I walked up and down the aisles picking up food: a carton of milk, a head of lettuce, a tomato, and a container of cottage cheese. I picked up two baking potatoes from the bin and then put one back. I was choosing simple things with tastes and textures that wouldn't surprise me. I didn't want to savor my food now; I'd eat because I was hungry and needed to be filled up. I bought a package of Jarlsberg cheese, a box of graham crackers, and a bag of popcorn that I started eating in line, chewing it, crunching down on the hard kernels, smelling the butter, thinking of my old nanny, Marie, who in her own way was gone now, too, like Gabriel was gone.

I shouldn't have been in a grocery store that afternoon, I should have been at a cemetery, but there wasn't going to be a burial. Gabriel had wanted to be cremated, like his father had been when his plane blew up. And also like his father, he had his ashes thrown over the sea. I hadn't been invited. I wasn't family. I tried to imagine the proceedings but my mind couldn't form the images.

Back in the loft, after I'd put away the food, I noticed the message light blinking on the answering machine and pressed the play button: my friend Tory had called. So had Ham, asking me please, to call him. And there were messages from my associate producer and several friends of Gabriel's whom I'd gotten to know over the last year that we'd been together. When the last message ended, I lifted the lid and put out my finger to press the erase button that was positioned between two other buttons: the one on the right was marked outgoing message record and the one on the left was marked outgoing message play.

Tentatively, I depressed the play button.

The tape hissed as I rewound it and then— "You've reached the studio, but no one's here so leave a name and number and I'll get back to you as soon as possible." The voice was gravelly, sliding down rocks, traveling through time to get to me. Gabriel's voice. As I played the message over and over, listening to him say those words, I tried to hear him say other words, but I couldn't.

After playing the message six or seven times, worried I'd wear it out, I popped the small plastic cassette out of the machine and carried it—as if I were carrying his heart—into the bedroom. Emptying my jewelry out of a velvet-lined box, dumping rings and necklaces on the still unmade bed, I carefully laid the tape down on the thick green velvet and closed the lid. Lifting the box in my hands, I held it against my chest.

In my life, I had been without him far more than I had ever been with him. Now, he was gone again.

TWELVE

I'd taken a leave from work and for fourteen days all I'd done was sit and stare at Gabriel's paintings, first one and then another, yearning for the day to be over and have it be night because the only feelings I had came while I slept.

Hating how much I craved my dreams and how much I resented waking from them, I fought sleep and courted it at the same time. During those nights, in my sleep, those first three weeks after Gabriel's death, I had violent orgasms. My hands clenched between my legs, the sheets pushed down exposing my skin, I moved up and down, my face buried in the pillow, my heels kicking the air. Drenched in sweat I felt his weight on me. His fingers, not mine, made me come. When I woke, my lips would be bruised as if we had been kissing and I could smell his scent on my skin.

That Wednesday morning, when the downstairs buzzer rang, I ignored its invading signal—there was no one I wanted to see—I was lost in a painting, a deep maroon garden, its night-blooming flowers illuminated by Gabriel's luminous light.

The intercom buzzed again and finally I answered it. "Hello?"

"Manhattan Art Transport, can you let us up?"

I pulled my hand away as if I'd been burned, but immediately the buzzing started again. My father hadn't warned me, hadn't given me enough time. I wasn't ready to let him take away the paintings; they were all that was left; they were heart-beating, breathing, fucking, laughing Gabriel alive.

The assertive buzzing continued. I imagined the man in the vestibule downstairs where the paint has peeled and the building shows its hundred years. He must have been leaning against the button, a small round black button no bigger than those candy buttons that came on skinny rolls of paper, row after row of different rainbow colored dots of sugar, that you peeled off and let melt on the tip of your tongue when you were a kid. Actually I didn't like that kind of candy. I loved the big red wax lips.

My father always laughed at me when I wore those lips. Laughed and asked me to dance. Then he'd bend down low enough to take me in his arms, hum a waltz, and swirl me around the room, lightly, expertly, and gracefully. He'd end the dance with an amorous kiss on those red waxy lips. A long movie star kiss. Then he would lick his own lips and in a mock theatrical voice say, "My dear, how sweet you are."

The man downstairs was still buzzing, not like most people do with evenly spaced taps, or staccato rhythms. He was leaning on the button—one long incessant pressure.

What could I do? Would ignoring him make him go away? And if it did, how long would it be before he came back?

"Hello?" my voice was unusually loud.

"Miss Haviland, please, let us up."

"I didn't make an appointment with a moving company. You didn't make an appointment with me. Did you?"

"I only make the pickups, Miss Haviland, I don't do the appointments. Is there a problem?"

Yes, there was a problem. "There's been a mistake. I didn't arrange to have anything moved," I said and hung up.

I'd have to call my father and convince him to wait, but what if he insisted? Could I hide one or two of the smaller paintings from him? Which ones? Suddenly I was lost in the landscapes around me.

There were almost forty paintings there, at least two dozen done in a ten-month frenzy after the accident. And those were the ones that most attracted me.

God, when you looked at these paintings you smelled the gardens, felt the wind, and sometimes you could even hear the fibrillating wings.

Stand in front of almost any other artist's work and you are aware of looking at the canvas—but these paintings invited you in and entering them you were absorbed by their light—Gabriel's luminous light—that in those last months had become some kind of messiah to him.

These were the paintings that had so angered my father when he had first seen them because they challenged what Gabriel had done before. Now he coveted them to satisfy the demand Gabriel's death had created for his work.

To my father it had become as simple as supply and demand.

Almost a half hour had passed and then the buzzing started up again. I was determined not to answer it and after a few more futile blasts, it stopped. Only to be followed, within minutes, by the phone ringing.

Since Gabriel's death, I preferred to let the machine take my calls. Screening enabled me to be invisible, to hide in the loft away from everyone's questions and theories. Except for my parents, I called most people back during the day when I knew they'd be out—it was easier. Answering machines couldn't ask me how I was doing, when I would be coming back to work, or why the police hadn't cleared up the mystery the papers were still reporting—and finally found the note.

The machine made a series of clicks and then a voice came through the microphone. "Genny, it's Benjamin Marks, I'm across the street. Please pick up the phone. Genny?"

His office had called twice that morning and I'd forgotten to return either call. Now, his voice was urgent.

I picked up the receiver. "Yes, Benjamin?"

"I'm downstairs. Can you let me up?"

My father and I had met with Benjamin Marks the day after the funeral in his modest downtown office, only two blocks from the court buildings. A big, boisterous man with intelligent eyes, and a stellar reputation, he'd asked questions for the better part of two hours and then agreed to take my case if I was charged.

I buzzed Benjamin up and waited for him by the front door. He followed me in, barely glancing at the large canvases leaning against the west and north walls, blocking the loft's windows, keeping out the sunlight.

"I don't have good news, Genny. The district attorney's office has decided to charge you," he said.

"Why?"

"Can we sit down?"

We pulled out seats next to each other at the dining table, and Benjamin shifted his chair so he could look at me. Behind him was a painting of a garden with gray green trees and a nebula of light clearing the darkness.

I pressed the ring I wore—the carved oval gold ring Gabriel had always worn until he had given it to me—into my cheek, feeling the edges of the metal depress my skin, hit my jaw. It was not enough pain, I pressed the ring deeper into my flesh.

"You said they wouldn't think assisted suicide was worth prosecuting. You said you'd be able to make a deal."

"They're not charging you with assisted suicide. This has caught me completely by surprise. . . . Genny, I'm sorry but the district attorney's office is charging you with murder." A catch in his voice made it sound as if he were asking me instead of telling me.

"They think by helping Gabriel kill himself I murdered him?"

"No, they are charging you with murder in the second degree. Murder in the second degree is intent to kill, Genny. They don't believe Gabriel had any intention of committing suicide."

I moved my chair back, scraping the legs against the wooden floor. And then moved it even farther away.

The gray garden was filled with ancient trees, gnarled branches, withered leaves. An animal howled, a strong wind whipped through the branches, snapping them. Glass shattered.

The animal was me. The glass had been full of water and sitting in front of me on the dining-room table. Benjamin bent over and picking up the shards, carefully put the smaller pieces inside the larger ones.

"What is going to happen to me now?"

He put the broken pieces on the table. "The police will formally arrest you, they can come here—"

"No!"

"Or I can take you to the precinct and you can turn yourself in."

Finding the distance again, I watched myself at the table with Benjamin Marks surrounded by Gabriel's paintings. My palms started to itch and I rubbed them on my knees. The light glinted on the broken glass. I could slit my skin open with the sharp edge of that glass. It seemed a plausible alternative, not the first time nor the last time that I earnestly thought about killing myself and escaping.

"Will I go to jail?" Jail, murder, suicide, killing; were these words describing events in *my* life?

In detail, Benjamin explained what procedures would take place during the next twenty-four hours and what I could expect after.

Before we left the loft, I went to the bathroom and in the mirror, noticed the red brand on my cheek, the imprint of Gabriel's ring. I touched the indentations on my skin and an hour later, when the police took my photograph, the red mark still hadn't disappeared.

Benjamin had told me the police would take away anything I brought with me to the station but I didn't take off Gabriel's ring, I wanted it with me until the last possible moment, until I had to give it up. And I wanted something else with me, too.

From the bathroom I went into the bedroom area, opened the closet, and searched through the shelves, throwing underwear and socks on the floor, overturning boxes, shifting through scarves, finally finding a clump of twisted leather belts, pearls, beads, and chains. It took several minutes to untangle, but I extricated a black onyx cross on a gold chain that Marie had given me.

Freed from the mess, I held out the cross and let it dangle in the air. Then lifting it over my head, I put it around my neck and dropped it inside my sweater. It hung down low beneath my breasts, cold against my flesh, but it connected me to Marie, to a time in my life before there were unspeakable memories and only the promise of miracles.

In the cab, on the way to the precinct house, Benjamin asked me the same question he'd asked me every day since I'd first met with him two weeks before: "Genny, are you sure you've searched everywhere for Gabriel's note?"

"In every sketchbook, through all the papers, through all the drawing pads, it's not there! It's just not there. I saw it though. I saw the envelope—stamped and addressed. Doesn't his losing it or forgetting to send it prove what I said is true? Doesn't it show how truly sick he had become that he could have forgotten the one thing that was the most crucial? The suicide note?"

"Yes it does," Benjamin said confidently. But I knew what he was doing, I knew how men sounded when they were protecting me. But he couldn't protect me from the procedures that awaited.

It was Detective King who escorted Benjamin Marks and me through a series of dingy hallways at the 10th Precinct house and into a small cubicle where he offered both of us plastic chairs. For the next fifteen minutes he asked me questions and filled out forms. My answers came automatically: my full name, where I lived, my date of birth, where I worked. After that another policeman came and took a Polaroid photograph of me to prove I hadn't been roughed up.

A female officer took me to yet another room and patted me down and then returned me to King who escorted us back outside, where Benjamin and I got in a blue and white police car and were driven uptown to another police building on 35th Street between Eighth and Ninth Avenues.

The street was littered with papers and bottles, garbage overflowed wire garbage cans. Despite the ten or eleven police cars parked in the street and up on the sidewalk, a group of middle-aged black men loitered by a hydrant, sharing a bottle from a brown paper bag.

Inside the station house another policeman took my fingerprints. There were so many of these men, all rendered the same by their blue shirts and navy pants. They all ate and drank and fucked and laughed when they were out of these uniforms, but in their official dark blue they were cut off from their feelings. The flash went off for my official police portrait: my mug shot.

While they processed my paperwork, Benjamin tried to talk to me but I couldn't concentrate on any of his words. I tried to think of a prayer to say. Once I had believed in God . . . once I had believed in my father . . . and in Gabriel. . .

"We're going to have to lock her up until the arrest report comes back from Albany," a policewoman was saying to Benjamin.

"It won't be long, Genny. I've checked and the computers are up so there won't be any excessive delays. As soon as the report comes in, they'll transfer you to the Criminal Court building for your arraignment and I'll be there waiting for you. Do you understand? Everything will be all right."

That morning, I was trying to believe in Benjamin Marks.

As the policewoman led me away down a long sloping hallway I tried to separate, to leave, to live behind my eyes. Pressing my palms together tight, I inhaled the pain. The policewoman opened an iron door and I walked into the holding cell.

Benjamin had taken me through every step of what would happen. But what was different about the prison, the procedures, and the police was that now it was real.

Gabriel had argued electronic technology was the only new arena for art, that virtual reality would redefine our society, making human interaction—even sex—unnecessary. We would communicate on a screen and be fulfilled. But neither film nor tape can create the stink of a cell, can confine you to seven square feet of space, can give you the feel of the greasy iron bars or the unforgiving hardness of a jail cell bench.

Two women talked in the cubicle across from mine. The white woman wore a bustier that exposed most of her abundant chest and a short, tight, spandex skirt that exposed her legs and some of her crotch. The Hispanic woman wore a purple catsuit, which showed the bulges of her belly, thighs, and breasts. An open zipper ensured that no one missed her cleavage. Their sweat and cheap perfume commingled with a pervasive smell of urine and stale body odor left over from women who'd been here before.

"You some kinda uptown girl?" the Hispanic one asked.

"Lookit how scared she is. Shit, man, she's gonna pee in her pants. You never been in jail before? Hey, this your first time? You a virgin?" The white woman laughed at her own joke.

"You think she's a virgin?"

"Shit. Just lookit her shaking. Of course it's her first time. She's no pro."

"You're no pro?" the Hispanic woman asked me.

Slowly, I shook my head no.

She leaned her head against the bars and inspected me more carefully than she had before. "So what'd they get you for?"

When I didn't answer, the white woman, who was lying on the bench with her arms dangling down, picked up her head and asked me if I'd stolen something.

I should have lied. It would have been easier to say, yes, I stole a silk scarf from Sak's Fifth Avenue at eleven o'clock this morning and got caught.

"Fucking bitch. I asked you a question. What'd you get caught on?"

"Murder," I whispered through the bars.

The white woman wasn't sure if she believed me. Lifting her head, she examined me, searching without shame for some physical evidence, stripping me down to see if the word fit.

I turned my back to them and faced the dirty gray wall. Lowering my lids, listening to my own breathing, I stopped seeing and hearing the two women.

Gabriel would—no, don't think of Gabriel. Not here! Don't think about what's going to happen next. Don't think of the fear knotting in your stomach. Don't feel the cramps. Think of . . . the books my nanny Marie gave me about the lives of the saints and read to me every night before I went to sleep.

Saint Teresa was a favorite. Violently in love with Jesus Christ, she beat herself with a whip and wore a hair shirt. Blood dripped down her stomach, scars formed on her flesh, and then she reopened them all to show Him how much she was willing to suffer in His name. During the night, she interrupted her sleep to wake and say prayers to Him. Kneeling on the hard stone floor in the convent, she pressed her hands together and lowered her head. Teresa had a single black habit, one nightshirt, a Bible, and a rosary. She lived in a tiny room that contained an iron bed with a rough horsehair mattress and one blanket and, except for a chest of drawers, there was no other furniture. The walls were blank except for her beloved crucifix. And yet, believing her pathetic cell was still too comfortable, she slept on the cold stone floor. Stripping her room of every comfort, she lived as harshly as she could bear, proving with her sacrifice how great was her passion. She gladly gave up the world to be with Jesus, her dead lover.

Would I be as glad to give the world up to be with mine?

"Here's your lunch." A guard slid a plastic tray through a slot on the floor: a carton of milk and a bologna sandwich on white bread. An interested roach skittered toward the food.

Somewhere nearby, a woman farted. Someone shouted at her. I stopped breathing through my nose.

About fifteen minutes later, a policewoman opened my cell door, handcuffed me, and ushered me back out through the halls. On the street she led me into the backseat of a blue and white police car. I gulped the outside air, forgetting all except that I could breathe again without gagging. But then I noticed people on the street peering into the car. Bystanders became inquisitors with the same questions in their eyes the two women in the other cell had asked: What have you done? Why are you here?

A neon clock glowed in the window of a deli. Was it only three o'clock? People in the street walked, swinging their arms freely, unconscious of the movement. My palms were pressed together lightly. I separated them slowly . . . an inch apart, an inch and a half . . . I could go that far . . . two inches . . . three . . . then the metal cut into my wrists. I started again from the beginning, palms pressed together, then slowly separating, tricking myself into thinking there was nothing holding me back until the cuffs stopped me. I'd worn bracelets and watches, known the feel of gold and silver against my skin, but no metal had ever been as cold or had weighed as much as those handcuffs.

The police car pulled up to the iron gate in front of the side entrance of the New York City Criminal Court building. A freckle-faced cop came over, leaned into the driver's window, asked for my name, checked it against a list, and then walked back to his post where he pressed a button that started the gate groaning open. He waved us in.

We drove into the concrete courtyard where the back of the Criminal Court building rose up around us. The car stopped at the dirt-streaked glass-enclosed booth and we waited as the cop spoke to someone on a phone, his lips forming the syllables of my name.

A pigeon swooped down in front of the car and flew back up, up past the dingy walls, the grimy windows, up to where the sky must be. I stared until I lost sight of the wings and then a female cop opened the car door and helped me out.

She led me into an old building with cracked white tiles on the walls and floors. After the fresh air in the car, the stale human smell made me gag. Once again, I started to breathe through my mouth.

Although Benjamin had warned me there might be a wait here and that I might have to go into another holding cell, the policewoman led me through a wide door into a courtroom, where, among a dozen other people sitting on wooden benches that reminded me of pews, Benjamin sat, watching for me.

There was a malaise in the room and an undercurrent of chatter; officials and guards carried on different conversations in both English and Spanish while spectators read books, stared straight ahead, or slept.

In the front of the room a court stenographer and a bailiff whispered to each other while the judge, in his official black robes, sat behind his desk, reading that day's *New York Times*. A case was called and a young black boy in sweatpants and a leather jacket and two lawyers all met in front of the judge. I tried to understand the proceedings so I'd know what would happen to me, but everything happened too quickly.

Soon my name and docket number were called and the police-woman who'd escorted me in, told me to get up and go stand in front of the judge. Benjamin and an eager young man wearing a boxy brown suit and a beige striped tie met me there.

The assistant D.A. read the charge of murder in the second degree and requested bail be set at $500,000.

"My client has no previous record, Your Honor. She is not a flight risk and, except for this charge, she has never had any altercations with the law. We request no bail and that she be released on her own recognizance."

I concentrated to stay focused, but my glance ricocheted around the courtroom, from the judge, to the flag, to the clerk typist and her fast moving fingers, to the late afternoon light coming through the window.

Someone's feet shuffled on the wooden floor, a purse snapped open. I heard a sneeze behind me, then I heard my own breath, strangely even and controlled. I hadn't been prepared for my bizarre detachment: the absurd sense that I was in a theater watching some-one else's drama unfold.

The judge set the bail at $100,000 and while Benjamin made arrangements with the bail bondsman so that I could be released, I waited patiently, my hands folded in my lap, the words *flight risk* re-peating in my head.

The only place I would run if I could was into one of Gabriel's paintings. Run deep into his luminous light and never leave.

THIRTEEN

New York City Criminal Court Building, Room 1317
Friday, December 4, 1992, 4:30 P.M.

There is a sense of hyper-reality to these court proceedings. If they were paintings, the people would be larger than life, their expressions exaggerated to the point of the grotesque, the colors intensified and saturated.

Linda has asked for a five-minute recess to confer with her cocounsel and while we all wait, I avert my eyes from the jury, the twenty-four-eyed monster that follows my every move, notes every twitch, and registers each sigh.

I'll never get to talk to these men and women outside of this courtroom, never meet their husbands, wives, lovers, parents, children, but they will meet mine and will know things about me when we are finished here that I have never told anyone else—all without my consent or my desire. And after my life with Gabriel has been exposed they will declare me guilty or innocent. I can't even guess which. It doesn't matter.

Unable to stop myself, I look back at them. The businessman in the second row is clasping and unclasping his hands impatiently as he does during every break, and the foreperson, a black woman in her fifties, is unconsciously playing with her charm bracelet, counting and recounting the five baby booties hanging from the chain as if she is saying a kind of rosary.

Benjamin didn't want her on the jury, didn't think she'd be sympathetic, but there were others he wanted even less.

"I have no more questions for Detective King, Your Honor." Linda sits down at the prosecutor's table.

Judge Bailey asks Benjamin if he has any questions for the witness.

Benjamin stands. "I'd like to ask you, Detective King, if it is possible that the reason Genny Haviland's fingerprints were all over the vials of Seconal and the plastic bag and her hair was in the twine was because she helped Slade Gabriel commit suicide?"

"Based on the circumstances surrounding—"

"Detective, please, yes or no, is it possible she opened the vials, shook out the pills, and handed them to Mr. Gabriel?"

"It's possible but in my—"

"Detective, I asked you, yes or no?"

"Well, yes, but—"

"And is it possible Mr. Gabriel asked her to put the bag and the twine on his bedside table before she left the room?" Benjamin asks.

"Yes, but again—" Detective King answers reluctantly.

"And is it possible that a strand of Genny Haviland's hair got twisted in the twine as she laid it down?"

"Yes, but I really—"

"And is it possible that a man can tie a piece of twine the same way a woman can tie it?"

The detective's voice had lost some of its emphatic strength by now. "Yes."

"That's all, Detective. Thank you." Benjamin has no more questions. The bailiff tells the witness he may step down. Judge Bailey glances at the clock and calls a clerk over. While they confer, Linda talks to her assistant and beside me, Benjamin takes notes.

In the jury box, the man in the middle of the first row—who could be a sculptor, or maybe an architect, because he always makes shapes with his hands: steeples, boxes—even now he's making a spire—is frowning at me.

Two seats over, an older woman who reminds me of Marie, gazes at me with a sad smile that is as kind as if I were her child here at the defendant's table.

Finished with his conference, Judge Bailey adjourns the court and dismisses us for the weekend.

I leave the courtroom flanked by my parents who protect me from the press of reporters. Outside, in the cold wind, on the steps of the courthouse and on the street below the steps are even more members of the press, shouting questions, snapping pictures, and trying to get close to me with their video units. Resolutely, we march past them, ignoring them. I hold my breath and lower my eyes as instructed by Benjamin who's cautioned me that if I show them anything, it should be sorrow.

Even when we are inside my parents' car, the reporters press up against the window peering in, taking pictures, yelling questions, their breath fogging the windows, but Jerry, the chauffeur, adroitly maneuvers around them and drives off.

On the corner of Canal Street, we get stuck in gridlock and stop. Along the sidewalks, people bundled in heavy coats against the chill December night hurry in and out of Chinese grocery stores, carrying their string bags. The neon Chinese characters and Christmas decorations give the street a festive glow. I have forgotten about the holidays.

"Both of you don't have to come to court every day next week. There must be business at the gallery you have to take care of," I say.

"Brian is handling everything at the gallery," my father answers. This is the first time we've talked since our confrontation during the lunch recess and he's still angry with me.

But his cool tone has no effect on me. I don't try to cajole him out of it as I did as a child. My father's emotions are just one more thing I can't care about anymore.

The traffic moves.

"Is the gallery busy?" I ask.

My parents exchange an embarrassed look. My father defers to my mother.

"Yes, Genevieve, quite busy. There is much interest now for Gabriel's work. We receive phone calls and letters every day requesting information about what paintings are available, inquiring about the next show."

"When will the next show be?"

"After all this is behind us," my mother says too quickly.

I turn on her. "Why are you lying? You know exactly when it will be. You just don't want to tell me. You think it will upset me."

"Won't it upset you?" my mother asks. "It's upsetting you now just to speak of it."

"No, it's not." Yet another lie. What's upsetting me is knowing they'll have to take his paintings away from me for the show and that's what I'm trying to find out about.

"Fine, then, we're planning to open the second week in January," my father says.

I nod, imagining the paintings my father has so reluctantly agreed to let me keep until the end of the trial, paintings he never particularly liked, hanging on the walls of the gallery.

"Is Richard Finder still writing the monograph?" I ask.

"No, Walter Bloom is." My father has named the curator of Twentieth-Century Painting at the Museum of Modern Art. Gabriel would laugh to know how quickly death has elevated his stature.

"This trial is going to be good for the gallery, isn't it?" I ask.

"Why would you say such a horrible thing?" My mother seems shocked.

Now that we're midtown, the traffic slows down again.

"But it's true, isn't it?"

The astonished expression on my father's face silences me.

Has he just figured it out? Didn't he understand from the beginning? Is it possible he's only now put it together and realized this is not an open and shut case; that there is other troubling information that could lead to an entirely different motive and if the assistant D.A. discovers it and uses it, I might be convicted?

The silent interchange between my father and me lasts until my mother decides it has gone on too long. Has she seen the terror flicker in my father's eyes? Has she grasped its implications? Or is she just uncomfortable with another communication she is not sharing?

PART III

What if art is not the great power?
What if art is an excuse to hide from life?

—Helen Humphreys, *Afterimage*

FOURTEEN

104 Greene Street, Apartment 5
Sunday, December 6, 1992, 9:30 A.M.

Last night, like every night since the indictment months ago, I stayed by myself. Captive by choice. Imprisoned in Gabriel's space, his white walls, wide wood-planked floors, and high windows. I paid penance to the painting in front of me, to its deep colors, shining lights, to its mysteries.

I made a salad and scrambled eggs. I eat convenient food for sustenance, not delight. A bottle of wine lasts me almost a week. I allow myself one glass each evening. More and I would slip into an alcoholic daze and dilute my punishment, which I crave as much as I once wanted Gabriel's hands to stroke my body, to breathe his scent, to give myself up to being pleasured by him. This is all I have left of Gabriel that is real, that is tactile: my punishment and his paintings—and the paintings are mine only for the duration of the trial.

To pass the time after eating, I read. Nonfiction—for edification, not escape. Last night it was a book about the sweatshops at the end of the last century when this loft was an artificial-rose factory.

In the late 1800s, New York City was a society centered on production. The working conditions for the men, women, and children in the sweatshops were untenable. The hours were inhuman. Children often worked from seven o'clock in the morning to six o'clock in the evening in badly lit, poorly ventilated, crowded factories.

They made the same items, over and over, because those were the items that sold. Their minds became mechanized, their perceptions dulled, nothing disrupted their work. How different was Gabriel from these children who had to produce?

While I read, I play music written for church services; listening to requiems not for pleasure, but to honor the dead. I no longer watch television, not since the morning after my indictment when I turned on the news and saw an electronic version of Gabriel's face looking at me.

Not until I wake in the dark, feeling like I am falling through black space, do I give in to missing him, aching for him, as if one of my limbs had been torn off my body. Furtively, I try to make myself come picturing his face, his black eyes, the curl of his lips, imagining the smell of him, but I don't orgasm anymore. There is not even that relief.

This morning, remembering the night before and my pathetic longing with shame, I repeat over and over to myself that the past is irretrievably gone and somehow I have to let go, but how can I while the trial continues, while there are still many questions to be asked and answered. . . .

My friend Tory phones. She's called almost every day, always trying to be positive, disappointed when I don't respond. I'm not the same, I tell her, and she says she understands, but I can hear the frustration beneath her words. She doesn't know what to do anymore to try and shake me out of my somnambulist state.

This morning she tells me she was at a party last night and was talking to a friend of her husband's who had a friend Benjamin Marks represented and got off—and this friend's case had been hopeless, but I don't have the energy to react.

After I hang up, I grab my black overcoat off the hook by the door and go out to get the Sunday *New York Times*.

It's a gray, cold sunless morning, so windy I'm practically pushed across the street. It's almost a relief to feel the icy air hit my face, to feel the freezing sidewalk through the soles of my shoes, to feel tears coming to my eyes, so instead of just buying the paper and going home, I keep walking. Occasionally I pass someone walking his dog and carrying the thick bundle of the Sunday paper under his arm, but mostly I have the streets to myself.

On the corner of Mulberry and Houston is a stone church and from inside I can hear the familiar sound of an organ playing. Standing outside, I listen to the heavy chords, thinking of other Sunday mornings when I was growing up. While my parents slept late, recovering from whatever party they'd given or been to the night before, my nanny Marie took me with her to High Mass at St. Patrick's Cathedral.

I walk uptown, through Washington Square Park, which winter has decimated, leaving it ugly and bare. Despite the freezing temperature, I pass at least a dozen people bundled up in tattered blankets or plastic bags sleeping on hardwood benches.

My hands sting from the cold. I hide them in my pockets and continue up Fifth Avenue passing two churches, on 11th and 12th Streets. I slow down in front of each and listen for the music. At another church, a service has just ended. I watch the people coming out, satisfied expressions on their faces as they button their overcoats, pull on their gloves, take their children by the hand, and start home.

It's not until I reach 50th Street, my whole body chilled, stiff and hurting, that I realize I had a destination all along. I haven't come back to St. Patrick's Cathedral seeking solace—I don't think that's within my reach anymore—but maybe here I can find safer memories, familiar, benign.

Inside the church there is a hush I instantly remember, a heavy silence as if the air is weighted by the sonorous organ, the scent of the incense and all the prayers. It's High Mass, eleven o'clock on a Sunday, and there are almost a thousand people watching and listening to the priest in his princely white and gold robes. The purity of the church's lines, the columns and arches all leading high, higher, heavenly higher up to the large cobalt blue, purple, and deep red stained-glass window, create a vast airy space, so although the church is full it doesn't seem crowded.

I don't go inside, don't try to find a seat. Something keeps me back in the vestibule with a group of Japanese tourists.

Not having been to mass in over twenty-five years, I'm disappointed to hear the priest speaking English instead of the magical incantations I remember from my childhood. Did the Latin mass seem more religious because I was more religious then? Or is it because a sacred ceremony shouldn't be spoken with the same ordinary language used to report the news on television: "*Friday, in what is being called the Madison Avenue Murder Trial, the prosecuting attorney Linda Zavidow . . .*"

"Our Father who art in Heaven, hallowed be thy name . . . Jesus died for our sins, so that we might have a savior . . . who among you who is not a sinner, let him cast the first stone."

Marie used to tell me we were all God's children, all on the same road, all equal in his sight, all sinners, and all worth being saved.

Even the people who are evil? Who have killed other people? Or who have murderous nightmares? Nothing she said about Christ or forgiveness lessened my fears or assuaged my guilt about those dreams. It was only years later, when I started therapy, that I was able to work out and accept those terrible dreams and understand they were a way for me to take control. If I killed the people I loved, they could never leave me.

The priest offers communion and the parishioners stand and walk slowly to the altar, heads bowed, hands clasped together. I remain where I am. I can't take communion, can't confess, can't pray. More than out of practice, I have given up.

Leaving St. Patrick's, I take a taxi downtown and get out at the Korean vegetable market on my corner where I finally do buy the Sunday *Times* and a cup of black coffee.

Upstairs, I take the coffee and the paper into bed; the same bed Gabriel and I made love in, the same bed he lay dying in four months ago, and I read the entire paper searching for stories I might add to my files. I started them years ago thinking they might lead to a television show about miracles—now I keep them out of habit. I have twenty-seven articles substantiating miracles and over three hundred and fifty that decry their existence.

In my miracle folder is a story about a boy who never stopped believing that one day his lost dog would return home. Wanting to protect the child, everyone tried to convince him the dog had been taken in by some other family. But one night, while the boy was lying in the den watching television, he heard scratching at the door; after three years, the dog had found his way back.

In my proof-there-are-no-miracles folder is the story of a man who returned home after spending twenty months in prison, had sex with his wife, and then raped his eighteen-month-old baby girl repeatedly, almost suffocating her during the act. The child suffered severe brain damage, though she did not die.

Today, within half an hour, I find a story in the National section for the miracle folder about a father and son impossibly reunited after seventeen years. For the proof-there-are-no-miracles folder, I spot four inches of type in the Metropolitan section, and only have to glance at the headline to know I will cut out this one too: MADISON AVENUE MURDER TRIAL RESUMES TOMORROW.

Getting one of Gabriel's scissors from his worktable I cut gently. Sometimes newspaper is soft and rips no matter how careful you are, but today there are no jagged edges, no characters cut off, no tears.

At three in the afternoon, the buzzer rings. I don't get up. It might just be someone who has forgotten his or her keys. But then it rings again.

Getting up, I depress the button. "Yes?"

"Genny, it's Ham. Can I come up?"

I don't want company and I am about to tell him.

"I know you don't want to let me up. I know you don't want to see anyone, but c'mon, Genny. Besides, it's freezing down here."

How can I ask him to go away? He has been a good friend for years. He was Gabriel's friend. He has been at court every day for me.

I wait at the door, listening to the creaking sounds of the old building. A minute later he is there, putting his arms around me, not saying anything, just holding me in an embrace that would have been comforting if I could ever feel comforted again. All I feel is the cold he's brought with him from the outside,

"Get your coat, we're going out."

Ham has one of those genuine smiles that begins in his eyes before it shows on his lips. He is kind and intelligent, but I don't want to go anywhere.

When I do not move, he looks around, spies the coats hanging on hooks by the door and walks toward them. My coat and Gabriel's, side by side. I don't want him, or anyone, to touch anything of Gabriel's so I get my coat.

Ham takes it out of my hands and holds it out for me. Like a child who does what she is told, I put my arms through the holes.

"Where are your gloves?" he asks.

For a moment I think about how long it has been since anyone has asked me such a caring question and behind my eyes feel the beginning of tears.

"You can cry over your gloves if you want, but personally I think it would be a waste of tears. Everyone loses gloves," he teases.

"I've lost more than gloves."

He puts his arms around me again and holds me for a few more minutes. When he speaks, it is softly but with confidence and assuredness. "I know you have. And even though you won't ever find exactly what you lost, you will find something else."

I try to say no but am crying so hard I choke on my sobs.

"Deep breaths, Genny."

"My gloves are in my pocket," I finally say after what seems like hundreds of my tears have soaked into the shoulder of his coat.

On the street, Ham hails a cab and gives the driver an address on the Upper East Side. It is only then that I finally ask where we are going.

"To a concert." He takes my gloved hand and folds it in his arm.

Fifteen minutes later we pull up in front of a red brick building that I recognize as a private girls' school. "Isn't this where your daughter goes to school?" I ask, trying to remember how long it has been since I've seen Madeline, who had been born when Ham was working for my father.

"Yes, she's performing in a concert."

"I'll ruin it for her, for the other kids." I pull back at the door. "People will notice me, they'll stare."

"This is New York, Genny. Half the parents here are either famous or infamous. No one will give you a second glance." Ham takes my arm and ushers me inside. And he's right. No one pays any attention to me.

The music is unusually competent. For forty-five minutes I manage to focus on the young girls who are up on the stage playing their instruments. There is freshness here; an excitement from the musicians as they surprise even themselves with their accomplished playing. How full of promise they are. How untouched by disappointment or cynicism. They have everything before them.

Ham is riveted to his daughter as she holds her child-size violin up to her chin and plays her heart out. His heart is in his eyes and his gaze does not waver. Beside me, I am not even sure he breathes until the piece is over and then he is on his feet clapping wildly and I rise with him, clapping, too, for what his daughter and the others have achieved.

Afterward, we stand with Sandra, Ham's ex-wife, her second husband, and their son. We all fuss over Madeline and congratulate her. Flushed with the excitement of the performance, she's delighted with the fuss we all make over her.

"Come to dinner with us," Sandra says to Ham and me.

"You go," I say to Ham, not wanting to intrude on the family celebration, not knowing how I could possibly sit in a restaurant and pay attention to what is going on around me or take part in a normal conversation.

"No, you come, too, Genny," says Ham's daughter. "I really want you to," Madeline adds, giving me a sideways secret glance from under her lashes that darts off in her father's direction for a minute before returning to me.

"Yes, Genny," Sandra insists. And without waiting for my acquiescence, she takes my arm and walks with me out of the auditorium.

Their warmth and welcome settles over me. Obediently, I go with them to the quiet restaurant nearby.

The dinner I order smells delicious but I cannot do more than push the food around on my plate. The conversation flows easily around me and even though I do not contribute anything to it, no one minds.

When we say goodnight, Madeline kisses me and thanks me for coming. "Mom says you're going to be fine," the twelve-year-old whispers in my ear. "And I really hope so, Genny. I don't know what would happen to Dad if you weren't. You know he's never ever liked anyone as much as he likes you."

Before I can even process what she's said, much less respond to it, Ham comes over and interrupts.

"What are you two conspiring about?"

Madeline smiles at me; like her father's the smile starts in her eyes.

Ham hails a taxi, insisting on taking me downtown and dropping me off at the loft despite my remonstrance he lives uptown so it's out of the way and that I am perfectly capable of getting home on my own.

He ignores my protestations and gives the driver the SoHo address. What I hear is not so much his words, as the sound of his voice, smooth like liquid jazz, soothing.

It is warm in the taxi and we are sitting close enough to each other that I can smell his scent, which makes me think of sunshine, blue water, and sand.

It is shocking to me that I am capable of thinking these things. And I wonder about that the whole way downtown and long after Ham has dropped me off, kissing me goodnight gently on the forehead, and I have gone upstairs.

FIFTEEN

New York City Criminal Court Building, Room 1317
Monday, December 7, 1992, 9:30 A.M.

This morning, after a breakfast of toast and a cup of instant coffee, I showered and dressed: gray flannel trousers, gray cashmere sweater set, and around my neck, my black onyx cross on its thin gold chain. After brushing my hair, I tied it back, per Benjamin's request to soften my appearance. He'd suggested I wear something other than black and that I try to tame my hair. Checking in the mirror, I try to see what the jury will see. But the less harsh colors don't change my posture, my expressions, my gestures. Gabriel once said I moved like a wild cat— fearless and dangerous—which is what Benjamin wants me to hide. Can I?

I went downstairs at eight-twenty to find my parents waiting to take me to court in their chauffeured Mercedes. Uncomfortable despite the luxurious soft calfskin seat, I held my hands together on my lap, trying not to scratch my itching palms.

As the driver navigated the small cobblestone streets, and the car jostled along, my parents and I spoke to one another, but without substance and the words floated, sentences drifted off. Twice I started to say something and then forgot what it was. My father seemed shaken, sullen, withdrawn, and my mother attempted to fill in our silences, and then somehow managed not to speak of anything negative.

Fifteen minutes later, the car stopped at the tall stone Greek temple that passes for a hall of justice for the city of New York. It's a large, sweeping, dark, ominous building that looks as if it has been washed with dirt, as if that grime has rained down on it morning after morning for years.

A crowd waited. Mine is the kind of trial that entertains the city. It's high drama, the stuff the six o'clock news covets: art, sex, scandal, adultery, murder, and suicide. I play the lead and share the spotlight with a dead painter and his angry daughter; providing the tabloids with lurid headlines like this morning's SOHO SUICIDE OR MADISON AVENUE MURDER?

We got out of the car, I in the middle, my mother and father on either side of me, and fortified by our solidarity, walked the twelve feet from the curb to the courthouse.

If during my childhood I missed my mother, if she was absent when I craved her presence, she is here now, her arm linked in mine, helping me take every step.

Inside the courtroom, before we separate, she and my father to sit among the spectators, me to sit beside Benjamin at the defendant's table, my mother brushes my cheek with her lips and whispers to me in her French accent: "You will be fine, Genevieve, you will be fine."

Suddenly, for a moment, I am fine. Her words have empowered me. And my father? Trying to overcome his anger, he squeezes my hand, I squeeze back, and then we separate.

"O ye. O ye. The court will come to order. The Honorable Jacob Bailey presiding."

The unending witnesses who pass before us this morning begin with Detective King, who tells the jury my prints were found on the evidence. Then a lab technician reestablishes the same information.

The coroner testifies that Gabriel died as a result of suffocation but that the autopsy also revealed he had ingested—by force or by choice—a lethal dose of Seconal. He describes the time of death to be approximately ten o'clock in the morning.

The coroner is followed by a forensic lab technician who reconfirms the coroner's testimony.

Next a woman who lived in our building confirms she saw me leave the loft before ten o'clock on the Monday in question.

To corroborate that information, Boris Yeltich takes the stand. He is a beefy man in his late thirties, wearing a heavy cable-knit sweater, baggy blue jeans, and thick rubber-soled shoes. He speaks nervously, with a thick Russian accent. Linda establishes he is a cabdriver who was driving in the vicinity of the loft on Monday, September 18, and then asks him if he picked up a fare in that area.

"Ya," Yeltich says.

"Where?"

"Corner Prince Street, Greene Street."

"What time was that, Mr. Yeltich?"

"Ten-oh-eight."

"How can you be so precise?"

"Digital watch," he answers, proudly pushing up his sweater sleeve to display the watch.

"But how do you remember the time?"

"Wrote down on list."

Linda holds some papers up in the air. "The people would like to enter into evidence Mr. Yeltich's log for the morning of September 18." Once the papers are entered, she resumes her questions.

"Do you remember the passenger you picked up that morning on the corner of Greene Street and Prince?"

"Ya."

"Could you point the passenger out for us?"

Mr. Yeltich remains motionless, watching Linda like a child waiting for his mother's approval. She nods, encouraging him.

"Ya, that's the lady."

"I have no more questions, Your Honor," Linda says.

"Do you have any questions, Mr. Marks?"

"No, Your Honor."

While Mr. Yeltich steps down, the court reporter asks the judge for a break so she can change her paper.

Benjamin looks down at my yellow pad, the first page still blank. "Don't you have any questions?" he asks.

"No."

"Genny, you've got to start caring about what happens to you."

"It's already happened."

"No, there's more. As bad as you think things are now, prison is worse. Do you understand that?"

"Yes."

"Then act like it, damn it!" he hisses through his teeth, careful no one can hear him, so that the jury only sees him smiling at me.

"Mr. Marks?" It's my father, behind us.

Benjamin turns around. "Yes, Mr. Haviland?"

"Why aren't you trying to destroy any of this testimony?"

"I can't. It's true. Your daughter was there. She left."

"But the jury doesn't know what to think."

"I know, Mr. Haviland, I'm counting on their confusion. I want them to wonder why I'm not discrediting any of Linda's witnesses. They expect the defense attorney to vilify the prosecution's witnesses, not let them go docilely back to their seats. I don't want to do what they expect; I don't want this trial to fit their preconceived notions of how a trial should proceed. I want them unsure." Benjamin finishes up as the court reporter does and my father, though not quite satisfied, takes his seat.

Judge Bailey bangs his gavel to quiet the courtroom and asks Linda to call her next witness.

"The prosecution calls Claire Bowers, Your Honor."

Claire, a reddish-blond-haired woman in her early thirties, with freckles and fair skin, has been my associate producer for the last four years. We've spent months together on location, in edit rooms, and sound studios. I've never seen her lose her implacable cool, but she's come undone. Shaking as she takes the stand, her voice trembles as she takes the oath.

Linda approaches the witness stand and asks Claire to state her occupation.

"Associate producer for a TV series called *Into the Paintings.*"

"And how long have you worked there?"

"For almost five years." Claire's voice is barely audible.

"I didn't hear that," the court reporter says.

"You'll have to speak up, Miss Bowers," the judge says.

"Almost five years," Claire repeats.

"For those almost five years have you worked exclusively for Miss Haviland?"

"She's been my executive producer, yes."

"Prior to last winter had you ever discussed Slade Gabriel with your boss?"

"Yes," Claire answers.

"In what context?"

"He was an important artist and his name came up at a staff meeting as a subject for one of our episodes," Claire says.

"And what happened to the suggestion?"

"Genny said she didn't think he was appropriate, and we went on to discuss someone else."

"Was it unusual for Genny just to kill a suggestion like that?" Linda asks.

"Well, umm . . ." Claire stammers.

"Was it unusual, Miss Bowers?" Linda insisted.

"Yes, I guess."

"How so?"

"Most of the time we all come to a consensus about who will be a good subject. It isn't that often that Genny feels that adamantly against any one artist."

"Where you aware then that she knew him personally?"

"No."

"When was the first time you became aware that Genny knew Gabriel?"

"It was in November of last year."

"That's November of 1991?" Linda clarifies.

"Yes." Claire nods.

"What happened?"

"Genny and I were in a sound studio on 57th Street listening to the mix of the Piet Mondrian episode of *Into the Paintings*; we were just finishing up—it must have been about ten-thirty at night—when a call came through from Paris, from Genny's mother."

"There has been an accident, Genevieve."

I held my breath.

"Your father has been hurt. Not seriously. But he is at Mount Sinai Hospital there in New York."

My father had been working late. At about nine o'clock he left the gallery and was walking from the building to the curb to get into his car, when an explosion sent him flying. A gas jet under the city street blew up.

Talking half in French, half in English, my mother sped through the story, relating what had been told to her over the phone by my father's chauffeur and then by the doctor.

"Your father landed on his arm. It is broken in several places. They have just finished operating."

"I'll go right away," I said as the long distance connection spit and cackled.

"Did you go with Genny to the hospital, Miss Bowers?" Linda asks.

"Yes. She was so shaken up, I thought I should."

"And what happened when you got there?"

"We went up to the information booth where the guard told us visiting hours were over. I explained Genny was there to see her father and he let her up."

"Did you wait for her?" Linda asks.

The hospital smelled of antiseptic and fear. As I walked down the hall I heard a nurse bitching about a doctor and saw a doctor too exhausted to stand.

My father was in a double room with a curtain drawn around him, creating an illusion of privacy. I'd been so frightened, but he looked all right, tired certainly, but whole. I kissed his cheek, and instead of his familiar scent I smelled disinfectant.

"Oh Daddy, I'm glad you're all right. How bad is the pain?"

"They gave me some painkillers. I don't feel a thing. I just can't believe it happened. Genny, I was actually in the air staring down at the street. You know what I thought of, it's so absurd, I thought, My Lord, I am a flying figure that Chagall paints, and then I hit the ground."

I squeezed my father's free hand and noticed the angry scratches on his chin. Without letting go of him, I sat down gingerly on the edge of the bed.

"I'm fine Genny, really fine."

"Do you need anything?"

"Not now that you're here."

"Are you uncomfortable?"

"Just terribly tired . . ." With his eyes closing, his head lolling to one side, my father seemed so vulnerable and something protective rose up in me. But how do you protect the man who is supposed to protect you?

"That's all right. Go to sleep. I'll be back first thing in the morning and Mama will be here by early afternoon."

"Wait, Genny, find out for me, before you go . . . find out about Gabriel. . . ." There was a long pause. My father was fading.

"Slade Gabriel?"

"He was with me . . . Find out . . ." he said, and was asleep.

My heart accelerated, my pulse throbbing in my neck. My stomach cramped tight like a fist. Gabriel had been with my father? Was he here? Hurt? What if he was worse than hurt?

It was quiet in the hall. Seven was an orthopedic floor. Hip replacements. Broken bones. Calmer in the night than other floors.

I ran over to the night nurse. "My father . . . Mr. Haviland in seven-oh-four . . . when he was brought in there was another man with him. Where can I find him?"

"Is he on this floor?" she asked.

"I don't know."

"Neither do I. You can use that phone over there," she said pointing to a hospital phone on the wall near the waiting room.

The woman who answered my call could only tell me that Mr. Gabriel's condition was critical. He was in Room 340, but wasn't allowed visitors. I couldn't imagine Gabriel in critical condition: he was too big, he was impervious . . . he had been impervious to me.

Dazed, I walked to the elevator, got in, pressed 1 and watched each number as it lit up: 6, 5, 4, 3 . . . 2, 1. But when the doors opened on the first floor, I didn't get out. I stayed in that laminated fake-wood elevator staring at the black plastic button imprinted with a white number 3.

What harm would there be in seeing him? Years had passed, it wouldn't be the same. I wasn't the same. No longer susceptible, no longer yearning.

Gabriel's door was partially open. It was easy to wedge myself into the doorway and peer in. The glow of the red and green blinking monitors illuminated the room but all I could see was a plump nurse, sitting, reading in an armchair.

Seeing me, she frowned, got up, and came over. "Can I help you?" She wasn't whispering. Why wasn't she whispering?

"What's wrong with him?"

"I'm sorry, but Mr. Gabriel's not allowed visitors."

"Please, just tell me, how bad is he?"

"He's suffered head injuries in a fall and he's in a coma."

"What does that mean? How bad is he?" I was moving forward, trying to push my way in.

"We just don't know yet," she said, effectively blocking me from going farther.

"Please, can I please come inside and just be with him for a minute?"

She was about to say no, but it was late and she must have been tired, so she acquiesced.

I suppose I expected him to look sick or damaged or as vulnerable as my father, but he didn't. It was the first time I'd seen him in almost twenty years. Had he changed? I suppose he was pale, but in that red and green light it was hard to tell. Some of his harder edges had softened. Gray streaked his thick black hair, lines creased his face, but Gabriel looked the way I'd been remembering, despite myself, for so damn long.

"I'm sorry, but you'll have to go now," the nurse said.

"Good night, Gabriel," I whispered to him and with one finger touched the fine black hairs on the back of his hand.

Linda, who's wearing a navy silk suit, crosses her arms on her chest. "And when Miss Haviland came downstairs from having visited with her father, how was she, Miss Bowers?"

"Much more upset than when she went up. I was worried that he was worse than her mother had said, but Genny said no, her father was fine. And then she told me about Gabriel."

"What did she tell you?"

Claire shifts uncomfortably in her seat, her cheeks redden to almost the same color as her hair. "She told me a man . . . she had known once . . . whom she cared about had been with her father and had been badly hurt."

"Is that all she said, Miss Bowers?"

"Yes," Claire mutters. "I think so, yes."

"Are you sure?"

My mother returned from Paris. For the next two days she spent all her time with my father in the hospital and I came up after work. I never stopped by Gabriel's room again.

On the third day when I arrived, my father was in the process of being discharged.

"We must check on Gabriel before we go," my father was saying to my mother when I walked in the room.

"Genevieve, will you go with your father while I pack up these things?" my mother asked.

"No, I'll stay here and pack. You go with Daddy."

"Please, there are papers I have to sign and too much I need to do here."

A violent accident makes you wary. As we walked toward the elevator, my father moved slowly and watched that other people didn't get too close.

Getting off the elevator, we turned toward Gabriel's room in time to see a nurse run out. Something must be wrong, I thought, taking my father's hand. It must have seemed to him that I was offering support, but I wasn't, I was seeking it.

"What's happened?" My father intercepted the nurse. I turned my head away, unwilling to watch her say the words.

"Mr. Gabriel is creating an uproar."

Suddenly forgetting his injury, my father rushed ahead of me and ran into Gabriel's room. I hung back, propping myself against the wall. I'd decided to wait in the hallway until my father came out. Gabriel was all right. I didn't have to see him.

A thin Chinese nurse struggled as she wheeled a huge piece of equipment down the hall and in order to get out of her way, I had no choice but to step inside Gabriel's hospital room, where he was sitting up in the bed as if nothing had happened.

"Get these tubes out of me!" he yelled at a middle-aged black nurse who was ignoring him as she studied the readout from his monitor.

I turned to leave, just as Gabriel turned and saw me. "Genny?"

His voice saying my name made me shiver. Even after so long. How could that be?

"We're so relieved you're better." In my own ears my words sounded flat and false, but he didn't seem to notice, he just stared, stroking me with his gaze the same way he had so long ago, the way I'd been waiting for someone to during all the intervening years.

Gabriel is delirious, I told myself. Still recovering from almost dying, he doesn't realize what he's showing in his eyes. I turned toward my father. Had he noticed Gabriel gaping at me? No, my father was oblivious to everything but that Gabriel was all right.

"Can't you take this fucking IV out of me?"

"Not until your doctor says so," the nurse answered, calmly unaffected by his temper.

"Well, where the hell is my doctor?"

"He'll be here in an hour or so."

"Why so long?"

"Mr. Gabriel, he's not on duty now."

"Why haven't I seen him before today?"

"He has been here, every morning, but you've been unconscious for three days," the nurse said.

The room became silent as Gabriel flopped back against the bed, resting his head on the pillow and shutting his eyes, nodding to himself as if he finally understood something that had been unclear.

"I thought they were dreams," he whispered. "I thought they were all dreams."

The nurse ushered us out of the room. "It happens sometimes," she told us in the hall. "They don't know and when they find out they get alarmed. That's all, he's just scared now."

That night I couldn't stop thinking about Gabriel lying back on the bed, scared, saying over and over "I thought they were dreams."

I'd had a recurring dream about Gabriel when I was married; a nightmare from which I would awaken in a cold sweat. My husband, Nicky, and I were at some kind of large social gathering and in the distance I'd spot Gabriel. Giving Nicky some excuse I'd break away and fight the crowd, pushing ahead until I reached Gabriel. Once he saw me, Gabriel grabbed me, kissed me, stroked me—in full view of whoever was around—and then made love to me, fiercely, violently. (Often upon waking I'd realize I'd orgasmed in my sleep.) After making love, Gabriel would insist I leave Nicky and be with him. I tried to respond but no longer knew how to form words. And while I tried again and again, my body began to change shape—every bone and muscle stretched and ached as I became something inhuman. I knew that to save myself I had to get away from Gabriel's voice, that somehow his voice was responsible for my altered state. But I didn't know how to escape.

I had the same dream that night after talking to Gabriel in the hospital. It woke me up at two in the morning and after that I was afraid to go back to sleep. I stayed up all night and before going to the office fooled myself into thinking I'd feel better if I got some exercise. So I took a long walk in the freezing cold—winding up at Mount Sinai Hospital.

Gabriel sat up in bed, drawing furiously. Page after page of drawings were scattered over the floor and piled on the bedside table. Standing in the doorway, watching him, I no longer saw a man overcome by demons. This Gabriel was at peace with his work, like the boy Callahand had known years ago in the Botanical Gardens.

When I knocked, his head jerked up, but for a moment he didn't see me, hadn't surfaced yet. He was still in the drawings.

"I know how horrible hospital food is. I thought you'd like some muffins, some fresh juice, good coffee."

"I was drawing."

"Yes, I see."

"Been drawing all night. I can't wait to get out of here. Come, see what I've done."

I approached the bed slowly, but he was impatient and as soon as he could, he reached out, grabbed my hand, and pulled me closer. My skin burned where he touched me.

Those drawings, like all his others, suggested gardens, but unlike anything he'd done before they were not abstracted to the point of destruction. These were sleeping rather than wasted: lost dream gardens waiting to wake up.

"I know what's been missing . . . what I have to do . . . to bring . . . the wonder back." The years had not changed that much about him.

His eyes were still fathomless, his voice was still low and scratchy, and I still felt it deep down in my stomach.

During the past twenty years I had followed Gabriel's growth as a painter by what I saw in my father's gallery. In the '70s when we met, his abstract gardens exploded as if grenades had been thrown in among the flowers. He commingled mangled blossoms with spilled blood. Then after the Vietnam War ended, the blood disappeared. The destruction was replaced by lushness. He stopped taking risks and the gardens of the '80s became exuberant, hedonistic. The brushwork was excessive, the colors oversaturated—all too rich—like the times.

But the drawings I saw that morning in the hospital were not debauched or extravagant. They were masterful and spiritual.

If I hadn't known who had made those drawings, I would have wanted to meet him and at the same time would have been afraid for fear the man would not live up to the artist.

Now I was afraid he did.

Finally, he put down the pencil and took a long look at me. "So, Haviland's daughter," he said at last. "I've been hearing about you all these years. Funny we never ran into each other."

"Not so funny."

"I wondered if you stayed away on purpose."

I nodded.

"Good for you."

"Good for me? What does that mean?"

"It was good for you to have stayed away from me. I use people up, remember? Haven't been any damn good for anyone. Only good as a painter, and not good enough at that, if you ask me. But I've kept track of you." He laughed. "It was easy. Just a simple 'How's Genny?' was all it took. Do you know your father loves to talk about you even more than the sales he makes?

"I know how well you did in college, about all those boys you went out with—every one of whom he hated—about your first job with that film company. What was it called? Doesn't matter. At first, Jonathan felt betrayed when you went into television, but then he was so proud of how fast you moved up the ladder.

"Did you know he invited me to your wedding? I had to plan a trip so I could decline without insulting him. Jonathan liked your husband, told me all about Nicky. Sounded a bit tame to me, but I kept my opinion to myself.

"All those years, I never told him about what had happened between you and me, and since he never said anything, I figured you hadn't either. I've seen a lot of your shows, Genny, they're good. Jonathan always hoped you'd do an episode on one of my paintings. I always hoped you wouldn't—"

"Why are you telling me all of this?" I finally asked, interrupting him.

"Always questions." Gabriel laughed. "I thought about you, that's all. I wanted you to know."

Listening to him, all I could think was that I had to get out of this room while I still could.

"You know, I'm late, have to go. We're finishing up a show. I only came because it seemed important to let you know . . . I wanted to tell you . . . I forgive you."

"You forgive me? What the fuck for?" he asked.

"For throwing me out that night, for closing the door, for not . . . no—never mind."

He was laughing. The same laugh that always drew me in, like a warm wave.

"But have I forgiven you? Genny, didn't you ever think about what I'd given up while you were feeling sorry for yourself? Do you think I wanted to stop seeing you? Jesus! What choices did I have? You were jailbait. Seventeen. Only six years older than my daughter. I've always been brave, but I've tried not to be stupid and it would have been stupid to do anything but stop seeing you. We had one of those crazy connections. It doesn't happen easily or often. But I had to stop. For your sake, for mine, for the sake of my career."

What of the waste, I wanted to scream at him, what of the years of longing? No, I was going to leave, I was going to save my life.

It took all my energy to pick up my bag and my coat. Being with him had exhausted me.

"I've never lost sight of you, Genny," he said to my back as I walked out of his hospital room, trying not to hear his voice or listen to his words as I shut the door behind me.

SIXTEEN

New York City Criminal Court Building, Room 1317
Monday, December 7, 1992, 4:00 P.M.

My father looks down at me from the witness stand, a slight slick of perspiration on his forehead and a gray cast to his face. He was not supposed to have been called.

At times, our faces are naked, when we let the truth show and do not hide the secret stirrings of our hearts. His face is naked now, here in the courtroom, as he sits where he doesn't want to sit, forced to give answers he doesn't want to give. No matter how angry I may be with you, I will lie for you if I have to, if I can, his eyes say. I wonder if the jury can read them, too.

It isn't just about love, the thing between my father and me. It is about the two of us, conspirators, both lost, searching through the darkness together. I want to turn away from him, but I don't. I accept my father's gaze until his muscles shift back into place and his face is naked no longer.

"Mr. Haviland, how many years did you know Mr. Gabriel?" Linda asks.

"Over twenty."

"Would you describe your relationship?"

"We were friends and business associates. I handled his paintings in my gallery."

"Would you say you were close?" Linda asks.

"Do you mean were we good friends?"

"Yes, Mr. Haviland, were you and Mr. Gabriel good friends?"

"Why didn't you just ask me that?"

The judge interrupts, "Please answer the question, Mr. Haviland."

"Yes. We were good friends."

"Did Mr. Gabriel tell *you* he had Alzheimer's disease?"

"No."

"Did he imply he had Alzheimer's?"

"No."

"How do you interpret that, Mr. Haviland?"

"Are you asking me if it meant that he didn't have Alzheimer's or if it meant that he and I weren't good friends?"

The judge bangs his gavel at the titters in the courtroom. "May I remind you that you are here at the court's discretion?"

I put my hands together in my lap and stare at the angel on my ring. As I listen to Linda's next question a certain coldness creeps along my spine.

"How important was Slade Gabriel to your business, Mr. Haviland?"

"He was one of my artists."

"Please answer the question, Mr. Haviland."

"Each of my artists is important, Miss Zavidow."

"What percentage of your sales come from Mr. Gabriel's work?"

"I would have to check my records."

"Can you approximate the number, Mr. Haviland?"

"I would imagine that Mr. Gabriel's work, in a dollar amount, signifies about twenty percent of the gallery's earnings."

"Isn't it more like thirty-five or forty percent?" Linda asks.

My father doesn't answer.

"I can subpoena your books, Mr. Haviland."

Benjamin stands. "I object. There is no reason to threaten the witness. Mr. Haviland might need some time to figure this out, Your Honor."

"Sustained." The judge speaks a bit harshly, "Give the witness a chance, Miss Zavidow."

"Mr. Haviland." Linda lets my father's name hang in the air, lets the refinement of the syllables echo, then repeats it as if the name were some kind of curse. "Mr. Haviland, what kind of financial damage would it have done to your gallery if Mr. Gabriel had left to go to another gallery?"

"It was not under discussion. Mr. Gabriel was happy with the gallery. We were, up until the time of his death, working toward his next show."

"Please answer my question," Linda insists.

"I object, Your Honor. Irrelevant line of questioning."

The volley rivets the jury. Does it occur to them that Linda has deviated from the plan she set forth in her opening statement when she said she'd prove I'd murdered Gabriel because he'd been cruel to me and forced me to have an abortion?

"I will prove, Your Honor, that this is indeed relevant."

"Go ahead." Judge Bailey wipes invisible dust off the gavel in front of him.

"Mr. Haviland, what would have happened if Gabriel had left your gallery?"

"We would have lost an important artist."

"Would it have hurt you?" Linda asks.

"Do you mean personally?" my father asks again sarcastically.

"No, Mr. Haviland, I mean financially. Would Mr. Gabriel's leaving have hurt you financially?"

"Yes."

"Mr. Haviland, could you tell us how much you recently paid to settle a matter, out of court, in regards to a forged Cézanne painting that you sold to the Van Arsdale Trust?"

Benjamin jumps up. "Objection."

"On what grounds, Counselor?" the judge asks.

"May I approach the bench, Your Honor?" Benjamin asks.

Judge Bailey calls both lawyers up to the bench for a sidebar.

The shock of the Cézanne forgery came so close on the heels of the gas explosion and my father's accident and hospitalization, you might have thought our luck had turned, if you believed in luck. Suddenly, my parents' lives and mine, which had been relatively tranquil, were thrown into chaos and aspects, which until then had remained and should have remained separate, were irrevocably intertwined.

About a week after my father had been released from Mount Sinai, I went to see my parents and have dinner with them at their apartment.

As soon as I walked into the foyer and my mother kissed my cheek hello, I knew something was wrong. I could smell it.

"Is Daddy all right?" I asked.

"Darling, come inside. Have some wine."

"Where is he?"

"In the study with Samuel."

Samuel Ryser is my father's lawyer. I'd known him since childhood. That he was there was not in itself suspect. It was the atmosphere, the overcharged electricity in the air, that alerted me.

In the living room, my mother poured two glasses of Pinot Grigio, handed one to me and sat down opposite me on the velvet settee.

"I don't want you to worry, but we have received what the lawyers call a claim letter from the Van Arsdale Trust accusing your father of selling a forged Cézanne."

"That's crazy," I said, instantly certain it was a mistake.

"Yes, crazy. You father just got out of the hospital, now this. It is crazy." A strand of gold hair came loose from her bun and she pushed it back into place. "We don't want you to worry."

"What's going to happen?"

"Hopefully it can be settled with lawyers."

"And if it can't?"

"Then it will be taken before the court."

My mother has always had the most incredible posture. Taught as a child by her governess to sit ramrod straight, she has never relaxed her pose; she did not relax it then.

"Daddy . . . didn't know about the Cézanne, did he?"

If my mother thought it odd that I could doubt my father she didn't say so. She just answered my question. "*Mais non,*" making a familiar gesture with her hand, as if she were throwing something away, dismissing my concern. "As usual, he consulted several experts. The Cézanne had been authenticated."

"This could be bad for the gallery, couldn't it?" I asked.

Usually my mother refused to become embroiled in my endless questions. That night was no different. "It is too soon to talk of things like that." She lifted her wineglass to her lips and sipped.

"But it could damage the gallery's reputation. If the press gets ahold of this you could lose clients, artists—"

Interrupting, she said: "The gallery has an untarnished reputation, Genevieve, like Marlborough before the Rothko scandal. They survived that."

"But Marlborough had enormous reserves. And the stakes weren't as high in the '70s."

"What do you want me to tell you? Yes, we might lose some

clients, some artists. Yes, it would be a disaster. Does that satisfy you?" my mother asked.

I shook my head no. "I'm sorry. It's just that I know how the press works. I can't help but imagine how they could make Daddy into an example of '80s excess, yet another businessman driven by greed."

My mother stood up. "Dinner must be ready."

I followed her into the dining room. There were only two places set. She sat at the head of the long gleaming mahogany table, and I sat on her right.

"Isn't Daddy having dinner with us?"

"No, he and Samuel will join us for coffee."

Neither of us had an appetite but we both made an effort to push the white food—Dover sole, cauliflower florets, and herbed rice— around on our plates.

About an hour later my father and Samuel joined us for coffee in the living room. My father sat beside me on the couch, close enough so that at one point the cast on his arm rubbed roughly against my cashmere sweater. My mother and Samuel sat in the Ruhlmann chairs facing us.

"We think we can get them to agree not to disclose the forgery as long as we buy back the painting. Obviously they're open to negotiate, or they wouldn't have sent the letter."

I didn't believe either my father's calm voice or Samuel's confident smile.

Out the window, across the park, lights twinkled in hundreds of apartments. A New York City landscape doesn't show you the dirt on the street, the grime that's built up on the millions of windows, the undercurrents, the covert illegal activities, or the rot and the deceit. I gazed at the skyline of glittering lights and tried to reassure myself of my father's innocence.

Although I had been in his orbit my whole life, a lesser star circling a greater one, a brighter one, a hotter one, I barely knew the man who

was my father. What if he was lying? What if the forgery did make it
to the papers? Would my father's artists leave? Would Gabriel?

After several minutes, the sidebar over, Benjamin returns to his seat
and Linda is allowed to ask my father to explain to the jury and this
roomful of spectators—including several members of the press—the
exact details of the forged Cézanne settlement, which until now he
had managed to keep private.

"So, Mr. Haviland," Linda says after my father has finished his
recitation, "in light of the five-million-dollar claim, you settled out of
court with the Van Arsdale Trust and in light of a very depressed art
market, wouldn't Slade Gabriel's defection have put you in very bad financial shape?"

"It wouldn't have been good," he agreed.

"Now, Mr. Haviland, after the scandal broke and the newspapers
suggested you had knowingly sold a forged Cézanne, how many of
your artists informed you that they would be leaving when their contracts were up?"

"None."

"None at first, but within a month?"

"A couple," my father offers grudgingly.

"How about four?" Linda persists.

"Yes, all right, four."

"And, Mr. Haviland, if Mr. Gabriel had been the fifth don't you
think more would have followed?"

"But he wasn't leaving!" My father bangs his hand down on the
wooden ledge in front of him.

"But if he did leave, mightn't other artists have followed his lead?"
Linda asks.

"I doubt it."

"Was it possible?" Linda moves closer to the witness box, leaning in. "Yes or no?"

"Yes, but I don't see how it could matter since—"

"Now, Mr. Haviland," Linda interrupts, "could you tell me, I'm not sure my numbers are right on this, how much was one of Slade Gabriel's paintings worth before his death?"

"Approximately $200,000."

"Wow. That is a lot of money. Is it true that when an artist dies his paintings go up in value?"

"I object, Your Honor. Calls for conjecture," Benjamin shouts out.

"Overruled. The witness is an expert in this area."

"Sometimes," my father answers.

"What about in this case? Mr. Haviland, have you sold a Gabriel since his death?"

"Yes."

"For how much?"

My father breathes deeply. "For $500,000."

A hush settles over the courtroom which Linda allows to play out like a long piano chord and then she dips her head slightly.

"Are you close to your daughter, Mr. Haviland?"

"Yes."

"So you'd say you have a good relationship?" she asks.

"Yes."

"If your daughter were in danger would you do anything in your power to save her life?"

"Certainly," my father says.

"Would she do the same for you?"

"Yes," he answers, then realizes the implication of his answer and adds, "within reason."

But his words overlap Linda's next question and I doubt the jury hears them.

"Who is the beneficiary of your estate, Mr. Haviland?"

"My daughter."

"Did you approve of your daughter living with Slade Gabriel?" Linda asks.

"Genny is an adult."

"But did you approve?"

My father glances at me. "Yes," he lies.

"So you had no reservations whatsoever that your daughter was involved with a man twenty years her senior?"

"No," my father lies once more.

"Thank you, I have no more questions, Your Honor," Linda says and sits down at the prosecutor's table.

The judge nods at Benjamin who gets up and approaches my father.

"For the record, Mr. Haviland, did Slade Gabriel ever discuss any plans with you whatsoever to leave your gallery?"

"No."

"Did you ever discuss any fears with your daughter you might have had about him leaving your gallery?"

"Absolutely not."

"Can you tell us, Mr. Haviland, in rounded off numbers what your net worth is?"

"More than several million dollars."

"So even if your gallery went under and you never sold another painting for as long as you live, your lifestyle would not be affected in the slightest?"

"That is correct."

"Thank you, Mr. Haviland."

But it's not about money. Without his gallery, without his coterie of artists, without his deals, my father would be less than himself, lost, living for what?

"I can see that it's getting late, so we will adjourn for the day. Thank you, ladies and gentlemen," the judge says.

As he rises, Benjamin leans close to me and tells me we need to talk.

Half an hour later, we are in his office, surrounded by piles of briefs. Books are scattered everywhere, including on the lumpy couch where I sit. His secretary brings in mugs of coffee and a plate of butter cookies. Benjamin wolfs down three.

"Linda was way out in left field asking your father about Gabriel's dissatisfaction and possible defection from the gallery. Surprises stink. I need you to fill me in, Genny. What's she found out? Where the hell is she going?"

SEVENTEEN

"Gabriel," I whispered. I lay in my bed, imagining his large hands, his craggy face, his hair, grayer, but still curling down his neck and over his ears. I had noticed his foot sticking out of the hospital bed, his long bony foot under the sheets. How many times had I rubbed my cheek against his foot before sucking on his toes, making him shiver.

"Gabriel," I said aloud, a moan. I had forgotten what it was to want like this. I got out of bed and with a shaking hand, like an addict giving in despite the best of intentions, called the hospital and asked for Slade Gabriel's room. The operator put me on hold, then came back on the line and told me he'd been released days before. I replaced the phone in the cradle. What had I been thinking? Was I crazy? What if he had answered the phone?

Gabriel was my poison.

But what would it have been like, I thought, after so long, to make love to him? To have him make love to me?

A week later, I was holding a production meeting in my office when the phone rang.

"Hello."

"Genny?" It was Gabriel.

My body temperature dropped, my bowels liquefied, my heart held midbeat. Shifting in my seat, I angled my body away from everyone sitting across the desk from me.

"Is this a bad time?" he asked.

I wanted to ask everyone to leave my office so I could stay on the phone, scared to sever the connection now that it had been made, but instead I told him I was in the midst of a meeting and asked if I could call back.

He gave me a number. I started writing it down and then realized it wasn't a phone number, it was an address. His address on Greene Street.

For the rest of the day, I functioned on two levels. As I worked on the Mondrian rough cut, suggesting dissolves, clipping the ends of some scenes, elongating others, I continued to reexperience the shock of hearing Gabriel's voice on the phone.

Despite my anticipation, or more likely because of it, I worked late that night and didn't finish up until almost eight-thirty. By then I'd convinced myself to go home, that there I'd be able to shut out the sound of his voice and put him back in the shadows.

Outside, a freezing rain was making the sidewalks slippery. Walking was treacherous and I had to wait five minutes for a cab. Ice settled in my hair, hit my face, stung my lips. I tried to shield myself from the rain but I had no umbrella. A car skidded, its wheels losing traction on the icy slick, and it spun out of control barely missing the cab that had just stopped at the curb. A man carrying a shopping bag got out. I got in and heard myself give the driver Gabriel's SoHo address.

During the ride downtown I sat up straight, keeping my back away from the plastic seat and my hands in my lap, not wanting to touch anything around me, or have anything touch me. I was aware of every sensation: the warmth coming back to my face, the shape of my breasts under my sweater, the pressure of my lips touching, the sweat running from under my arms, the dampness between my legs. Christ, I was as nervous as I'd been that first time I'd taken a cab down to Gabriel's loft twenty years before.

What of my promise to myself to turn him away, to make him

suffer? Not abandoned, only postponed. First I would talk to him about his work, have my private viewing of his paintings, even allow a sense of awe to overwhelm me if that was what his work did to me. And yes, before I would take my revenge I would touch him, feel him, have him touch me, bring him to the edge, and then I would leave him there.

Using a small mirror, I examined my face. In twenty years circles had developed under my eyes and the frown lines no longer disappeared when I stopped frowning. I brushed my damp hair, stroked on more mascara, slid on some lipstick. In my bag, I carried a small silver flask of perfume, Golconda, a dark scent of roses and cinnamon. Dabbing some on my fingers, I touched the back of my neck, the skin between my breasts, and, through my tights, the backs of my knees.

The cab bumped over the cobblestones, coming to a stop in front of the familiar five-story building. I paid the fare and took my change, dropping some of it on the floor by accident but not stopping to retrieve it.

In the street, I shivered in the cold as the sweat dripped down my back.

Inside the vestibule the same yellow paint peeled off the walls and the elevator still creaked on its way up. When I got to his door, I stopped. It wasn't too late. Gabriel need never know I'd been there. I could turn around and leave and probably catch the same cab cruising the block, hoping for a fare. I pushed the doorbell.

Gabriel opened the door wide for me and I walked past him into the loft. I hadn't taken more than five steps when he put his hands on my hips and turned me around so that we faced each other. Lifting his hand, he extended his forefinger and traced the outline of my lips in the air. I sighed in defeat, finished before I'd begun.

"Took your time, didn't you?"

I nodded.

"Did you get pleasure out of knowing I was waiting?"

"I didn't know you were waiting."

"The truth, Genny. This time we start with the truth."

"Yes, it gave me great pleasure to know you were waiting."

Then he leaned down and I lifted up my face. Oh God, how fast it came back, all the same pressures and pulls as his tongue licked my lips and his hands gently cupped my face.

After a long kiss Gabriel let go of me and I swayed on my feet. "Why am I here?" I asked, sitting down on the same old Jackson Pollock couch.

"Do you have to ask?"

"Yes."

"Genny with a million questions still needs to know all the answers."

"Why am I here?"

It did not surprise me that he responded not with words but with touch, brushing a wayward lock of my hair off my face, combing my curls with his fingertips, keeping his eyes locked on mine.

"Why don't you answer me?"

"Your questions aren't always easy."

"Gabriel, why am I here?"

"You're here because I called you and you came."

"Why did you call me?"

"Another question." He tried to pull me to him but I held back.

"Okay, I'll try an easier question: Where is your wife?"

"We're living apart."

"Why do I always seem to meet you when you're separated from your wives?"

"We weren't separated. I woke up in the hospital."

"How is the second Mrs. Gabriel taking the separation?"

"Happily. The unhappy part was living with me. Last question."

"What happened in the hospital to make you decide to call it quits?" I asked.

"Saying your name out loud."

A vein throbbed in his forehead, his dark eyes glinted.

It was a short distance for him to lean over and take me in his arms. We didn't rush, didn't pull off each other's clothes. Gabriel pressed his lips to my forehead, my eyelids, and in the hollow of my throat. He unbuttoned my shirt, unhooked my bra, and pressed his lips to the flat space between my breasts.

Too aware of every sensation, I couldn't float, not yet. I kept thinking of how long it had been, how many times I'd imagined this, how poor my fantasies had been without his smells, the feel of his skin. And I kept thinking, too, of how dangerous it was for me to be with him.

He took off his clothes and sat facing me on his bed, rediscovering my body with his eyes, with his hands.

How long had it been since I'd felt that wonder when someone touched me? The truth, he had said. All right. I hadn't felt it since the last time he had touched me. What furies was I unleashing?

The lights were on, the lights had always been on when Gabriel and I made love, so he could watch me and see how much I enjoyed it, he said. After Gabriel, with other men, I insisted on having sex in the dark and even during the day I lowered shades and pulled covers up, shrouding myself.

Gabriel put his hands on my hips.

Covering his hands with mine, I felt him feeling me.

I was different than I'd been twenty years before; this time I held back, shaking, trembling, unwilling to open myself up to him so quickly.

"Am I scaring you?" he asked. "You're trembling."

Unable to answer, I nodded.

"I remember the girl who wouldn't scare," he said.

"I've changed."

"No, you haven't. Not really."

He made me lie back and do nothing but allow him to touch me. Closing my eyes and resting my head on the pillows, I smelled his scent on the bedding and inhaled deeply.

He sat on his heels between my legs, then starting at my temples he traced the bones of my face, my lips, my neck, my breasts, my stomach, my thighs, my calves, my ankles, my feet with his fingertips. Painting me with his fingertips. Up and down, he stroked me, and I just lay there, arms at my side, palms up, shivering.

The only place Gabriel did not touch was between my legs. Even when I reached out and tried to put his hand there, he pulled it away.

"Do you know how long I kept seeing you like this? I went back to Nina, to other women, but I kept seeing you."

None of his touches ignited me the way this revelation did. With furious fingers I grasped his hips and tried to pull him on top of me. Resisting, he pushed my hands back down and held them by my sides. I struggled against his hold, thrusting my hips, trying to push myself up so close that he couldn't help but slip inside me. But not the wild thrashing, kicking, or biting made him release me.

"Please, now."

"Not yet, Genny." His voice was so low it scraped the floor. And keeping me pinned down with his hands, he used his tongue to touch me, traveling from my forehead down to my lips down to my neck, down to my collarbone, down my breastbone and around my nipples, down across my stomach circling my belly button, down and then— oh no—around—damn him!—to my right thigh and then I shifted my hips and opened my legs and snapped them together like a vise trying to trap him but he just laughed and sat up.

"You have to want it," he said.

"How much more can I want it?"

"We'll see."

Much more.

"I'm going to come, without you even going in me," I finally whispered.

"The hell you will," he said and let me loose at last. My hands were all over him, and then all twisted up in each other we stopped, separated, and changed positions. Gabriel lay down and I straddled him and slowly lowered myself on him feeling every inch of him going inside me. The whole time each of us watched how it felt on the other's face.

Gabriel grabbed my legs by the ankles and wrapped my feet around his neck so that he was far inside me. Had I ever been that open to any other man? Had I ever been that open even to him? The sensation was close to pain, but I had no desire to stop. We still watched each other, and he was smiling. He was so far into me . . . so far into me . . . but now I didn't want to come because then it would be over and how would I bear that? Maybe we could just die like this, I thought, and then he shifted his hips under me and I lost any sense of separation between my body and his. It wasn't until he asked if I was all right, that I realized I was crying, and that my hot tears were falling on him like some crazy summer shower.

The next morning Gabriel showed me the painting he'd been working on since being released from the hospital. Like the drawings he'd done after the accident, the painting was not as abstract as his usual work. And there was a new light shining in these canvases: a luminous magical cadmium white Godlike light.

In the loft, other paintings, done before the accident, paled in comparison. There was no depth to them, no possibility of rebirth, no musing on what happens once we wake, no hope to hold on to.

It was a bold, brave painting. Not just because of the brushstrokes he was working with, or his darker jewel-like palette, but because he was mixing poetry in with the colors.

It had been out of fashion to speak of poetry and painting for over a century but there was nothing anachronistic or passé about Gabriel's paintings.

"So you've become some kind of romantic at last," I said to him over breakfast.

"Yes." He laughed. "A postmodern romantic."

"Well, I like it."

"As much as that blue Picasso of yours?" he teased.

"The Picasso is gone. My father sold it."

"When?"

"While I was in college. My father didn't want to miss the boom in the market when Picasso died and sold it without asking me. I'm not sure I've ever forgiven him."

"It's good to lose things. People shouldn't become so attached . . . to things . . . to each other. Forgive him, Genny."

"Are you satisfied with your new painting?" I asked, too busy with my next question to have really heard what he had said.

"With this painting, yes. But not with painting as an art form. There's still nothing I want to do more than paint, but I can't justify my obsession. Paintings are unnecessary in this world. There's no need for these canvases. For any more canvases."

"Why?"

"We've explored this medium to death. If I were starting now, I'd go into film. It's open and accessible. People know how to respond to celluloid. I'm tired of fighting to be understood."

As much as he believed what he was saying, he was staring at the unfinished painting on his easel, chafing to get started on it.

I poured myself a second cup of coffee. "Go ahead. I'd like to watch you paint."

Soon, he was lost in his gardens.

After an hour he came over to me, pulled me up, and held me.

"There have only been two places I've ever felt I really belonged," he said. "In front of a canvas and inside the circle you make of your arms. Genny, move in with me. We've lost so much fucking time already."

If I let go of hating and resisting him, and then he changed his mind again, would I ever be able to regroup? I had suffered over this man for too long. I had to say no while I still could.

"It's too late, Gabriel. Too dangerous. I shouldn't have come. Now I'm going to have to forget about you all over again."

"Wouldn't that be nice: If we could forget about each other? How prosaic. If we could just grow old and only think of each other as a pleasant memory. How dare you? It can't be like that. Not with us."

"Why not?" I whispered.

"I can't explain. Just like I could never explain how I heard your voice right before the cab careened toward me, or how I just knew how to draw. What happened to your courage, kid? I remember you as being so fucking brave."

The next morning at my office, my father called and, after talking to me for a few minutes, insisted I meet him and my mother after work for dinner.

Having hardly slept the night before, I was tired when I walked into the restaurant, angry with myself for having agreed to meet them. Passing through the front room at Petrossian, past the glass cases full of smoked salmon, pâtés, and tins of caviar, I stopped at the maître d's stand and gave him my name.

Ushering me past the long mirrored bar into the intimate dining area, he showed me to the table where my parents waited, sipping flutes of champagne.

As soon as I'd kissed them both, said hello, and sat down, my father spooned some glistening black beads on a triangle of toast and offered it to me. While I popped the caviar eggs on my tongue, the waiter poured me a glass of champagne.

"Have you heard anything more about the Cézanne?" I asked after we'd covered all the benign topics.

"Not yet," my father said.

"Are you sure you shouldn't just let the Van Arsdale Trust take you to court? What's the risk? You know you'd win."

Neither of them answered right away and I couldn't help but read into the silence.

My mother lifted her glass to her lips and took a single sip. As a child I tried, but failed, to mimic her grace. Even after so many years of living in America, she was still so French.

"You shouldn't be worrying about this," she said.

"I'm not worried," I lied.

"You sounded upset on the phone; you look exhausted. Is something wrong?" My father was concerned.

"No, I'm fine."

"Is it work?" my father asked, dissatisfied with my denial.

"No, work is fine."

"Leave her alone, Jonathan," my mother reassured him.

"No, Maguy, something is wrong. Genny?"

Toying with the stem of my glass I said: "I'm seeing someone. . . ."

"Is it serious?" my mother asked, smiling.

"It's Slade Gabriel," I blurted out.

My mother lifted her eyebrows and her shoulders at the same time as if to say, So what is the trouble? However, my father's forehead creased with concern.

"You know he's married," he cautioned immediately.

"He's separated and asked me to move into his loft with him."

"That's insane. You can't know him well enough to take a step like that," my father said, his voice taut, tense.

And then turning his back to me, my father caught the waiter's eye and gestured to the champagne. Within seconds our glasses were topped off.

I'd never asked for their permission, had never involved my parents in whom I'd dated or even married. So why was I involving them—my father really—now? Was it because these two men were connected? Or was it because I knew my father would try to stop me? Was I hoping he could?

"A man like Gabriel doesn't know how to take care of anyone but himself. For Christ's sake, Genny, he barely takes care of himself. He's too busy being a painter. That's all his life is. Do you understand?"

"Yes," I said.

"It's unnatural for you to be with Gabriel. Don't you see that?"

"Why?" I answered his question with my own.

"He's almost my age, Genny, old enough to be a—"

"Jonathan," my mother interrupted. "Genevieve doesn't need anyone to take care of her. She never has, regardless of what you've always thought and she's certainly old enough to make up her own mind about whom she wants to be with. She's not your little girl anymore. Tell him, *mon chou*," she said to me. "Tell your father not to worry."

"Genny." My father put his hand on mine. "Please, look at the man's track record. Be sure this is what you want, because you might have to pay for it, dearly."

I already have, I wanted to tell my father. I've been paying for half my life.

Thinking back on it now, I doubt anything my father could have said would have convinced me to stay away from Gabriel, even if he'd told me I'd go on paying for the rest of my life, too.

EIGHTEEN

New York City Criminal Court Building, Room 1317
Tuesday, December 8, 1992, 9:15 A.M.

Judge Bailey wipes at something on his desk, compulsively rubbing with his finger until satisfied he's gotten it off, then he says good morning and asks Linda Zavidow if she's ready to call her next witness.

"I call Mr. Hamilton Lane."

As he takes the stand several of the women on the jury perk up, responding to his thick curly hair, his athlete's body, and his light green, intelligent eyes. They don't know him, so they can't tell that there is anguish in his eyes, too, but I can.

"I hate that I have to testify," he had told me when he called me last night. "Of all people, I don't want to be the one to say something that could damage your case."

After Linda has asked Ham to describe his respective relationships to my father (mentor), Gabriel (friend), and me (ex-lover and current friend), she asks him the question Benjamin has been dreading, the one which will send this trial spinning off into a different, more dangerous direction.

"To the best of your knowledge, what were Mr. Gabriel's plans with regards to his career up until his death on September 18 of this year?"

"He was planning to leave the Haviland Gallery and come to my gallery when his contract came up for renewal."

Behind me an angry "No" escapes from my father's lips and washes over me.

So my father really had *not* believed Gabriel intended to leave.

"Why was Mr. Gabriel going to move to your gallery?" Linda asks.

"He had a different idea of how he wanted to pursue his career. Unable to handle the constant pressure of promoting and marketing his paintings, he wanted freedom to pursue new ideas. He had a feeling that he had *produced* art for too long. The whole system of produce-sell, produce-sell was getting to him. That plus Mr. Haviland was insisting Gabriel continue painting in his old style. It was suffo—"

Realizing what he has said, Ham breaks off midword.

"Yes, Mr. Lane?"

"It was inhibiting him."

"Didn't Gabriel care about making money anymore?"

Benjamin stands up. "I object. Calls for conjecture."

"I'll rephrase," Linda offers even before Judge Bailey has a chance to rule. "Did Mr. Gabriel have occasion to discuss his finances with you?"

"Yes. He told me he'd made a lot of money and could handle it if nothing sold for a while. Doing something new was more important. Having discovered what was missing from his art, he felt compelled to at least try and put it back, even if that meant making a financial sacrifice. I understood that. I wanted to help him find what he was searching for. I'd seen his new work. He was on the brink of doing something so worthwhile."

"Well, well, well. That's all very sophisticated and erudite. As far as you know, are those the only reasons Mr. Gabriel wanted to leave Mr. Haviland's gallery?"

"As far as I know."

"Come on, Mr. Lane, wasn't Mr. Gabriel also bothered that Mr. Haviland was involved in the Van Arsdale Trust debacle?"

I can see from the expression on Ham's face that he isn't prepared for this attack on my father. Although they have differed philosophically about how to nurture artists and sell art, Ham has never wanted to cause his mentor pain.

"No. He simply felt that he wanted a different environment," Ham says.

"Please explain that."

"I think I already have."

"For the edification of the court, please explain it again."

Benjamin stands, "Your Honor, I object, Miss Zavidow is badgering the witness."

"Overruled. The witness will answer the question."

"Gabriel said he and Mr. Haviland didn't agree on the new direction Gabriel's work was taking. He told me they had been arguing about it."

"What about the Cézanne forgery? Wasn't Mr. Gabriel highly principled? Hadn't he left his previous gallery, Marlborough, because they, too, had been involved in a scandal?"

"Calls for conjecture, Your Honor."

"Sustained. Once again, Miss Zavidow, rephrase your question," Judge Bailey admonishes.

"Mr. Lane, did Gabriel ever tell you he was disturbed by the negative media attention the Haviland Gallery was attracting?"

"I still object," Benjamin says sternly.

"I'll allow it." The judge looks at Ham. "You may answer the question."

"I don't remember."

"You don't, Mr. Lane?" Linda asks sarcastically.

"No, I don't."

"At this point I would like to introduce a document, labeled exhibit E, to be entered as evidence."

The document is logged in and read aloud. It is a preliminary letter of agreement between the Hamilton Lane Gallery and Slade Gabriel. On the bottom, in Gabriel's handwriting was a note:

Ham—this works for me. Let's talk timing. S.G.

"Your Honor, I would like to be able to examine the evidence and have Mr. Gabriel's handwriting verified," Benjamin says.

Like other things she is trying to surprise the jury with, Linda never mentioned this letter in her opening statement. She saved it for its shock value. Now that the jury's aware of the agreement, there's an almost collective gasp as everyone makes the leap and finds the foothold: Gabriel was leaving my father's gallery and I killed him before he could make the switch, killed him not just because he'd hurt me so badly, but because now he was going to hurt my father, too.

"Mr. Lane," Linda continues her cross-examination. "Can you tell us how this letter, this preliminary agreement between you and the deceased, came about?" Linda asks.

It was mid-March, the morning of a Sotheby's auction, and I'd been living with Gabriel for a few months.

I came out of the bedroom, dressed to go, and found Gabriel still painting. "Maybe you should get ready. We have to leave soon," I said.

"Where?"

"The auction. Did you forget?"

He looked at me, perplexed. "The auction?"

On his easel were half a dozen yellow Post-it notes—one reminding him about the auction. There were more on the refrigerator, the bathroom mirror, and on the front door. Little reminders of what he needed to buy at the art supply store, or meetings he'd made.

But then he'd forget to look at the notes.

When I was seventeen and he was thirty-seven, I never thought about the age difference between us, but I thought about it now. Gabriel had never been so distracted or forgetful before. Maybe the accident had affected him. Or perhaps he was simply getting older.

What would happen to us if he turned into an old man? Stop, I warned myself. Don't create yet another fantasy of what will go wrong, of how Gabriel will leave this time.

We took a taxi uptown to Sotheby's where one of Gabriel's paintings was to be included in an auction of Twentieth-Century Art. Despite my parents' efforts, rumors about the Cézanne forgery and my father and the gallery had been in the papers for days; damaging, nasty pieces questioning a possible conflict of interest in my father's lawyer being on the board of directors of Sotheby's as well as being chief counsel for the Association of Art Dealers of America. Each article exposed something else supposedly wrong with the unregulated business of selling art. So when Gabriel and I walked into the stone and glass building on the corner of 71st and York, we weren't surprised to find the press buzzing around my parents.

Compared to the auctions of the last decade, this one was subdued, the audience serious rather than hyper, the clothes outfits not costumes. There was no crush of spectators, the fanfare replaced by a businesslike atmosphere. All but the hard-core investors had disappeared in a market that had not just weakened but almost dried up.

The sale got off to a solemn start when Jeff Koons's basketballs—two Spauldings floating in a store-bought aquarium, filled with twenty-two gallons of distilled spring water, not tap water, according to the auctioneer, sold for only $101,000—the same price a collector had paid for it in 1989.

There were many mediocre works for sale. A few years before each would have been fought over. That morning, few of them even met the reserve. It was only the best examples of the most established names that got a rise out of the audience and went for more than the estimate.

After an appropriation of Duchamp's urinal didn't sell, Gabriel whispered to me, "Wasn't it Duchamp who said when everything becomes art, art becomes nothing?"

I didn't have time to answer because his canvas was up on the block. A lush abstract garden from the mid-eighties, joyful and excessive. The bidding started at $50,000 and climbed steadily to $150,000. Several people were putting their paddles up and the action in the room moved swiftly.

One of the bidders, two rows in front of us, looked familiar. But so did half the people in the room. I'd probably met most of them at my parents' parties. I failed to remember where I met this particular bidder.

The bid was with him; he nodded. Another bid in the back. Another on the side. The bid was at $200,000, when there was a momentary lull.

"Going once and—" the auctioneer intoned.

The man in front of us raised his paddle and the bidding continued, ending with a portly gentlemen in the back of the room who got the Gabriel for $250,000.

Stifling a laugh that threatened to overtake his body, Gabriel shook his head. In my father's gallery the largest paintings were selling for $100,000—$250,000 was a record.

On one side of me, Gabriel was amused. On the other side, my father was triumphant. The sale would not only enable him to raise the going price of Gabriel's canvases but increase the value of gallery-owned Gabriels. My mother was nonplussed. It was déclassé to focus on the price, but I knew she had to be pleased by it.

When the auction was over, we followed my parents out into the lobby where a reporter waylaid my father. Gabriel walked away, but I remained with my mother, by my father's side.

"Do you have a comment on the sale, Mr. Haviland?" the reporter asked.

"Yes, I'm thrilled. This proves there is a steady market out there."

"And what can you tell us about the Cézanne controversy? Is it true you've offered to buy the painting back from the Trust?"

"No comment." My father turned away to exchange greetings with a client. I went in search of Gabriel, whom I found standing with Hamilton Lane near the front entrance.

As soon as they noticed me, they both fell silent.

"What's going on? You two look like a couple of schoolboys in cahoots," I teased.

"Hello, Genny." Ham kissed my cheek, smiling and responding too quickly. "We were just talking about Gabriel's quarter of a million dollar record. Quite a coup in this climate."

Until that afternoon, I'd never been uncomfortable around Ham. Our friendship had survived our short-lived dating attempt and we had drinks or lunch together every few months.

But for the first time, standing there after that auction, I was aware of the nights we'd spent together. And I knew Ham was, too.

Of course we were too courteous, too well bred to even obliquely refer to it, but we didn't have to. It was there in the way we avoided each other and focused on Gabriel.

And for the second time that day, I was conscious of how much older Gabriel was than either Ham or me. There were lines in his face I'd never seen before, lines subdivided by other lines.

Out in the street, my father invited himself and my mother to the loft to see Gabriel's latest canvases. In the car on the way downtown, my father treated Gabriel and me as if resigned to our relationship, but there were subtle signs that warned me otherwise: My father flinched every time Gabriel leaned close to me or touched me. My mother, on the other hand, seemed completely at ease, accepting us as a couple without any trouble. What was the last thing I had done that she'd minded?

I remember exactly how my father stood in the loft, without saying a word, appraising Gabriel's work. He wore a handmade olive green suit, a black cashmere scarf around his neck, and soft, black suede Italian loafers. His gray hair curled just above the collar of his cream colored shirt.

Gabriel's hands were shoved in the pockets of his Levi's. His white shirt was clean but his shoes, broken-in moccasins, were spattered with green paint. He'd worn a jacket to Sotheby's but had taken it off and hung it on a hook by the door as soon as he'd walked into the loft.

My father's stance was rigid; Gabriel's was relaxed. There was so much information in the backs of those two men; the way they stood only four inches apart, sharing the same small space, comfortable with each other after twenty years of doing business, and uncomfortable because after so many years things had irrevocably changed. Together they stared out at the same paintings, but they each saw them so differently.

My father is a tall man; Gabriel was several inches taller. Together they could have formed a fortress around me but I didn't stand near them. I stood back. My mother was beside my father, but deferring to him, as she usually did in public.

"Gabriel." My father's voice was subdued as if he were offering condolences. "More than anyone, I can understand your desire to forge ahead, to progress, but I told you weeks ago when you showed me the first of these, that we need a transition from what you were doing before the accident to this. The '90s are not as brave as the '70s were—"

"Bullshit," Gabriel said.

"Listen to me. This change in style is too abrupt. It will frighten people away. They are challenging, spiritual. They are not what we ex-

pect from a Gabriel. We expect an easy exuberance, if you will, deca-
dence, an escape."

"So these paintings won't be easy to sell? So what? Will you go
broke? Will I?"

My father pressed his lips together, showing his displeasure. His
mouth disappeared into an angry line. "Can't we compromise? Include, say, three or four of these new paintings in the show along with
some of the older work."

"I've been . . . without . . ." Gabriel's most fluid expressions had always been with paint and brushes, with blazing colors, glazes and gels,
not with words, but too often lately he really had to search for the
right phrase. "Shit, Jonathan, you know I've always worried that if I finally found what I was searching for I wouldn't be good enough to
paint it, but I *have* found it and I *can* paint it. And I'll be damned before I go backward. I'll leave the gallery before I go backward."

My father waved away what Gabriel said. It was inconceivable to
him that he might ever lose him.

"As your dealer, I'd be remiss to hang a show that wouldn't sell. Especially after what happened today at Sotheby's. We've got to keep the
momentum going, keep the museums interested, keep the collectors
drooling."

Was there subtext here? How much of my father's discomfort with
these paintings was because they had been painted since I'd become
Gabriel's lover?

"This is my best work," Gabriel said, not to my father or my
mother or to me, but to the paintings. "I can't go back. It would be
like imitating myself. Fuck it, Jonathan." Gabriel hurled the words as
if he were throwing paint at a canvas. "No!"

The afternoon sun shifted and shined through the multipaned sky-
light. My father paced. With the threat of the Cézanne controversy
and his integrity as a dealer hanging over his head, he was not going to

back down. "I sold my soul to get Richard Finder to write the mono-graph of your catalogue, and I will not abide a text damning you with faint praise which is what you'll get if the show includes only these canvases."

"How the hell do you know what he's going to say? He hasn't even seen the paintings."

"Yes, he has. He came down the other afternoon," I said.

Gabriel glared at me as if he'd been betrayed.

"Finder was here? When?" he asked me.

"When you were lecturing at Cooper Union. I told you about it."

"No you didn't."

I knew I had, but this wasn't the time to argue the point.

"Well, I don't give a fuck what Finder thinks," he muttered.

"But I do, Gabriel. He's an astute critic, he's influential, and he feels your new things aren't as painterly as your previous work. He thinks you're trying too hard to imbue these canvases with a message and not leaving enough room for interpretation."

"Like I said, I don't give a fuck what Finder thinks."

My mother stepped forward. "Gabriel, do you have so little regard for your success? For the time it has taken to build your career? For how much energy Jonathan has devoted to—?"

My father interrupted her, straining to keep his voice level. "You can't just throw a new style at your audience. You have to ease them into it when the time is right. You don't act on instinct for Christ's sakes and blunder ahead. Who willingly walks into a house on fire?"

"Is what I paint completely irrelevant to the money it brings in?" Gabriel asked. "Listen to me, Jonathan, these are the paintings I'm showing."

"Even if the show sets your career back?"

Gabriel's laugh was cruel.

In an effort to get away from the bitterness and indignation criss-crossing the room, I moved closer to the wall.

"When the fuck did you stop loving the paintings, Jonathan? Did I miss the announcement? When did you stop caring about the art?"

"How dare you insult my husband! It seems to me you've enjoyed quite a nice life with the checks he's given you in exchange for that art," my mother hissed.

Gabriel walked over to a taboret stand where a corked bottle of wine sat beside a few glasses. He splashed some of the wine in a glass and drank it down in two furious gulps. "Painting is my job. It's all my job is."

"In a perfect world, yes." My father had regained his composure and now was trying to placate Gabriel. "But in this world it's not all your job is. Your job—the job you've been doing for the last twenty years—is to make paintings I can sell."

My father turned to me with an exasperated sigh. "Genny, see if you can talk some sense into him." He walked to my side, kissed me lightly on the lips, then went to Gabriel, rested a fatherly hand on his shoulder, waited for my mother to say good-bye, and together my parents left.

Sadly, Gabriel poured another glass of wine for himself and one for me.

"He's impossible," Gabriel said.

"I know, but—"

"Genny, you're not going to try to talk me into changing my mind, are you?"

I didn't answer.

He searched my face and I could tell he wasn't thinking about the paintings now but about me.

"I don't want to be in the middle of this. Can't you understand that?"

"You are not in the middle of this."

"Of course I am. Didn't you hear him ask me to talk some sense into you?"

"Well, just tell him you tried and I'm past being sensible." And then he laughed.

"I don't think it's funny."

"I know that, sweetheart."

"Why does it have to be all or nothing, Gabriel? Would it really be so awful to do what he asked? To compromise?"

"You tell me," he said.

I sipped my wine slowly. There was no chance of him capitulating, not when it came to his painting.

Seeing that he had won, he smiled and gently brushed a strand of hair off my face. Deep in my stomach, I felt the throb of wanting him. No matter how difficult things ever were, I never stopped wanting him.

He pulled me toward him and I fit into the familiar hollows and bumps of his body.

"Genny, do you know what it's like to always be so damn lonely . . . ?"

I nodded.

"Not to have anyone understand except you?"

It was like a benediction.

Yes, I understood.

But only to a point because although Gabriel was my lover, Jonathan Haviland was my father and I prayed that I would never have to choose between them. The thought chilled me and I shivered even within the temporary shelter of Gabriel's arms. Unaware, Gabriel let go of me, picked up his brush, and began painting again.

Slade Gabriel, at that point in his life, was finally free to explore the limits and boundaries most of us fear. It made him dangerous and that made me afraid.

It also made me want him even more.

NINETEEN

New York City Criminal Court Building, Room 1317
Tuesday, December 8, 1992, 12:15 P.M.

Before Benjamin has a chance to question Hamilton Lane, the judge adjourns the court for lunch. As the jury files out several of them look over at me.

Are they starting to decide what I can't decide—whether I'm guilty or not? I've tried to count which of them, from their body language, their stares from across the room, seem to be on my side, but this game, adding up my supporters, moving them like beads on an abacus, provides no satisfaction.

Besides, they won't decide alone. They'll be together in a single room, fighting it out until they all agree. I'm the one alone. Despite my parents, friends, despite Benjamin always by my side, I experience my aloneness as if it were an affliction. My separateness is so total I'm severed from the ordinary world, able to connect only with my physical being.

I look at the windows and picture bars on them. Turning in my seat, I pretend the closed courtroom doors are locked. I try to imagine what it will be like in jail. Putting my hand up to my face, I try to remember what Gabriel's touch felt like.

How long can I live without being touched?

How long might I be forced to?

"Benjamin, I have a question."

He turns. "Does this mean you've finally decided to join us?"

I'm almost sorry to disappoint him. "What is the maximum sentence for murder in the second degree?" I ask.

In that voice that I have come to recognize as being protective, he tries to assure me, "You're not going to be sentenced, Genny."

When I was charged, there was some discussion about my pleading insanity. What would those headlines have said? CRAZY WITH LOVE TV PRODUCER MURDERS LOVER.

"Maybe we should have pleaded temporary insanity?"

"C'mon Genny, let's go have lunch. We can talk about it once we're out of here," he says.

My parents, who have been waiting at the back of the courtroom, join us and we make our way out the door and into the crowded hallway and past Ham. There is so much distress in his eyes.

I want to stop and tell Ham that what he said on the stand was important. That people need to hear about idealism and integrity. Even if it is bad for my case, even if it hurts my father's pride.

What Gabriel infused in his paintings, what my father missed seeing, what Ham recognized—it's worth some sacrifice.

Down the hall in this small room, my parents, Benjamin, his associate Sam, and I sit down on the unmatched chairs around the wood table where the food has been laid out.

It's so cold today the heat has been turned all the way up, making the air dry, staticky, almost suffocating. I get up and try to open one of the windows, but it won't budge. I try another. Neither will open. Shifting my weight, I lean in and try again. Both my father and Benjamin get up to help me at the same time, but Benjamin is closest. He uses both hands and pulls up from the bottom. At first nothing, he tugs again, and then with an enormous *whoosh* that nearly throws him off balance, the window rises. Wintry air blasts into the room.

Once or twice in the courtroom, I've heard something, not words, but a sound that is like a whisper of wings or the first words in answer to a question or a prayer. I hear those wings now, coming in with the wind but apparently, no one else does.

"Mr. Haviland, did you know Hamilton and Gabriel were even talking?" Benjamin asks my father, preparing for his redirect of Ham Lane.

"No, and I'm not sure I believe that they were."

"Did you ever offer Gabriel anything not to leave?"

"I didn't do anything to try and stop him because I didn't know he was going." My father drains his coffee cup and pushes it away disdainfully.

Benjamin asks my mother if she knew anything about Gabriel's possible defection and like my father she says no.

"All right, Genny, tell me once more, when did Gabriel first mention leaving your father's gallery?"

A week or so after the Sotheby's auction, I was walking home from work on West Broadway. As I passed by an Italian restaurant called I Tre Merli, I happened to look through the window and see Gabriel sitting at a table with Ham.

Something warned me not to stop. When Gabriel came home, I didn't ask him where he'd been, but he told me.

"I had drinks with Ham."

"Oh yeah? How is he?"

"Genny, there is something I want you to know." The trepidation in his voice was out of character: Gabriel was never afraid. "Your father had someone at the auction bidding up the price of my paintings."

Turning on Gabriel, I accused him of being disloyal to my father, of buying into the bad press, of being influenced by what other people were saying instead of standing by his dealer, but all the while I screamed and shouted, I remembered other auctions where I'd seen that same man bidding on my father's other artists.

"Even if true, it goes on all the time," I said, full of bravado.

"Do you remember why I left Marlborough?"

"Everyone bids up paintings. Dealers have been doing it since the '70s."

"My work was tainted by the Rothko scandal; every artist's work there was tainted."

"Don't tell me you didn't know paintings get bid up?"

"Genny, it's . . . it's not just the auction, or this thing with the Cézanne. Your father is pushing me to go back to safe paintings that will sell. Doing what's fucking fashionable. I'm not some factory worker cutting out the same piece of plastic over and over. I can't paint a certain way because that's what people will buy."

"If you go, everyone else will, too. He'll lose everything."

"I wouldn't go now, Genny. I'd never break my contract."

I turned away. My father. My lover. My lover. My father.

"But you're going to leave when your contract expires?"

"Yes, I might. I suppose it depends on whether or not your father finally accepts this new work. On whether or not I can reconcile what he did at Sotheby's. On how this Cézanne mess turns out. I just don't know."

"You'll go with Ham, won't you?"

"Yes, he likes what I'm doing. It doesn't scare him. He's a good man, Genny. I know you understand that."

I knew then that every time I saw my father I'd be thinking about what Gabriel had said . . . if the Cézanne case didn't resolve itself . . . if he pushed Gabriel too hard . . . my father's carefully constructed life would slowly break apart. My mother would be in Paris nursing my grandfather, while my father remained in the large apartment on Central Park West, alone with only the paintings on his walls.

"You can't leave the gallery. You can't leave my father."

"It's crazy to talk about this now. My contract isn't up for months."

"How many months?"

"It's up in November," he said.

Benjamin, my parents, and I are out in the hallway, making our way along with everyone else, back to the courtroom. To shield me from the crowd, Benjamin stands in front of me, my mother on my right, my father on my left. It's inappropriate here, surrounded by so many people but this is where my father suddenly stops, and turns to me and asks: "Genny . . . tell me . . . did you do it?"

When Benjamin first accepted my case, I asked him if he thought I was guilty. Instead of answering he explained the presumption of innocence to me; he would never ask me, nor should anyone else during this process, if I'd killed Slade Gabriel, because under the constitution everyone is innocent until proven guilty.

Of all the people who might have asked, I never expected it to be my father, least of all here in this crowded hallway, on our way back to the courtroom, while strangers' faces pass in a blur.

"Do you think I could have?" Using his old trick, I answer his question with my own.

Subtly and with the old kind of love he used to have for me before I started seeing Gabriel, he imperceptibly nods his head yes.

If my father thinks I could have killed Gabriel for him, what will the jury think?

TWENTY

New York City Criminal Court Building, Room 1317
Tuesday, December 8, 1992, 1:33 P.M.

CROSS

In his redirect, Benjamin deftly dilutes Hamilton Lane's testimony, making it appear Gabriel was only flirting with the idea of changing dealers. He ends the redirect by asking why, if Gabriel were planning CROSS on joining Ham's gallery, didn't he go ahead and do it?

"I don't know," Ham answers.

"Do you know why he didn't continue negotiations with you, Mr. Lane?" Benjamin asks.

"No, I don't know that either."

Now, at least some doubt has been introduced.

"I have no more questions of this witness, Your Honor," Benjamin says and sits down beside me.

Ham looks right at me as he leaves the witness box and I can read the questions in his eyes. Has his testimony hurt my case? Has he done damage when all he has ever wanted to do was help?

Even though I don't know the answer, but because he's my friend, I force my lips into a smile I do not feel.

He straightens up and his step quickens and he walks down the center aisle.

Benjamin whispers my name to get my attention and I turn back and face forward.

"Miss Zavidow, would you call your next witness?"

"My next witness is Officer Wylie. He's in the building, Your Honor, he should be here in a few minutes."

So now this woman, in her practiced law school voice, will ask more questions to elicit the responses that will lay bare yet another part of my life. What if I just got up and walked out now? Followed Ham out of the stuffy wood-paneled room and into the cold winter air.

I shift in my seat. An officer stands by the door; would he stop me? Force me back here? How bad would it be for my case if I tried to run away? Does it matter?

Benjamin is looking at me. What does he read in my eyes that makes him so worried he takes my hand, not to comfort me—which is how it must seem to the jury—but to restrain me?

In the last week of March, Gabriel and I were walking home one evening when a disheveled man weaved toward us mumbling a request for money. Automatically, I reached into my pocket for change. After taking my nickels and dimes, the man shuffled off.

Gabriel watched his retreating back.

"Nice way to honor our vets, isn't it?" I said.

"We have to stop this war."

I was confused. "The war? Gabriel?"

The streetlight shone on his panicked face.

"What war?" I asked.

A moment passed. "Sorry, what did you say?"

"What just happened?"

"Nothing."

"It was like you spaced-out in the middle of a conversation. And you were talking about the war. What's wrong?"

"It's nothing, Genny. You can't keep asking questions. There aren't always answers."

But there are answers, even if you don't like them, even if you don't want to confront them or believe them.

When we got back to the loft Gabriel went to work painting and I got into bed on the side with the books piled high around it: stacks of books filled with information, filled with answers, books about Zen Buddhism, lapsed Catholics, atheism, books written by Joseph Campbell, Nietzsche, de Beauvoir, autobiographies of the last czar, Georgia O'Keeffe, Picasso, psychology books—one by Jung, one by Freud—a novel by Edith Wharton, a mystery by P. D. James.

I reached down and picked up the mystery, started reading, and at some point fell asleep, the book still in my arms, against my chest like a shield.

A circus made its way across the water, floating on some kind of raft. A red clown juggled sparkling balls. Flying high on a trapeze, a lady in an emerald outfit swung over the ocean and then back again. Acrobats in glittering black leotards jumped high over each other's backs into the air. The wind picked up, the water got rough. Waves built up far offshore. I called out to the performers to warn them, but they couldn't hear my shouts over the ocean's roar and continued their magical performance, even as the waves rolled in, swelled, and devoured them.

Did the dream wake me or was it Gabriel finally coming to bed? My eyelids were heavy and I didn't open them as he slid in beside me, kissing me while I drifted in and out of sleep, almost drugged. His hands stroked my body, lulled me. Rough skin rubbed me. Fingertips up my legs, across my stomach, circling my breasts. Night moves. Silent gropings. His lips pushed me into a new dream and while I struggled to stay on the surface instead of swirling off into darkness, something silken slipped between my legs. In my half-sleep state, I felt petals of flowers falling on my face in a soft rain. Then release and then a deep sleep.

I woke up in the morning and took a shower, remembering Gabriel making love to me only when I soaped between my legs and found the stickiness there. After dressing, I joined Gabriel in the kitchen. He was standing beside the coffee machine, a baffled expression on his face.

"What is it?" I asked.

He turned to me, startled for a second, then grinned. "Ah, Sleeping Beauty."

"What was wrong just now?"

"Nothing. Did you sleep well?"

"Except for this dream I had of being ravished."

"But I was gentle, Genny."

He turned back to the coffeemaker, poured the water in the top, and then switched the machine on. Whatever had troubled him had passed.

Over breakfast, I felt a familiar twinge in my stomach and realized I was ovulating. "You know, I wasn't wearing my diaphragm last night," I told Gabriel.

"Fucking diaphragm. I hate that piece of plastic between us. It's not really making love when I feel that thing there separating us."

"Lovely sentiment if you don't mind where it leads."

"There's always abortion."

The word landed on the table along with the dishes and the juice and the coffee and the cereal and rattled everything. "Have them scrape out my insides so that you don't have to fuck into a plastic dome? Abortion is a solution, Gabriel, but for Christ's sake, it's not an alternative to birth control."

Two and a half weeks later I discovered I was pregnant. At first, elation; then fear. I'd been pregnant twice when I was married. I'd felt the fullness in my belly, the tenderness of my breasts. But both times I had been pregnant I'd miscarried and after endless doctor appointments, sitting in overcrowded waiting rooms, reading dog-eared out-of-date magazines, I was told over and over there was nothing medically wrong. Now I was afraid it would happen again, and this time I would lose Gabriel's child.

It was seven-thirty at night. Gabriel had just opened a bottle of wine and we were sitting on the Jackson Pollock couch.

"I'm pregnant," I told him.

Uncomprehending at first, he stared, and then got up and walked over to the studio area where he began cleaning the day's brushes. The smell of turpentine, which I usually liked, made me gag. This was not how I imagined the moment; I cursed myself for having imagined it at all.

I shut my eyes and leaned against the back of the couch, listening to the sloshing of the brushes in the paint thinner. Gabriel was methodical with those brushes, spending a full half hour cleaning them each evening, getting all the paint out of the bristles and cleaning the handles with a cloth. "Genny, you can't have the baby," he said finally, from across the room.

"I can have it."

He walked over and sat beside me. "But you won't if it's not what I want, will you?"

"Why don't you want it?"

"I don't want to share you with a baby. Even our baby. I've tried it once and it doesn't work for me. Genny, we belong together, you and I, like this, in this place, for this time. Don't fool with it."

"You selfish bastard. *You* fooled with it. That night. Practically raping me in my sleep. I wasn't wearing my diaphragm and you knew it, but you fucked me anyway."

"So, you're going to have the baby to make me pay?"

"No, I'm going to have a baby because I want to."

He took my hands in his much larger ones; my hands disappeared. I felt them but couldn't see them. "Aren't there enough children in this fucking world to absorb its pain? Feel *my* hands, Genny. I'm already alive."

Imploring me with his eyes, he was sucking me in. I wanted a baby, had always wanted a baby. I wanted Gabriel, had always wanted him. It was as if he could read my mind.

"I hate saying it, making it sound like an ultimatum, but you can't have both of us. Either you'll have me or the baby and I'm asking you . . . please . . ."

There were tears in Gabriel's eyes. Despite myself, I saw his pain, much worse pain than he brought to the canvas. I couldn't yet feel the baby in my stomach, but I felt Gabriel's tears wet my skin.

For the next week I prayed I would have another miscarriage, that the decision would be taken out of my hands. At the same time I tried to change Gabriel's mind. But he was adamant.

I finally confided in my friend Tory and we talked about it for hours. She'd had an abortion in college with no regrets, but admitted this was different. "You have to figure out whom you want more; whom will you be able to forgive yourself for giving up?" she said.

Would I forgive myself if I had an abortion? Would I forgive myself if after waiting so many years for him, I walked away from Gabriel?

My confusion worsened. Nervous, sick, both mentally and physically, I'd make up my mind, then change it again.

I had plans to see my parents for lunch. It was easier than having dinner with them and making excuses for why Gabriel wouldn't be there. He didn't want to see my father socially while they were still battling over the paintings.

When I got to the gallery my mother and father seemed strangely quiet. Lunch was set up in the same conference room where, years before, Mimi and I had sorted through Gabriel's slides.

"We got some news today," my father said and then stopped to take a long drink of his ice water.

"Bad news?" I asked.

My mother picked up some breadcrumbs that had fallen on the granite table.

"Yes," my father answered. "But not about the Cézanne. This morning, Ed Blackmore told me that when his contract expires, he isn't going to renew."

Blackmore had been with the gallery since the early '60s. This was the kind of story that could wind up in *New York Magazine* or on "Page six" of the *New York Post* and cause reprisals, have repercussions. This could start an exodus of artists.

"Can't you do anything to stop him?"

My anxiety was a blow to his pride and he made an effort to laugh and be reassuring. "One artist leaving is bad, but it's not a disaster, Genny. "

But he did not seem very sure. For the first time he sounded like a sixty-seven-year-old man who was uncertain of his future.

"I am trying to convince your father this is a good time to retire. He doesn't have to leave the gallery world entirely. We could go live in France. He could revitalize your grandfather's gallery."

What my mother said made sense to me, more sense than all the time my parents spent living apart, he in New York, she in Paris. As their child, I was pleased at the thought of them being together. My mother had been going off to France more and more in the last few years, leaving my father in order to take care of her father. Why was it so difficult casting her as the dutiful wife? Because she was too independent. She couldn't even allow me to depend on her when I was growing up. My hands up in the air grabbing for her skirts had scared her. I remember wanting her to just bend down and pick me up so I could nestle in her arms, look into her pretty face, play with her curls, but she would call for Marie to come and tend to me. My mother was a whiff of perfume left in the room after she was gone.

"No, Maguy. That's crawling away and I won't do that. I made these artists. I will make more if I have to."

He'd never said it quite that way before and I didn't like how it sounded. Yes, he'd grown artists, like flowers in a garden, but now he was claiming to be more than the gardener. He was saying he could create the seeds.

Beside him was a pad of paper that he pushed toward me: a list of all the gallery's artists ranked in order of how much money they brought in, and beside that the dates their contracts came up for renewal. Gabriel's name was first.

"Three contracts are up within the year. Four next year. By then I can find new artists. I can weather this," he said. "I'll just give up the SoHo space, that will help."

The SoHo space was a large street-level gallery my father had renovated in 1986 for over a million dollars, but since then the art market had softened and it was evident by now the drop in sales was not an aberration but a trend.

"I've been foolish," he said. "Thinking a city in a recession could support two Haviland galleries."

My father had wanted that space because being in SoHo allowed him to go head to head with Ham Lane, Castelli, and Boone. Being downtown kept him fresh. "Yes, I'll let go of the SoHo space." He neatly folded his used napkin and laid it beside his plate.

My mother turned to me. "Tell him to close up here, too, and come to France with me."

"And live how, Maguy, in whose shadow?" my father asked.

I didn't understand—my grandfather's shadow? My mother's?

"You are terribly upset, Jonathan. You don't understand what you are saying," my mother said.

I pushed my salad away; some lettuce fell on the table. My voice seemed far away to me. "What is he saying?" My mother ignored my question.

"I've had enough, Maguy," my father said.

"What is going on?" I asked again.

My mother got up and walked toward the door, then stopped and turned around. "Why don't you just tell her already, Jonathan? Tell her whose shadow you referred to and stop using it as a threat."

"That's enough, Maguy," my father said. She left the room and he turned to me. "It's nothing, Genny. You know how we fight about your grandfather. Your mother has this idea about me going to France. Ridiculous. Can you see me, at this point in my life, being ordered around like your grandfather's stock boy?"

It sounded logical, but it didn't have the ring of truth.

"Is that really all?" I was remembering him tucking me in at night, telling me stories about a little girl named Abacazoo who had access to artists from all ages who painted for her.

"Yes, darling. Don't worry. Your mother is just trying to protect me from what might happen if things get any worse."

Before I left the gallery, I stopped at my mother's office to say good-bye.

"Come in for a moment," she said and then surprised me by asking if I was all right.

"Well . . ." I hesitated. What good would telling her do? She'd just shrug and say she was sure I'd do the right thing.

"Are you pregnant?"

"How did you know?"

"You didn't eat. You're pale. I remember how I was. How you were the last two times."

I told her the rest. Her response to my dilemma was so objective it chilled me, but it was the only advice anyone gave that helped me. My mother said if the passion I had for Gabriel was as strong as it appeared, no child would be able to carry the burden of proving to me that I'd made the right choice.

A week later, without knowing my decision, she left for France. "All you have to do if you need me is call and I'll come back. You're all right, aren't you?" she asked as she kissed me good-bye and I felt her slightly cool lips against my cheek.

"Yes, I'm fine," I lied, enabling her to go.

After almost a month of sleepless nights, I made an appointment with my doctor for an abortion. Gabriel offered to go with me, but I didn't want to be with him. He was the enemy, had been for weeks. Instead, I called my father and asked him to take me to the doctor.

TWENTY-ONE

New York City Criminal Court Building, Room 1317
Tuesday, December 8, 1992, 1:40 P.M.

"Officer Wylie, could you tell us where you were on the morning of April 26 of this year?" Linda asks.

Along with Linda, everyone in the courtroom listens to him recite his schedule. "I was responding to a call at a Doctor Nash's office on Park Avenue and 72nd Street. One of the doctor's nurses had called 911 when protesters began taunting the patients. In front of the doctor's office were approximately ten men and fifteen women carrying pro-life signs and chanting pro-life slogans."

In the car on the way to my doctor's office that morning, my father took my hand and said, "Come home and have the baby, Genny. We can help you, we can be a family again."

Did I consider it? Yes. I allowed myself to picture the life he was offering: he and I and the baby with visits from my mother when she flew in from Paris. If I were more depraved (for wouldn't it have been perverse with all that was unacknowledged between us to play house like that?) perhaps I would have accepted his offer.

He was furious when I didn't. "Damn Slade Gabriel. Goddamn him."

"Why shouldn't he have a choice?"

"Why shouldn't you?"

"This *is* my choice."

We rode the rest of the way to the doctor's office in silence, but when we got there, to the good Park Avenue doctor's office, we were greeted by the loud angry shouts of a group of pro-life activists. It had been happening more and more around this city, other cities, determined zealots who picketed the National Organization of Women's recommended doctors, trying to scare away abortion patients.

Linda Zavidow asks the witness if he remembers any of the slogans the protesters shouted and Benjamin objects: "I suggest that is immaterial, Your Honor."

"Sustained," Judge Bailey says as he takes off his glasses and wipes them with his handkerchief.

But I remember what the placards said and what the protesters shouted as they broke out of formation and surrounded us, blocking our way to the doctor's door.

"Baby killer," one man shouted.

"Baby killer! Baby killer! Baby killer!" The cry was taken up by all of them.

My father shouted back at them with all the anger he felt for Gabriel, "Leave us alone, you bastards."

A young man, about thirty, who seemed to be the leader, jeered. "Murderer," he hissed and spat at my feet.

"Murderer!"

"Murderer!"

"Murderer!"

They'd all picked up the chant, repeating the same three syllables until they stopped having any beginning or end. Frozen to that spot of sidewalk, I was doomed to watch their mouths move, shaping the accusing word over and over, while my father shouted at them to let us through.

"Officer Wylie, what did you do when you arrived at the scene?" Linda asks.

"There had been an altercation between one of the protesters and a gentleman escorting his daughter into the clinic. I attended to him while my backup arrested the protesters."

"Do you know that gentleman's name?"

"Yes, Jonathan Haviland."

"And his daughter's name?" Linda asks, dramatically lowering her voice.

"Genny Haviland."

I can still see my father striking out, hitting the man in his solar plexus hard enough so the man doubled over. But not for long. He came up even angrier and punched my father, the blow landing on the side of his head. My father fell to the ground and I dropped down beside him to see if he was all right. I wiped up the blood dripping from a cut on his forehead with the cuff of my shirt. Then I heard the sound of a police siren and was so relieved to see the dark blue uniforms, the shining silver badges, the bulges of their guns.

"Did you have reason to talk to the defendant and her father?" Linda Zavidow asks.

"Yes, I took their statements."

"And in the course of taking their statements, did you discover why they were at that particular doctor's office that particular morning?"

"Yes," Officer Wylie says. "In explaining what had happened, Miss Haviland told me her father had been goaded into striking a protester who had been trying to block her way into the doctor's office. Her father was upset, she said, because she was there to have an abortion."

"Thank you, Officer." *CROSS*

Benjamin waives his redirect.

Linda's next witness is my gynecologist, Dr. Nash. After he's been sworn in and she establishes who he is, Linda asks him to tell the court if I had an appointment with him on the morning of April 26.

"Yes." *(SO IS THIS PRIVILEDGED.)*

"Did you perform an abortion on Miss Haviland?"

"That is priviledged information."

Inside the doctor's office, the nurses offered to reschedule, but I decided to go through the abortion then. I did not want to prolong the process. My father could lie down in one of the examining rooms and rest. By the time I'd be finished, he'd be fine, too, the nurse said. But I knew I would not be fine. The scars of an abortion are invisible, on the inside of your body where no one but you can see or feel them. It's a blessing that you don't know how your womb looks scraped, but it bleeds for days.

It was my choice—I worried about it, feared it—but in the end, I made it myself.

During the abortion, my love for Gabriel crossed back over to hate; the two emotions are that close. I was seventeen again and Gabriel had refused to let me explain, slamming the door in my face. My hate quickly became a hard stony thing inside of me, replacing the fetus. Yet, I also saw Gabriel's eyes on me and felt his arms around me during the operation. Although I hadn't let him come, he was with me anyway. And when I lay in the doctor's recovery room, waiting for the cramps to subside, curled around myself, my knees up against my stomach, I rocked myself back and forth, hating him, loving him. How strange to feel both emotions at once.

TWENTY-TWO

Judge Bailey carefully writes something on a slip of paper, hands it to the bailiff, and then smooths down the sleeves of his robe with the flat of his hands. He always appears absolutely sure of what to do next, of the proper procedure; nothing to ponder, to question, to doubt. With a nod of his head, he instructs Linda to call her next witness. She asks my mother to take the stand. Beside me, Benjamin's body goes rigid. Behind me, my father says, "What the . . . damn it, Maguy, you're not going up there."

"The prosecution would like permission to treat Mrs. Haviland as a hostile witness."

"So noted," Judge Bailey says and searches out my mother in the crowd. "Mrs. Haviland, would you please take the stand?" His voice is polite, but stern. My mother, head erect, posture perfect, walks to the witness stand and is sworn in.

"Mrs. Haviland, I am sorry to have to ask you to take the stand. I can only imagine how difficult this must be for you."

My mother bows her head slightly, acknowledging Linda's comment.

"Are you and your daughter close?"

"Yes," my mother answers.

"Would you say you are as close to her as she is to her father?"

"I'm sure my daughter has quite different relationships with both of us, Miss Zavidow."

"Will you admit your daughter and your husband have a very close relationship?"

"They love each other very much."

"When Genny was growing up did you spend a lot of time away from her, in France?" Linda asks.

"Not a lot. No."

"You don't think leaving your only child for two weeks at a time every other month or so is a lot?"

Benjamin calls out his objection. "I fail to see any relevance here, Your Honor."

"Miss Zavidow, where is this going?" the judge asks.

"It will prove relevant, Your Honor."

"It better," he says.

Linda repeats her question.

"I didn't leave her alone. She was with her nanny and her father."

"I see. Mrs. Haviland, did Genny have trouble starting school?"

"No."

"Let me refresh your memory. Didn't she have such separation anxieties that your husband had to stay at school with her for several weeks before she was willing to let him go?"

"That happens to many children." My mother shrugs.

"Would you tell us your religion, Mrs. Haviland?"

"I am not religious."

"Fine. Were you baptized or christened?"

"Yes?"

"In what faith?"

"My family was Catholic. But I think religion is an old-fashioned concept."

"And your husband's religion?"

"He was raised as an Episcopalian, but, like me, he is not religious."

"So we can assume you raised Genny without any religious training?"

"Yes," my mother says, "that is true."

"Then why does your daughter sit there day after day at the defendant's table wearing a cross around her neck?"

"That was a gift to her from her nanny," my mother answers.

"So it has no religious significance?"

"You'd have to ask my daughter."

"But I think you know. Doesn't Genny's cross have deep significance? Wasn't Genny indeed raised as a devout Catholic? Not by you, or by Mr. Haviland, but by her nanny, Marie Javernu?"

When my mother saw this cross on me the first morning of the trial, she cringed. The only god either of my parents believed in was the one painted on the ceiling of the Sistine Chapel. With art, they had never needed another religion.

But Marie only had Catholicism. She'd lost a husband in the war, a son had drowned when he was only seven years old, and she'd fervently turned to her church to supplant them both.

Every morning she was with us, Marie walked the mile from our Central Park West apartment to St. Patrick's Cathedral. When it rained or snowed, she took a taxi—the only luxury she ever indulged in. And secretly she took me with her. From the time I was a baby in a carriage, she told my mother she was taking me to the park but instead sneaked me into the church and exposed me to the mystical world of the Catholic liturgy.

Like a nun in a parochial school, Marie taught me the catechism and the prayers. Twice a day we said the rosary together; my little fingers moving from bead to bead to the silver crucifix, our two voices joined in unison.

"In the name of the Father, and of the Son, and of the Holy Spirit. Amen. I believe in God, the Father Almighty, Creator of heaven and earth; and in Jesus Christ, His only Son, our Lord, who was conceived by the Holy Spirit—"

"Marie, why can't I see the Holy Spirit?"

"*Shh.* No questions while we are praying."

"But how do I know the spirit is there if I can't see him?"

"Pray, Genevieve, pray with me."

I learned to know the rosary in the dark, to tell where I was, to discern the body of Christ on the cross—which ridges were his sinewy arms, his legs, the undulating folds of his loincloth.

A few years ago, coming across a photograph of me as a child, wearing a veil, pretending to be a nun, I asked my mother why she'd allowed Marie to sneak me to church and covertly teach me Catholicism.

"You obviously knew what she was doing, why didn't you stop it?"

She waved her delicate hand, sloughing away any responsibility, and in that accent that makes even ugly words sound beautiful, said she didn't see any harm in Marie teaching me about God. "After all, your grandfather had been a Catholic."

"But you let it become something illicit," I reproached.

"What was the harm?"

The enormity of the secret. The magnitude of the guilt. It made the church's seductiveness that much more attractive. Too early I learned the thrill of the forbidden and saw my parents accept, even condone, lies.

"So, Mrs. Haviland, would you say that Genny adopted the precepts of the Catholic Church as her own?" Linda asks.

"Yes, I suppose so. What was the harm?" My mother seems slightly annoyed.

Benjamin stands up, "Your Honor, I have been patient up till now but I fail to see how any of this information has any relevance here."

"I am equally confused, Miss Zavidow," Judge Bailey says. "Could you please get to the point?"

"Certainly, Your Honor. Mrs. Haviland, what is the Catholic Church's opinion of abortion?"

Now Benjamin leaps up. "I object, Your Honor. Only minutes ago this witness stated she is not religious. How can she know the church's opinion on anything?"

The judge gives Benjamin a sorry look. "Overruled. Go ahead, answer the question Mrs. Haviland."

"The church believes abortion is a sin."

"Which means, according to your daughter's beliefs, Slade Gabriel asked her to commit a sin?" Linda asks.

"I object, Your Honor!" Benjamin yells out.

"Sustained."

"Mrs. Haviland, did Genny tell you how she felt about committing a mortal sin?" Linda persists.

Before my mother has a chance to answer, Benjamin objects again. Again, the judge sustains the objection, warning Linda Zavidow to watch the phrasing of her questions. Linda says she has no more questions and Benjamin is asked if he has any.

"Yes, Your Honor." He stands and faces my mother. "Mrs. Haviland, did Genny tell you how she felt about the abortion?"

"Yes, she said she was sad about it, but she told both me and her father it was what she wanted."

"Did she ever, ever refer to it as a sin? Did your daughter ever tell you she thought that by having an abortion she committed a sin?"

At ten when I first confessed to Marie that I was having sexual fantasies, she chastised me and gave me several prayers to say. But no matter how much she tried to convince me, I couldn't connect my sexuality with sinning. Still, I might have remained religious if Marie had not left me.

Her mother had become ill and she was needed at home in France, she explained, telling me that I was so grown-up and that at twelve, I needn't have a nanny anymore.

I prayed all the prayers she had taught me, begging Jesus to make her mother better so that she could stay with me, promising to make all kinds of sacrifices if only I would not have to sacrifice Marie. I went to the church she had taken me to for so many years, dropped my coins in the metal box, and lit dozens of votive candles while I repeated the prayer, "Please, dear Jesus, let Marie stay with me."

I spent hours kneeling on the padded prie-dieu, staring into flickering flames and praying that when I went home Marie would tell me that her mother had gotten well and her plans had changed.

I was sitting on my bed reading when she came to say good-bye to me. She wore a new coat my mother had given her as a going-away present but the handbag on her arm had been the same one she'd been carrying since she'd come to work for us when I was a baby.

I had always known this woman and I didn't know how to say good-bye to her.

"Genevieve, you must remember to pray every day," she said as she slipped her own black onyx cross over my head and kissed me.

I threw my arms around her, crying, hanging on and not letting go. Was this what happens with the people you love? Either they remain beyond your reach or they leave you?

What about all the prayers, the sacrifices that I'd promised God I would make? The candles I had lit? Why hadn't they worked?

Marie disentangled herself from my grip.

"No!" I shouted, holding onto her sleeve.

She wept as she undid my fingers and then she lifted them up to her mouth and kissed each one. Like I was still a baby. Her baby.

"Good-bye, Genevieve," she said, and then turned and was gone.

Sobbing, I ran to the window and watched her emerge from the building. She didn't look up, but walked straight toward the taxi the doorman had hailed and got in.

Her leaving had been a topic of conversation for weeks so I should
have been prepared, but it's hard to prepare a child for loss and its
fathomless bottom.

Once Marie's cab drove off and had become a distant speck of yellow I pulled my camera case out from its secret hiding place under my
bed. Inside was every gift she had given me: the mother-of-pearl Bible,
the medal of St. Mary, the statue of the baby Jesus, the prayer cards
laminated in plastic.

I took the case to the open window.

Even though it was early March, the wind blew in warm on my
wet cheeks. It would get cold again before it turned spring. I un-
snapped the case and threw, one by one, everything Marie had given
to me out the window.

The Bible hit the pavement and a car rode right over it. The prayer
cards caught the wind and floated out toward the park. The medal was
too small for me to see where it landed, but I was sure I heard it hit the
ground.

TWENTY-THREE

104 Greene Street, Apartment 5
Tuesday, December 8, 1992, 6:30 P.M.

After my mother's testimony, court adjourned for the day. I refused my parents' offer to have dinner and they dropped me off at the loft on their way uptown. Closing the door behind me I am greeted by the pervasive smell of turpentine, linseed oil, and oil paint. Gabriel's supplies have not been removed. The bottles of solvents, oils, and glazes, the primers and paints still sit out on the long wooden worktable, the brushes rest in their can of turpentine, their stems sticking up in the air. They're all waiting for him. Shutting my eyes, I inhale the oily sharp scent.

Searching through the stacks of canvases, I pull out two and choose between them. Carefully I drag the five-by-seven-foot canvas into the middle of the studio and lean it against the easel.

Alone in the cavernous loft, I pour my single glass of wine and sit down on the floor in front of the painting. *Garden #113* . . . done in May. Seven months ago. Sipping the wine, gazing at the painting, I find the courtroom disappearing in the dark green trees, the black night sky, and the sleeping flowers. In the painting the ever-shining white light descends, hovers, and showers the garden in possibilities.

*   *   *

On May 16, I started preproduction on a new episode of *Into the Paintings* featuring Poe Linden's experimental sky paintings. I came home that night to find Gabriel working on a new painting: *Garden #113*.

"Come inside with me," he said, putting down his brush. "I have something for you."

Strewn all over the bed were packages gift wrapped in gold and silver foil paper.

"What's all this?" I asked.

"You're the romantic and you don't know what day it is?"

I had to think.

"Genny, it's May 16."

"How did you ever remember?" There were so many things he did forget those days, how had he remembered that?

"How could I forget the day you saved my fucking life?"

In the first box was a dark purple velvet shawl from the 1920s. Gabriel pulled my black sweater over my head and draped the shawl across my bare shoulders. A green crushed velvet skirt spilled out of the next package and Gabriel insisted I take off my black slacks so he could wrap it around my waist. In the third box I discovered large teardrop-shaped amethyst earrings, which I slipped into the holes in my ears.

"Look in the mirror," Gabriel said, so pleased with his creation. "These are the kind of colors you should wear, not all those beiges and blacks." Pushing me in front of the mirror, he showed off what he'd created. "Like a gypsy." He laughed and put his palm in my hand. "Now, tell me my fortune."

With the tip of my forefinger I traced what I thought was his life line. "You will have a long life—" He reacted as if I'd burned him, pulling his hand away, and when I questioned him, he said the touch of my finger on his skin was driving him crazy. As if to prove it, he bent over and sucked my finger into his mouth.

"Now touch yourself."

I did what he asked, keeping my eyes on him. Seeing how much I could excite him aroused me.

I thought the abortion would quench some of my ardor for Gabriel, but it didn't happen. My body refused to obey my intellect. Around him, I was always ripe, ready. As time passed, I'd almost convinced myself a baby would have been an unwelcome disruption in our lives.

"Make me come," I pleaded.

"No. I want to watch you do it to yourself."

So I did what he'd asked—brought myself to the edge and over while he sat and watched, his lips curled into a smile. And then he went back to this painting, absorbed by it, oblivious to everything else going on around him.

If only I could, like the characters in my show, really disappear into one of these paintings now—just step into his garden and remain there permanently. Inside the painting, I could escape the jury's prying eyes, which despite myself, I bring home with me every night. We've become connected and even after they have heard all the questions and answers and made their decision and have walked away, we will be allied. My story, how it ends and their part in it, will remain with them. They'll always know that once they sat on the jury in the trial of a woman named Genny Haviland and decided her future.

Or will they? There's another option. Tonight, or tomorrow night, or maybe the night they spend deliberating on the verdict, I could decide my own future.

There are no pills left, but I could slit my wrists with one of Gabriel's razor blades or jump out of the window. Would dying like that be an admission of guilt? What about accidentally driving across a divider line into oncoming traffic the way Gabriel had? People would accept that as an accident, wouldn't they?

We'd been going to his house on Long Island for the weekends; not the same house his wife and daughter had lived in the summer I was seventeen. This larger house sat alone on a large parcel of land edging the bay.

It was a Friday night in the beginning of June and we were driving home from the movies in East Hampton when Gabriel crossed the yellow divider line and drove into oncoming traffic.

There was a loud blast of horns and the screeching of brakes and bright lights streaking by and then Gabriel maneuvered the car back into the right lane and off the road. We were both physically all right, but badly frightened.

"What the hell happened?" I asked.

Gabriel's face was pale and bullets of sweat popped out on his forehead. He didn't say anything.

"We're lucky we're not dead," I said.

He didn't respond.

A week later we were in the supermarket, walking down the aisles, when he just stopped and stared blankly at the jams and jellies.

"Gabriel?"

He turned and looked at me. He was frowning and perplexed. "Why are we here?"

"We're shopping." I tried to keep my voice calm despite the panic I felt building.

"Gabriel?" I touched his hand and that seemed to refocus him. His eyes cleared. When I asked him what had happened he'd told me he'd just been day dreaming, but it was more than that. At first he refused my suggestion that he see a doctor and then admitted he had already seen one and that he was experiencing some residual effects of the accident back in February.

"Why didn't you tell me?" I asked.

"It's not important."

"Is it serious?"

"Absolutely not," he lied.

That afternoon, he sat in front of a canvas for a long time without picking up a brush. It was taking him longer to finish each painting. During February, March, and April, he'd been doing two a week. Now it was taking two or three weeks to finish one. When I asked him that day in the Hamptons if he was all right, he complained I was putting him under a microscope and insisted we take a walk.

We took the moss-covered brick path past lilac bushes set off by deep red and purple azaleas—brash choices, strong decisions. Reaching the pool enclosed by a ten-foot-tall manicured boxwood fence, we sat on a weathered bench and Gabriel pulled me close. I rested my head on his shoulder. Overhead, birds chirped, and in the distance gulls cried and waves slapped against the shore.

Gabriel unbuttoned my blouse and cupped my breasts. He leaned over and kissed them. He unzipped my jeans and pulled them down, letting them fall on the grass. My skin had goose bumps, but not because it was cold. He got down on his knees and put his face between my legs.

And then—when? How long? There is no way to know. He took off his own clothes and his erection led us into the water. Submerged, our skin turned to some other finer material, more like silk. After we swam, we wrapped ourselves in one big towel and we made love, standing up, by the side of the pool—Garbriel moving quickly, urgently, as if proving something. I didn't understand until we were walking back to the house, and with a laugh, he asked me if I was still worried about him. And if his voice hadn't been so melancholy under his laugh, I wouldn't have been.

The next morning, we got up early, drove to a little deli on Fireplace Road, picked up two coffees, two buttered rolls, the Sunday *Times* and drove to the beach.

The ocean was as still as a pond, the water a sheet of glass reflecting the exact bright blue of the sky. Exquisite and yet disturbing. The blustery ocean had been quelled. Where was the constant roar of the waves? This was an alien quiet, a silent warning.

"I've never seen the ocean so still," I said.

"It happens like this only two or three days each summer."

We ate our breakfast, sipped our steaming coffee, read the paper, and then took a long walk on the sandy beach; Gabriel close to the water, letting it wash over his feet, me on the dry sand, the hotter the better even if it burned my soles.

When we went swimming it was like being in a pool without boundaries. Effortlessly, we stroked straight toward the horizon, brave without the waves and the dangerous undertow. Yet I feared this subdued ocean more than a violent one. With a turbulent sea I knew what to expect.

Back on the beach I lay down on my towel while Gabriel drew in the sand. Watching him through half-closed eyes, I was mesmerized by his intensity. Even at the beach, just playing, his whole body was taut and he concentrated completely on what he was creating.

When he pulled me up I saw that he had drawn me as an odalisque, a giant nude etched in the sand.

"It's beautiful." I walked the length of the eight-foot sketch and then back. "*I'm* beautiful."

"This is all that matters anymore, not the success of your effort, but that you made something that pleases you. That pleases the woman you made it for. Now, right now, does this please you?"

"Yes."

Then, running through the sand, Gabriel began to obliterate the lines he spent so much of the morning on.

"You're ruining it!" I screamed.

But he just ran crazy through the drawing, zigzagging back and forth, kicking up the sand, until there was nothing left of the drawing, nothing left of me.

TWENTY-FOUR

While we went back and forth from Manhattan to Long Island, my parents were staying in the South of France with my grandfather. In mid-July, he died there in his sleep, while taking a nap on the patio overlooking the sea.

Gabriel traveled with me to France for the funeral. It was held on an obscenely beautiful day: blue skies, no clouds, eighty degrees—the kind of day to be down at the beach, not in an old churchyard. Afterward everyone went to my grandfather's villa. Built in the early 1900s, it stood on a point jutting out over the sparkling Riviera. French doors opened onto wide terraces where lemon trees grew in terra-cotta pots. The inside of the house had pale blue walls and fine Provincial furniture. There were few paintings of value. Those were in Paris at the gallery, while here were sketches and prints.

Many friends of my grandfather's and my mother's arrived, as well as several American artists vacationing in France. There were times that afternoon I wasn't sure if I was at a wake or an opening. My mother was subdued, not so much grieving as lost (it both frightened and reassured me to see her fragility), so I offered to act as hostess. She took my face in her hands and kissed me gently on the lips. "*Merci*, Genevieve," she whispered. And so I was the one who greeted the guests, made necessary introductions, refilled glasses, saw to the kitchen staff, and made sure everything ran smoothly.

We had arrived back from the cemetery at about one o'clock, so it must have been an hour or two later when I noticed the woman walk in.

About my mother's age, she was tall and thin, with pale skin and pale red hair that ended in a blunt cut just below her shoulder blades. Wondering why she seemed familiar, I watched her seek out my mother and embrace her. Behind me, someone said she was a painter.

As the afternoon wore on, people continued coming, filling the terrace, crowding the living room, clustering in threes and fours, drinking, eating, and talking. My father and a group of his French associates sat around the coffee table, deep in conversation, many of them smoking cigarettes. Gabriel was in a corner with two painters he knew, drinking wine.

Suddenly I realized how tired I was. How much I yearned to get away from the heat and the light and the brightness. Everyone was taken care of, there was enough wine and cheese and fruit. Certainly I could disappear for fifteen minutes and find someplace dark to lie down.

Walking inside the house and up the stairs, my feet dragged. My jet lag was bad and for the last few nights, I'd only slept for an hour or two. Dreams startled me awake, terrorizing dreams where I ran down long corridors only to stop short at the same sheer drop of a hundred feet above an endless canyon. I'd shout for help but hear only my lonely echo answer.

I was so tired as I opened the door, I didn't realize I was in the wrong room. It was cool and dark inside, that was all that mattered, but as I stumbled forward toward the bed I saw shadows. Streaks of red and blond hair. My mother's face in that woman's hands, her eyes shut tightly against the grief of the afternoon. My mother and this stranger making love. On such an inappropriate occasion. Especially for my mother, who had always seemed so appropriate.

The women were still kissing each other—one loving the sadness

out of the other—when I walked out, shutting the door silently behind me. Unable to stay on my feet, I slid down to the floor in the
hallway, so close to the room I could hear their soft moans.

And then I understood my mother's elongated trips. This woman,
not my grandfather, was why my mother had returned to France so
many times. Was this woman the only one or had there been a series
of them?

A memory surfaced. I was eleven. My mother had left for Europe a
few weeks before and my father waited with me until my school
recessed and then we flew to join her. On the plane was a young
boy traveling with his parents who kept smiling at me from across the
aisle. I crossed my eyes then stared down at my feet while my father
teased me.

Arriving in Paris, we went to my grandfather's apartment, which
had already been shut down for the summer. Sheets shrouded the furniture; the drapes were drawn. It was early in the morning and my father
and I walked up the grand staircase quietly so we wouldn't wake her.
Opening the door to the room he and my mother usually shared, my
father stepped inside. I was behind him so I couldn't see what he saw
and though I heard my mother's whisper I couldn't discern her words.

He backed out of the room, shut the door, took me by the hand,
and pulled me away.

"Your mama is not feeling well. She needs to sleep so let's you and
I go out to the bakery for croissants."

It wasn't far, but we walked very slowly and on the way back
stopped at a café where he had coffee and I had hot chocolate.

Approaching the apartment, we passed a beautiful woman on the
street. She was tall and thin with red hair and wore a wonderful fra-
grance. As she strolled by she smiled at me.

It was this same woman. Now I knew where I had seen her before.

Not wanting my mother and the red-haired woman to come out of the room and find me there in the hall, I went back to the living room where many people were still eating and drinking to my grandfather's memory. It is never a tragedy when an eighty-five-year-old man dies swiftly, painlessly. The burial doesn't elicit heavy sighs and weeping, only a sweet melancholy.

But my grandfather wasn't a sweet man. He derisively called my father "the salesman" when he—despite his precise French accent—was exactly the same thing. My grandfather probably knew about the red-haired woman and encouraged it, pushing my mother to find someone in Paris so that he could hold her there.

I found my father on the terrace overlooking the glittering sea. "When I go back to New York in August, your mother will be staying on." I nodded, not questioning him, letting him continue. "She's going to take care of your grandfather's gallery."

"Is she going to live here then?"

"For the time being."

"Without you?"

He nodded.

"Are you getting divorced?"

"Of course not. Why would you think that?"

My father seemed as shocked by my suggestion as he seemed indifferent to my mother's desire to stay here. What moved him? For Christ's sake, did he have someone else, too?

"He left your mother the gallery." My father was trying to make some point but I wasn't sure what it was.

"He didn't leave it to both of you?"

"No, he left it to his daughter." He paused. "Just as I am going to leave my gallery to you. Hopefully it will be something worth having."

"But it's not that—what would I do with it?"

"You don't have to take it over." He was angry with me again.

"Have someone else run it. It's just that I've worked so damn hard for it, I want it to live."

I nodded. It wasn't a hard promise.

"You're not sick, are you?" I asked.

"No. Why would you ask me that?"

"All this talk about leaving the gallery to me."

"That is because of your grandfather. I'm fine. Sick of some things. Certainly sick of some things. But I'm fine. Going to be fine for a long time."

Behind him I saw Gabriel cross the terrace and sit down next to a young woman whom I didn't recognize. She had pouty lips and blond hair. Soon a heavy gray-haired man joined them and put his hand on the woman's thigh proprietarily. His thick lips parted. There were sweat stains and creases in his shirt. He was sloppy, debauched, a man who smoked cigars and drank too much. The girl wore too many gold chains around her neck, too many gold bangles on each wrist. Leaning against the older man, she didn't hesitate to put a hand on Gabriel's leg.

I didn't want to think about sex, not then. Not any kind of sex, not between a man and a woman, not between two men, not between two women. My father was talking about the gallery as if no one had died two days before, planning his fall strategy, talking about—

"I don't feel well."

"Maybe you should lie down. Do you want me to help you?" my father asked.

I shook my head, afraid of him walking me to my room, afraid we would pass by the room where my mother and her lover lay wrapped in each other's arms.

A few minutes later I lay down on my bed and shut my eyes, but I could still see red hair, like flames consuming the pillow.

TWENTY-FIVE

The next day Gabriel and I left my grandfather's house and flew to Paris and then drove out to the countryside that afternoon so I could see my old nanny Marie.

"It's better than a museum," Gabriel said with a sweep of his arm once we were out of the city limits. "Look—that field is a van Gogh in the Modern. Don't you recognize his poplar trees, his undulating green hills?"

We drove past stretches of scenery without Coca-Cola billboards, factory buildings, or television cables to destroy the illusion that nothing had changed in the last hundred years.

"Forget you're looking at a tree or a house or a field, just look at that space of blue, that rectangle of brown, that splash of orange. Do you see the impression of the scene?" Gabriel hadn't taken his eyes off the vista. "What a wonderful time it must have been for all those painters—to be doing what no one before them had done. Think of it, Genny. That's what I want to do—not paint like the Impressionists—but find an unexplored world the way they did."

"There must be some breakthroughs left," I said.

"Where can you go with a tube of paint or a brush someone hasn't already been?"

"Do you want to start over? Is that what you mean?"

"Walking through museums, watching people trying to experience art . . . where is the fucking wonder? You have to participate to feel wonder and how the hell can you participate with the kind of painting most of us are creating?" He sighed. "Genny, it is so trite, so overblown, but there's no other way to say it—it's a dead art."

"No, not quite dead. To use your overblown phrasing, maybe more dead than alive—but there are artists like you who keep coming along and resuscitating it. And that's what matters. Not who is killing it, but who is breathing life into it. Because we need the hope of art even more than the art itself."

"We may be past that," he said.

"No, we aren't."

"How can you be so sure?"

"I've seen your paintings."

"There you go: saving my life again."

We'd pulled up in front of a small house in the village of Giverny. I got out of the car and rushed up the brick path and knocked on the door. In a moment a stooped woman in her late seventies opened it.

"*Bonjour,*" Marie's sister said and extended her hand. I kissed her and she hugged me and then I introduced her to Gabriel.

"I made coffee for you," she said in French.

Gabriel and I sat down and took the proffered cups of coffee. I kept watching the door, waiting for Marie.

"Is she out?" I asked in French.

"No, she's here," Jeanette said and then told me that she hadn't wanted to tell me over the phone but Marie had been sick. She'd had a stroke and was in bed. We could go up and see her, but first she wanted to warn me that Marie wasn't herself. She probably wouldn't even know me.

Following Jeanette up the staircase, we entered a low-ceilinged, whitewashed room. There, in the middle of a four-poster bed was a tiny shriveled woman. Vacant eyes stared out the window.

This was not Marie Javernu. She was too small. Shrunken.

"Marie?"

Her eyes were confused, occluded. Sitting down on the edge of the bed, I took her in my arms. She allowed me to hold her, but her body was stiff. There was no smell of butter. No folds of flesh. Just a sour staleness and dry, paper-thin skin. No Marie. Just a shell.

Gabriel backed out of the room. He bumped into something and then there was a loud noise of metal hitting the wooden floor. Then I heard his footsteps on the stairs.

Beside the bed was a night table with Marie's rosary on it, the wooden beads worn and shiny from her fingering them for sixty years. Taking the rosary, I intertwined it through her fingers and mine and began to say the Our Father with her, in French, the way she had taught it to me. Halfway through the prayer, her voice surfaced. Her voice, strong and real. And through the rest of prayers her eyes focused on me and shone.

During the time we held the rosary, she knew who I was and we were together, yet as soon as we stopped praying she ceased being aware. Just stopped. Her eyes went dead again.

Gabriel was waiting for me outside. Smoking. Pacing. I walked around to the driver's side of the car and started to get in.

"I need to drive," he said and got behind the wheel.

For a while we drove in silence. Gabriel was racing back to Paris, this time neither of us paying attention to the scenery.

"I had no idea anything had even happened to her," I said finally. "Oh, Gabriel, she used to be a big, fat, cozy woman. She used to be—"

"She's not dead," he snapped at me.

"What?"

"You're talking about her in the fucking past tense."

"What's the matter with you?" I asked.

"Nothing," he growled.

The blackness that had hovered around him for weeks fully descended. I was sick at having seen Marie like that and sick at having to deal with Gabriel in a mood I didn't understand, a mood he wouldn't explain.

"I'm the one who should be depressed. First my grandfather's funeral. Now Marie. You're acting as if all this is happening to you."

"I'm sorry."

"I don't care that you're sorry, Gabriel. I want to know what you're upset about."

"Was it hard to be with your old nurse today? Did it scare you?"

"Of course it did! She wasn't there. You said she's not dead, but except for the few minutes when we said the rosary, she *was* dead. How long can she go on living in that room? Not functioning? It's awful."

He nodded as if I was confirming something for him. "Callahand . . . do you remember my friend Ryan Callahand? He became like that, too, old and withered and unable to take care of himself. His daughter finally put him in a home. . . . I went to visit him . . . once . . ." He shook his head as if he were trying to get rid of the image of it. "If you could pick how you would die, Genny, how would it be? When would it be?"

"I don't know. Like my grandfather, when I'm old, after having lunch and taking a walk, during a nap."

Taking one of my hands, he held it up to his lips. "I haven't been sympathetic, have I? Preoccupied I suppose with . . ." His voice trailed off and he didn't finish his sentence.

"What?" I asked.

He looked confused. "What was I saying? I'm sorry."

"You were saying you were preoccupied. . . ."

He nodded, seemed relieved. "Yes, about the paintings for the show. I spoke to your father at the villa, he's still adamant about my showing mostly old paintings."

That night when we made love I felt the pressure of him between my legs and things that had been worrying me came like birds flying wildly in the dark, smashing into me: the image of Marie in her bed, the image of my mother and the red-haired woman in another bed, my grandfather in his satin-lined coffin, my father in his gallery with nothing hanging on the walls.

There are times when we turn to each other out of a need to connect, but that night our connection was incidental to our separate, desperate desires to escape. I bit Gabriel's skin. He squeezed my flesh. Bruising each other, we left marks. I ground my pelvis against his. I pulled his hair. Slicked with sweat, our flesh made smacking noises when we met. He thrust up so far into me he made me cry out. I wasn't sure I'd be able to tolerate another second of his assault, but then the feeling went past pain into pure intense sensation. It was like hate crossing to love and back again. I came when I felt the hot burst of him flood my insides and heard his long moan.

TWENTY-SIX

New York City Criminal Court Building, Room 1317
Wednesday, December 9, 1992, 11:30 A.M.

My friend since high school, Tory Cole, nervously takes the stand. Her gray eyes are wide and worried. All I can do is hold her gaze and listen to the bizarre trail Linda takes her down.

"Did Miss Haviland tell you about the abortion she'd had?" Linda asks.

"Yes."

"Did you talk about it often?"

"I don't know what you mean," Tory answers.

"How many times did you talk about it? Three times? Half a dozen? Twenty times?"

"I have no idea. Probably a half a dozen times. When it happened. Then after less and less."

"Did Miss Haviland confide in you about other aspects of her life?"

"Yes." Tory's eyes return to me, afraid.

"Did she discuss her relationship with Mr. Gabriel with you?"

"Yes."

"Did she tell you how much she loved him?"

"Yes."

"Did she also tell you how much she hated him?"

"It wasn't like that."

"Mrs. Lawson, please, answer the question. Did Genny ever tell you she hated Slade Gabriel?"

A whisper: "Yes."

"Did Genny ever tell you she went back with him for revenge?"

"No."

"Did Genny ever discuss any lesbian relationships with you?"

"I object, Your Honor." Benjamin's shout hurts my ears.

"Miss Zavidow." The judge is angry, too. "Where is this questioning leading?"

"May I approach the bench, Your Honor?" she asks.

"Both of you approach the bench," he says.

While the judge and the two lawyers confer, Tory waits, staring at me helplessly.

She does not know where she is being led. But I do. Linda wants to plant the possibility that I am gay and suggest that my entire relationship with Gabriel was a sham, just a way for me to get close enough to him to kill him and save Haviland's gallery.

But there is nothing I can do to explain what even Tory does not understand. It is not my secret to tell.

A week or so after Gabriel and I had returned from our trip to France, I was still uneasy, unable to settle down, to connect, to stop seeing secrets beneath every surface. So I made plans to have dinner with Tory. When she opened her front door, seeing her was like spotting the first familiar landmark that told you you were on your way home.

We had dinner with her husband and two kids in her Park Avenue apartment with its peach walls and comfortable furniture. It was all so soothing: the same china she'd had since her wedding, the same paintings on the wall, the same begonia plant on the windowsill.

After dinner her husband Jack went into his study to do some work and I flipped through an art book while Tory put the kids to bed. The paintings in the book were abstract color fields that acted like Rorschach tests for me. I kept seeing red hair fanning out on a pillow.

"So you want more coffee or anything?" Tory asked when she returned.

"No, thanks. But I have a crazy question to ask you."

"Shoot."

"Have you ever been attracted to a woman?"

"You mean sexually?"

I nodded.

"In college. Do you remember my roommate, Trina?"

"I met her, didn't I? She was Middle Eastern?"

"Lebanese, yeah. She wanted to be a writer and was as enamored of Anaïs Nin as I was. After we read all of her diaries, we read all of Henry Miller's books. The surprising thing was, Trina was a virgin."

In the '70s virginity wasn't a virtue, but something to overcome. "Because she was gay?" I asked.

"Well she said she was interested in men, but found the boys at school boring. Anyway, I guess I wasn't sure. And then one afternoon I was leaving, going to visit Peter at Penn for the weekend and went into Trina's room to say good-bye. We'd gotten in the affected habit of double kissing each other good-bye, the way Europeans do, so I leaned forward to kiss her but she turned her face and really kissed me. On the lips, open mouth."

"How did you feel?"

"Strange. Shocked."

"What was it like?" I asked.

"You know, when I really thought about it, it was physically no different than a boy kissing me. It was lips and tongue. No gender."

"Did you like it?"

"Yes. No. It was just a kiss, but it confused the hell out of me," Tory said.

"What did you do?"

"I left for the weekend. And when I saw Peter, I told him about it. Then—this is the odd part, one of those coincidences you're always looking for to prove nothing's an accident—we went to the movies at the Student Union. A French film was playing, *Murmur of the Heart*."

"About the mother who seduces her son?" I asked.

"Yes and, as it turned out, it made sense of everything. The mother loved her son so much she didn't know any way to express it other than sex. Sexual love but not for the sake of sex. Trina's kiss had been like that, love she didn't know how to express any other way."

"Was that the end of it?" She hadn't really told me anything that would help.

"Yeah, my one big experience." She paused, smoothed down the cushion on the couch, and then asked, "Gen, what's up?"

"I'm not sure."

"Did you meet someone?"

"Oh no. It's not me." I laughed, hoping to make the serious expression on her face disappear.

"Then what?"

But I couldn't tell her. I couldn't make the words come out.

In the cab home, I sat back against the seat, closed my eyes and saw the image of my mother wrapped in that woman's arms. My mother's pale skin. The other woman's paler skin. The faces damp with the effort of their lovemaking—or was it tears?

I had always wanted my mother to hold me—not sexually but with that much passion—and she never had. I'd spent my whole life missing my mother and had never known it until I saw her hand curved around another woman's hip.

I was tempted to call my father and ask him when it had started, how it made him feel, if it had anything to do with the mixed messages he'd given me about us? But how could I?

Judge Bailey allows Linda to finish questioning Tory who admits that I did talk to her about lesbian relationships. When Linda is done, Benjamin requests that since it is close to the lunch recess, he'd like to postpone his redirect until the court reconvenes. The judge agrees, and Benjamin asks me if we can talk. Once again I follow him to that small room, the confessional down the hall.

After shutting the door, he tells me Tory's testimony has created a big problem. "Linda Zavidow is overdoing it. Piling it on. Raising all sorts of ridiculous doubts in the jury's mind about your love for Gabriel. But the judge allowed her prosecutorial overzealousness and now I have to completely eradicate any possibility you ever had a homosexual relationship. Your obsession with Gabriel has to be completely believable. Now, tell me exactly what that was all about so I can figure out how to wipe it out of the jury's mind."

"I don't remember that conversation with Tory," I lie.

"Think."

"Benjamin, I just don't remember. Maybe I'd read some book and wanted to talk to her about it."

"Hey!" he starts to yell and for the first time I'm aware of how much pressure he's under and of how scared he suddenly seems. "What the hell is this crap? Your best friend's testimony just damaged you, Genny. We're living in a homophobic society. You and I can only convince the jury you didn't commit murder if they believe you were passionately and obsessively in love with Gabriel, not cheating on him with some other woman."

A knock on the door interrupts his tirade. When he opens it, my parents are standing there.

"Mr. Marks, I would like to talk to you," my mother says.

"This isn't the best time, Mrs. Haviland."

"Perhaps it is." She walks in and seats herself beside me at the round table. My father stands by the door as if guarding it.

"How bad for us was the implication that my daughter took a woman as a lover?"

"Very bad. As I was just explaining to Genny, I need that jury to believe her love for Gabriel was the most important thing in her life."

"Then you will need to put me back on the stand."

I turn to her, face-to-face with the woman I am so different from, and I watch her mouth form the words she plans to use when Benjamin puts her on the stand.

"It was me that Genevieve was talking about with her friend. My daughter was troubled about my sexuality, not her own."

"Jesus Christ. Who in their right mind will believe that crock? Excuse me, Mrs. Haviland, but this will appear to be like exactly what it is, an overwrought mother coming to her daughter's defense, perjuring herself to protect her kid. I appreciate the effort, but no thanks."

My mother's façade of control crumbles, the corners of her mouth droop.

"Mama?"

She looks at me.

"I . . . thank you."

Her chin trembles and she nods. My father, who has not said a word, now kneels down beside her and whispers something in her ear that seems to rouse her. Sitting up, her face once again composed, she apologizes to Mr. Marks for intruding and leaves the room on my father's arm.

"I'll handle this in the redirect," Benjamin says to me brusquely as we walk out the door, a few steps behind my parents. At the threshold he stops. "I'm sorry if I pushed you, but I needed to know."

"Yeah, so now you know. What good did it do?"

CROSS

Benjamin starts his redirect of Tory immediately after the lunch recess. "Mrs. Lawson, have you ever had any conversations with Miss Haviland, other than the one you mentioned before, to suggest she was involved with anyone other than Slade Gabriel?" Benjamin asks Tory.

"No," she answers.

"Did Genny ever tell you she was gay?"

"Absolutely not."

"During your conversations with Miss Haviland, have you ever discussed your relationship with your husband?"

"I guess so."

"Have you ever told Miss Haviland you're bored with married life?"

Tory squirms in her chair. "I may have said something like that."

"Have the two of you ever talked about other men you've met whom you found interesting?"

"I don't know."

"Yes or no, Mrs. Lawson?" Benjamin insists.

"I guess so, I mean, yes."

"Have you ever discussed how mad your children make you at times?"

Finally understanding where Benjamin's headed, Tory relaxes. "Yes."

"Do you think in the course of your conversation with your best friend you ever mentioned that you might like to *kill* one of the little monsters?"

"Probably."

"Have you ever in the course of your relationship talked to her about the plight of women in the workforce and wished you were a man?"

"Yes."

"So, am I to assume that because at some point you have discussed with Miss Haviland your desire for a man other than your husband and your frustration with your children and your disappointments with being a woman that you are a: having several affairs, b: considering a sex change operation, and c: plotting the murder of one or more of your children?"

The jury laughs.

"Of course not. Genny and I have talked about hundreds of crazy things."

"Thank you, Mrs. Lawson. No more questions, Your Honor," Benjamin says. Tory, much relieved, gets up, walks out of the witness box and returns to her seat.

TWENTY-SEVEN

New York City Criminal Court Building, Room 1317
Wednesday, December 9, 1992, 2:00 P.M.

"Next witness, Miss Zavidow," the judge says.

"I call Elizabeth Gabriel Rosser, Your Honor."

Gabriel's daughter has his black eyes and his dark hair. The resemblance between them is strong enough to make me wince when she takes the stand.

"Were you and your father close, Mrs. Rosser?" Linda asks.

"Yes, I think so."

"Did you see him much last summer?"

"Yes."

"What were the circumstances?"

"We met for lunch several times and once I went up to the loft," Lizzie says.

"Did you meet with him alone or was Miss Haviland present?"

"Except for the last time, alone."

"What was your father's state of mind last summer?"

"Calls for conjecture. This witness is not a psychiatrist, Your Honor," Benjamin objects.

"Sustained."

"Mrs. Rosser, did your father complain to you about his gallery representation last summer?"

"Yes, he was upset about the way Mr. Haviland was pushing him to stay with his old style."

"Did he tell you what he planned to do about that?"

"He said he had been thinking about changing galleries," Lizzie says.

"Did he tell you he had definitely made up his mind?"

"Yes, he did. He said when his contract was up he was not going to renew it. He no longer trusted Mr. Haviland."

"He said that to you?" Linda asks.

"Yes, he did."

"But he was living with Mr. Haviland's daughter, was he not?"

"Yes, and he was concerned about that, too. He was worried Genny would take it out on him if he left her father. Apparently she didn't want him to leave. They'd fought about it. He'd be alive today if he'd only trusted his instincts and realized how dangerous—"

"Your Honor, objection!"

"The witness's last remarks will be stricken from the record," Judge Bailey says.

"Mrs. Rosser, do you have any children?" Linda asks.

"Yes, I have a six-month-old little girl."

"So when you saw your father over the summer you were visibly pregnant?"

"Yes."

"How did Miss Haviland react when she saw you in the loft she and your father shared?" Linda asks.

"I was in my father's loft when she got home from work. We'd never met before so Dad introduced us and as soon as she noticed I was pregnant she ran into the bedroom. I could hear her crying in there and then calling Dad in to see her."

"Could you hear them talking?"

"Well, my father was talking. Genny was yelling and crying at the same time. She was hysterical, calling him selfish, saying it was his fault she wasn't having a baby, too."

"What did your father say to you when he came back out?"

"He told me Genny had gotten pregnant without talking it over with him—"

"Objection, hearsay," Benjamin says in an exasperated tone.

"Overruled."

"Go on, Mrs. Rosser," Linda encourages.

"Dad said he told Genny he'd prefer not having another child so late in life, and that she'd decided to have an abortion, but she couldn't seem to get over it. He was worried about her. He thought she was on the verge of a breakdown. He told me that the abortion coupled with the fact of him leaving the gallery was too much for her. He thought she needed professional help."

"I object, Your Honor."

"Overruled, Mr. Marks."

"So, Mrs. Rosser, he confided all that in you?" Linda asks.

"Yes."

"Did he also confide in you that he was planning—excuse me—to kill himself?"

"No."

"Do you think, if he was planning to kill himself, given how close you were, he would have told you?"

But before Lizzie can answer, Benjamin is on his feet objecting again. This time the judge sustains the motion.

"I have no more questions, Your Honor," Linda says as she takes her seat.

"Your witness, Mr. Marks."

"I have only one or two questions now but I would like the right to recall this witness, Your Honor."

"So noted, go ahead," the judge says.

"Mrs. Rosser, given how close you were, did your father confide in you that a leading specialist had told him he was suffering from Alzheimer's disease?"

"No."

"Do I have this right?" He sounds incredulous. "You are saying he told you he wanted his girlfriend to see a therapist, but he didn't happen to mention he was suffering with a debilitating disease?"

"That's right."

"Later this past summer, did your father tell you why he changed his mind and renegotiated his contract with Haviland after all?"

"No." Lizzie is angry now.

"Hmm. Maybe you weren't all that close after all, Mrs. Rosser. What do you think?"

When I came home from work that day, I did find Lizzie Gabriel Rosser sitting with her father on the Jackson Pollock couch and when Gabriel introduced us I did notice she was quite pregnant. How did I react? Not with hysterics. I suppose I was jealous, but what I remember more clearly is that Lizzie wouldn't make eye contact with *me*. I said I was making tea and asked them if they wanted some. Gabriel answered me, but Lizzie wouldn't. I excused myself and left so they could be together.

Did I begrudge Lizzie her child? Yes. But enough to kill Gabriel for refusing me my own?

That night, after Lizzie had gone, Gabriel apologized to me for her behavior, explaining she'd often been jealous of the women he saw. Then he went to paint while I went into the kitchen to make dinner.

It was warm out and all the windows in the loft were open and a strong breeze was blowing in. I boiled water for penne and chopped up the ingredients for a pesto sauce. We'd planted basil in the country and brought back bunches of it, filling the car with its heavy, green, minty smell. Now the whole loft smelled of garlic and basil.

Hearing a soft fluttering sound, I turned and saw a bird land on the couch. It was a young pigeon, all white with only a few brown feathers on his tail. He sat perfectly still. Unmoving. Unblinking. Staring at me as I stared at him.

With tiny jerky movements the bird inspected his new surroundings. He actually seemed to be looking at Gabriel's paintings of those dark flower gardens illuminated by that magical light.

Despite his size, the pigeon's wing span seemed wide in the loft as he flew closer to one of the paintings. Perching on a chair, he peered at the canvas's glistening surface. After a few minutes he took off again, flying from the chair to the couch to the rim of a lampshade. From one perch to the next and then the next.

"Like an angel's wings," Gabriel whispered as he came and stood behind me, watching the bird circling the room.

He was studying the bird's wings as if he were drawing each moment of flight in his head so he could remember it later with his brush.

"Do you believe in angels?" he asked.

"I used to."

"When?" His hair was tousled. He wore sweatpants and a T-shirt and as I leaned back against him and he put his arms around me, I smelled oil paint and turpentine and tobacco.

"When I was a kid."

The sound of the boiling water distracted me and the bird, who panicked and took off frantically looking for an escape.

"How do we get him out of here?" I asked.

"Maybe we should let him stay."

"A pigeon? Gabriel, pigeons are filthy."

"But he's beautiful, isn't he?"

And then a breeze wafted through the loft and the bird flew on its current out the open window and was gone.

Gabriel's eyes remained on the window. "Tell me about angels," he said.

"Marie used to say we each had our own angel who watched over us and guided us and helped us when we strayed too far from God."

"Think how much easier religion would be to swallow if it were goodness instead of God. Who wouldn't believe in goodness? Did you have an angel?"

"Of course. He was a fat baby with strong wings and when I prayed, I thought he flew my message straight up to God."

Gabriel slipped his gold ring off his finger and put it on the ring finger of my left hand where a wedding band would go, but it was too big. He tried it on my middle finger. It fit much better.

"Now, you have your own angel," he said.

I inspected the cherub, a fat baby with round legs and a round belly, feathery wings, and tiny penis.

"But it's yours."

"You take him—something of mine."

I could have had a real fat baby, something of his alive, kicking and screaming and drinking my milk, I thought, and had to press my lips together to stop myself from speaking.

I put our dinner on the table, but I wasn't hungry. As I watched Gabriel eat the pasta and drink the wine, I kept touching the ring he'd given me, feeling its weight, rubbing it against the palm of my other hand, getting to know its contours.

"Genny, you've been upset since we got back from France."

"I guess."

"It must have been hard to lose your grandfather and then see Marie like that."

"No, it's not about them. It's something I found out about my parents, that's all. Something I never knew."

He nodded wisely and I was grateful he didn't question me. I didn't want to talk about what I'd seen, didn't want to deal with what it meant.

After dinner we took a walk through SoHo into Greenwich Village where we stopped in an Italian café that had been there since the 1950s. We sat at an old marble table, with our feet on the cracked tile floor, and drank small cups of espresso.

"I didn't want to be the one to tell you, but now that you know the truth about the Cézanne mess, you'll understand why I'm going to let Ham handle my work."

"What truth? What are you talking about?"

"Wasn't that what you meant? What you found out about your parents while we were in France?"

I shook my head. That wasn't what I had found out at all. "Are you saying my father was guilty? Oh Gabriel, I didn't know."

"Shit, Genny, I'm sorry, I just assumed when you said—"

"You can't go," I interrupted him. "It will kill my father if he loses you . . . now . . . especially to Ham. My father has never done anything for you but good."

"But I can't ignore that he knowingly sold a forged painting. Or that he bid up my painting at the auction house. Or that he's fighting me so hard on my new work. I just can't stay."

"All these years you and everyone else stayed. All of you knew the kind of things he did—you all agree to give away paintings as gifts, to suck up to the curators and collectors at parties. Why all of a sudden is that a reason to leave?"

"Genny, think what he's asking me to do," Gabriel said.

He was being selfish. "What about what you're asking me to do?"

"You?"

"Did you forget he's my father? Gabriel, please. Give him a chance."

"To do what?"

But I couldn't answer. I didn't know.

We left the café and walked back to the loft in silence. Upstairs he went to work on a canvas; I went to the bedroom where I undressed, jerking down my jeans, pulling open my shirt. I threw my clothes on the floor, got into bed, and rolled over, as far from his side as possible.

If Gabriel left my father, other artists would follow. How long would it take before the gallery was denuded? My father had more than enough money to live on, but if he had to close the gallery, everything he had cared about and loved, the only thing that had never betrayed him, would be gone. He didn't have my mother, he couldn't have me, and he wouldn't have the artists.

I was leaving the next morning to film Poe Linden, the experimental artist, and his sky paintings at the observatory he'd built on the site of a crater in the middle of the desert in New Mexico. While I packed and had breakfast, I avoided Gabriel. My father was now between us.

When it was time for me to go, Gabriel insisted on helping me downstairs with my suitcase and waiting until the car came.

"Instead of you coming back on Friday, why don't I fly out and spend the weekend," he offered.

"I don't know." My voice was flat, expressionless.

"Call me. Think about it. There are places I've never seen in the desert. I don't want to miss them. I want us to see them together."

Reaching out, Gabriel touched my cheek as if he were wiping away my tears. Except I wasn't crying.

The chauffeur got out of the black town car, took my suitcase, and put it in the trunk. Another car coming down the block honked to get by.

"Why do you have to leave the gallery?" I asked Gabriel.

"Don't, Genny, this isn't about us."

"I can't pretend your dealer isn't my father."

"But you don't have to hate me because he and I are having problems."

The chauffeur faced away from us, stood by the car door, and waited.

"Why don't I go with you out to the airport? We could make up in the back of the car." Gabriel put his hand on my waist and tried to pull me toward him, to romance me out of my anger.

"I'm picking up Claire. I'll be late," I said and moved toward the car.

"I'll see you Friday then," he said.

I didn't argue. In the car on the way to the airport I thought it might be a good idea if he did come to New Mexico. Maybe there I could convince him not to leave Haviland's.

TWENTY-EIGHT

New York City Criminal Court Building, Room 1317
Wednesday, December 9, 1992, 2:30 P.M.

Linda's last witness walks up to the stand. While Nicky and I both work for the same parent company and are friendly when we run into each other, my ex-husband and I aren't close. We haven't had a real conversation since our divorce four years ago.

Medium height, steady blue eyes, Nicky is a long-distance runner who knows how to pace himself. He steps up to the witness chair with an athlete's ease and is sworn in.

"Can you tell the court how you make your living, Mr. Parrish?"

Nicky's voice is as calm as he is. "I raise funds for the Public Broadcasting System."

"Is that where you met Genny Haviland?"

"Yes."

"When was that?" Linda asks.

"In 1983."

"And when did you marry Miss Haviland?"

"In 1986," he says.

"And when did you get divorced?"

"Three years later."

"Short marriage?"

Nicky doesn't respond.

"Mr. Parrish, could you tell the court why you and Miss Haviland divorced?"

"I think perhaps we were too consumed by our individual work to work on our marriage. We simply drifted apart." It was the answer he gave all the time, the one he could live with.

"What about Miss Haviland's family? Were they a problem for you?"

"I suppose so." Nicky gracefully crosses one leg over the other, the first time since he took the stand that he's moved.

"Could you elaborate?"

"Genny was very close to her father. As far as I was concerned he had too much influence over her. I resented his attempts to interfere in our lives."

"How did he interfere, Mr. Parrish?"

"They talked on the phone at least every other day. She had dinner with him once a week. There wasn't anything about her life, our lives, that he wasn't aware of."

"How close was Genny to her father, Mr. Parrish?"

"I object, Your Honor!" Benjamin says.

"Sustained," Judge Bailey says.

"Did you talk over your feelings about Mr. Haviland with Genny?" Linda asks.

"Of course."

"Was she sympathetic?"

"She seemed to be, but regardless of what she said, her father had her loyalty, not me."

"If she had to, Mr. Parrish, do you think Genny Haviland could have killed for her father?"

"I object," Benjamin shouts out as the judge simultaneously instructs the clerk to strike Miss Zavidow's question from the record, tells Nicky not to answer, and warns Linda to watch herself.

"I have no more questions, Your Honor," Linda says apologetically and takes her seat.

"Mr. Marks, do you wish to question the witness?"

Benjamin says he does and gets up. "Mr. Parrish, how much money were you making when you married Genny Haviland?"

"Forty thousand dollars."

"How much was Miss Haviland making?"

"I don't remember," Nicky says without trying to remember.

"She was making the same as you were. Plus a trust fund her father had set up for her as a child was bringing in an additional hundred thousand dollars. Do you remember that, Mr. Parrish?"

"Yes."

"Where did you and Genny live during your marriage?"

"In an apartment on 78th Street," Nicky says.

"Owned or rented?" Benjamin asks.

"Rented."

"Isn't it true that Mr. and Mrs. Haviland wanted to buy you and their daughter an apartment for a wedding present?"

"Yes."

"So why were you living in a rented apartment?"

"We refused the gift," Nicky answers.

"We?"

"I refused."

"Why was that, Mr. Parrish?"

Nicky is steel. Nothing I ever said to him rattled him—he never lost his temper—so I don't imagine Benjamin will be able to upset him now. But I'm wrong.

Nicky clenches his jaw and speaks through his teeth. "Because I didn't want to be beholden to him."

"You resented Mr. Haviland's money, didn't you, Mr. Parrish? Isn't that what really came between you and your wife? Isn't that why you got divorced, because you were jealous of her financial independence?"

"All I ever wanted was for her to let me take care of her. Was that such an awful thing to want? To have her depend on me?" Nicky says and then angry with himself for having broken, bangs his fist down on his thigh.

"No," Benjamin says. Turns. Looks at me. Then turns back to Nicky. "One more thing, Mr. Parrish. You never were aware of anything unnatural going on between your ex-wife and her father, were you?"

"No."

Nicky Parrish was Linda's last witness.

For our first witness Benjamin calls Dr. Henry Davis.

Once the doctor has been sworn in, Benjamin establishes he is the Chairman of the Department of Neurology of Mount Sinai Hospital in New York City and that Slade Gabriel was one of the doctor's patients. "When did you first see him, Doctor?"

"On November 20, 1991," the doctor answers.

"Under what circumstances?"

"He had been in an accident, had suffered head injuries, and was brought, unconscious, to Mount Sinai. A few weeks after he had been released he came to see me because of some problems he was experiencing, mostly having to do with memory loss."

"And how many times after that did you have occasion to see him as a patient?"

"He returned for testing twice and the last time I saw him was in late January to go over my diagnosis."

"What was your diagnosis?" Benjamin asked.

"That Mr. Gabriel was suffering from a rapidly advancing case of Alzheimer's disease and had been for several years."

"In layman's terms, could you explain Alzheimer's to the court?" Benjamin steps away from the witness stand to allow the jury full view of the doctor.

"Alzheimer's is a progressive, degenerative disease that attacks the brain, resulting in impaired memory, thinking, and behavior."

"Could you summarize for us what symptoms Mr. Gabriel experienced?"

"Yes." The doctor leaned forward as if lecturing to a class. "He would search for words, or forget where he was in a sentence. He didn't remember where he put things, or how to use simple objects, like toasters and coffeemakers. His judgment was impaired due to his forgetfulness and in one instance he forgot simple traffic rules and almost killed himself and Miss Haviland in a car accident. All of these were classic signs . . . all devastating."

"Would you tell the court how you planned to treat Mr. Gabriel's disease. What medicine did you prescribe, Doctor?"

"There is no treatment available, Mr. Marks. No medicine, no cure."

"Is there any doubt now or was there any doubt in your mind then that Mr. Gabriel was suffering from Alzheimer's?"

"No."

"And can you explain the progress of the disease?"

"In elderly patients the disease can take years to develop to its final stages, which are catastrophic. But in younger patients, like Mr. Gabriel, it's not uncommon to see severe mental deterioration occur very quickly."

"How many years have you been treating Alzheimer's patients?"

"Well, there is no real treatment, as I explained before. But I've been diagnosing Alzheimer's for fifteen years."

"Now, Doctor, would you please tell the court what you told Mr. Gabriel about his condition?"

"I told him exactly what I have told you."

"And how did Mr. Gabriel react when you told him he had Alzheimer's?"

"He was obviously disturbed, but he had expected that to be the diagnosis. A good friend of his, a famous painter, Willem de Kooning, had had Alzheimer's for several years. Mr. Gabriel knew a lot about the disease. Most of his questions concerned when his independence and ability to paint would be impaired."

"And what did you tell him?"

"That he would be able to paint indefinitely."

"Why is that, Doctor?" Benjamin asked.

"There is a difference between mind memory and muscle memory, which exists in a separate neural network in a different region of the brain. And these muscle memories—which take a lot of practice to learn in the first place—seem to take longer to forget."

"What are some of the other muscle memories that last?"

"Walking down steps, kissing, typing, playing piano."

"So were you able to ease Mr. Gabriel's mind?"

"No. He said that unlike de Kooning's work, which is more about color and line, he needed to think through a canvas. He wanted some idea of how long he would have a real ability to reason, to understand what he was painting."

"And how did you answer him, Dr. Davis?" Benjamin asked.

"I told him what I had observed in others: his sustained reasoning power would eventually be impaired, but there was no way to know when that would start to occur."

"Did that reassure him?"

"Well, he didn't say anything for a few minutes, and then he asked me how long he would continue to understand the concept of creating. I wasn't sure if he was rephrasing the question or if he'd already forgotten he'd asked me one just like it."

"How did you answer him the second time?" Benjamin asked.

"I told him I didn't know. Then he asked me if I thought his disease would progress in a similar way as de Kooning's."

"Why did he think you would know that?"

"Mr. Gabriel was aware that my associate was de Kooning's doctor. It was one of the reasons he had chosen me as a physician. "

"How did you answer Mr. Gabriel? "

The doctor sighed. "I told him there was no way of knowing. But I pointed out that de Kooning was still painting and that there were even people who thought he was doing some of his best work since he'd been diagnosed."

"Did that satisfy Mr. Gabriel?"

"No."

"What did he say?"

"He burst out laughing and told me I didn't know anything about art. That the work de Kooning was doing now was being ridiculed. He called it a grisly satire of his earlier work."

"And then?"

"He said that . . ." For the first time, the doctor's professional demeanor cracks and his voice drops.

"Could you speak up, Doctor?

"I'm sorry. He said he would not let that happen to his work. That people would never mock or ridicule his paintings the way they were doing with de Kooning's."

"So he appeared suicidal?"

Linda stands. "I object, Your Honor. Mr. Marks is asking the witness to draw a conclusion."

"Sustained."

Benjamin rephrases the question. "Dr. Davis, did Mr. Gabriel talk to you about committing suicide?"

"Yes. He said he'd rather be dead and would take his own life before he would allow this disease to destroy his ability to paint."

"Thank you, Dr. Davis, I have no more questions."

"Miss Zavidow?" the judge says.

Linda approaches the witness stand. "Good afternoon, Doctor. I have just a few questions. Were you absolutely certain about your diagnosis of Slade Gabriel's disease?"

"At the time, not absolutely, no. The only completely certain way to diagnose Alzheimer's is to study the patient's brain tissue, which can only be done in an autopsy."

"So even though Mr. Gabriel was forgetful and often became disoriented you were not one hundred percent certain of your diagnosis?"

"One hundred percent? No, not one hundred percent. But pretty damn close."

"Did you explain that to Mr. Gabriel?"

"Of course. I explain that to all my patients." The doctor is indignant.

"So there was a possibility that Mr. Gabriel did not have Alzheimer's, that he was perhaps increasingly forgetful and distracted because he was undergoing a professional crisis?"

"Given the combination of symptoms, I did not believe so."

"But it was possible?" she insists.

"Possible, but not likely."

"Did you and he discuss the possibility of that?"

"As I explained, Miss Zavidow, I am careful to explain to every one of my patients that my diagnosis is based on my collective experience. That is why they come and see me. I have that experience."

"Yes, of course." She is being solicitous now. "But I just want to make sure I understand. Did Mr. Gabriel know there was a good chance he didn't have Alzheimer's?"

"No, there was not a good chance. As I already explained, he had been experiencing symptoms for several years. They were gaining in frequency and becoming worse. There was only a minute chance Mr. Gabriel was suffering from something other than Alzheimer's."

"But you and he did discuss that possibility?"

"Yes, we did."

"I'm sorry, Doctor, just one more question. If Mr. Gabriel did have Alzheimer's, how many more years do you think he had of lucidity?"

"It's hard to say."

"Did he ask you?"

"Yes."

"Well, what did you tell him?"

"Perhaps another year with sustained periods of lucidity. It's an inexact science based on previous case histories. Each patient is different."

"Thank you, Dr. Davis."

Outside the window, the first snow of the winter has begun, a disturbance that distracts the members of the jury.

Benjamin speaks more loudly than usual as he calls Fred Rasset to the stand, the first of several artists he's told me he will use to paint a portrait, in words, of Gabriel as a man totally obsessed with his art.

"Painting was Gabriel's life. He wasn't even disturbed that he was preoccupied by it. Gabriel took pride in his single-minded devotion."

"He pursued painting. He fed on it. I never saw him love anything the way he loved his work," Tisha Carraway adds when she's called.

"He was the consummate selfish artist," Bill Marra describes him. "It got in the way of our friendship, but not in the way of my respect for him as a professional."

And now, on the heels of these artists' testimonies, Benjamin recalls Gabriel's daughter to the stand.

"What kind of father was Slade Gabriel?" he asks.

"An excellent father." She's angered by the question and raises her voice.

"What were some of the things you did together when you were a child?"

"He . . . we . . . I used to go to his studio and he would let me paint with his paints."

"And what did he do while you were painting? Was he showing you how to paint?"

"No . . . he was painting."

Does the jury notice that whenever Lizzie's eyes drift in my direction, she averts her gaze and shifts in her seat to avoid me? Would I be like her if my father took a lover? I try to imagine if I would hate the woman, whoever she might be, enough to poison so many people's minds against her.

"Did he teach you how to ride a bike?" Benjamin asks.

"No."

"Did the two of you ever go to the circus or the zoo?"

"Your Honor, I object!" Linda yells out.

"I see no reason the witness should not answer the question," Judge Bailey says.

"No," Lizzie says.

"How old were you when your parents were divorced?" Benjamin asks.

"I was twelve," she says.

"And where did you grow up?"

"In South Miami, Florida." Lizzie bites her bottom lip.

"Where was your father living at that time?"

"In New York and then California."

"How often did you see him during those years?"

"I never counted, Mr. Marks."

"Well, count now, Mrs. Rosser. Did you see him every other weekend, once a month, once every six months, once a year?"

"At first about once a year, but when I got older we became closer." Lizzie bites her lip again.

"Why do you think that was, Mrs. Rosser?"

"My work gave us a common meeting ground."

"Oh, what do you do?" Benjamin asks, sounding as if he's actually interested.

"I'm the associate curator of Twentieth-Century Prints for the Museum of Modern Art."

"I see. So you take after your father?"

"Well, my mother is an artist, too, a potter," Lizzie answers.

"So you take after both of them. I suppose it made both of your parents very proud of you, to have you involved in the arts."

"Yes."

"Why didn't you pursue a career as an artist yourself?"

"It's too demanding, too all encompassing."

"You saw that from watching your mother when you were growing up?"

"No, she wasn't obsessed about art the way my father was—"

Lizzie has backed right into Benjamin's trap, and stops herself.

"You sound bitter."

Linda Zavidow interrupts. "I object. Counsel is badgering the witness."

The judge turns to Benjamin. "Please, Mr. Marks, get to the point."

"I already have, Your Honor. I have no more questions."

Court is adjourned for the day but Benjamin has asked me to stay for a few minutes and talk. I tell my parents to leave without me and follow Benjamin down the hall to our pathetic meeting/lunchroom.

"I want to put you on the stand tomorrow," he says and waits for a response, but I have no response.

"Do you want to go on the stand?" he asks.

I shrug. "If you think I should."

"Damn it, Genny, no. Not if I want you to. You have to *want* to. Don't you care what happens to you? Don't you want to be vindicated? Don't you want to get up there and tell everyone what really happened, so they'll all stop staring at you as if you killed someone?"

I know what kind of answer he's waiting for but after all the lies, I can't lie to him.

"Go home tonight and think about it. Your testimony is the only hope I have of getting you off. I know you're confused, Genny. I see it in your eyes every time I look at you. But what's done is done. You can't take back what happened. If you want me to try and save the rest of your life, you have to help me. I'll be home tonight. Whatever time you reach a decision, call me."

He takes a few steps toward the door. "Oh, just in case you didn't know, Genny, they don't let prisoners hang paintings in their cells."

Outside, everything is covered with a layer of white and the disorientation of walking without knowing which way is west or which way east is oddly comforting. Street signs are dusted over, traffic lights glow in the diffusion, people burdened by heavy overcoats, scarves, hats, and gloves walk tentatively, squint, and try to keep the snow out of their eyes. I give in to the confusion. Nothing is what it seems.

In minutes, my thin-soled ballet slipper shoes are soaked through. I shouldn't have refused the ride my parents offered. I should have asked them to wait while I talked to Benjamin, but I wanted to be alone, to go home by myself. It's work having my parents hovering: my mother convincing herself I'm fine, my father trying to put aside his anger and find a way to protect me.

I get on an uptown bus. Wet wool coats, red-cheeked faces, runny noses, people willingly crowded together, simply glad to be temporarily safe from the storm. None of these strangers has any idea who I am. Their eyes do not rest on me the way the jury's do. I could stay on this bus, let it take me as far as it goes and then get on another bus, and then another until I was far away. What would happen if I didn't show up tomorrow? After our conversation in which he asked me to take the stand, Benjamin would think I'd run because I'm guilty.

Back in the loft, I hang my wet coat on a hook and step out of my soggy shoes. I leave the mail on the table, go into the kitchen, open a can of soup, empty it into a pot, and heat it on the stove. I pour my glass of wine and sit down on the couch facing Gabriel's paintings, which by now lean against every wall and every window. Into the painting I go, where it's warm and green and trees bend in the fragrant wind and it's not until I smell the vegetables burning that I remember the soup. It's scorched. The bottom of the pot is burned.

The phone rings. It's Ham. He can tell from my voice that something is wrong and asks what it is. I tell him what Benjamin has asked of me.

"Will you do it?" Ham asks.

"Taking the stand, telling the story, answering the questions. It won't bring back Gabriel, will it? No, let them decide without me."

"But you're just giving up. Sentencing yourself."

It is just a string of seven ordinary words, but they resonate.

"Genny, you can't give up. Not yet. Aren't there still things you want to do? In your work? Don't you want to have your own children? A little girl with all your curiosity?"

I don't answer, but I am still listening. I could have hung up on him, but I am still hanging on to the phone.

"You know, I used to wonder why you and I didn't connect," he says.

"It was too soon after your divorce."

"That's what you said back then . . . but I don't think that was the reason. I don't think it had anything to do with me."

Outside my window a siren screams as it passes and I wonder what other tragedy has occurred.

Ham continues, "It was Gabriel. He was there in between us even though I didn't know it. He was probably there with you in your marriage, too. He's been with you your whole adult life, hasn't he? Preventing you from seeing any man clearly enough to know if—"

I interrupt, "I don't want to talk about him."

When he finally answers he sounds angry. "I'm sure you don't, but that's too damn bad. It's just an easy out."

"Easy? Are you kidding? Nothing about this is easy. It hasn't been easy for years!" I'm shouting.

"Genny, listen to me. If you don't get on the stand it will be like you're committing suicide. That would be two deaths. No, you can't do that for him, too."

After getting off the phone I move Gabriel's largest paintings into a circle around my bed. I crawl in and lay my head against the pillow. Now, no matter which way I turn, all I see are his paintings, his light, his landscapes, his darkness, his illusions surrounding me.

If they put me in jail, I will never see his paintings again.

I feel . . . what? A stab of fear? No. Pain? No. The terrible anticipation of loss? Of living without being able to see Gabriel's Edens?

My head throbs. My throat tightens. I feel the pressure of unshed tears.

It doesn't matter how unpleasant—they are feelings. Finally. Not numbness. Not anymore. And I realize if they put me in jail there will be even worse things than never seeing Gabriel's paintings again.

PART IV

Continue to laugh at those things that made us laugh together. . . .
Dry your eyes and don't cry . . . if you love me.

—St. Augustine

TWENTY-NINE

I have been on the stand for two hours. Benjamin asks his questions, I
give my answers. So far I've told the jury how Gabriel and I met when
I was seventeen, how I felt about him, why he stopped seeing me, and
then how we began seeing each other again last year.

"Were you ever pregnant by Mr. Gabriel?"

When we rehearsed this question, we were in Benjamin's office,
alone, and I did fine. But in this courtroom, I hear the reverberations
of the word *pregnant* and get lost in them.

"Genny? Were you pregnant this last year?" he repeats the
question.

This morning, Benjamin told me whenever I sense I'm close to losing control to think of how much I don't want to go to jail, to say it to
myself like a mantra—I do not want to go to jail, I do not want to go
to jail—and yet even as I sit here on this hard seat in this wooden cage
beside the judge and face the jury, I know that I am still conflicted.
Part of me does want to go to jail: to be punished and to suffer and to
do penance for the things I've done.

On the stand I look out into the audience and see Ham's face. His
eyes are focused on me and I become aware of a faint fluttering of

anticipation in my chest, a sudden sense of possibilities, so I steel myself, sit back, and with as strong a voice I can muster I answer.

"Yes, I was pregnant and I had an abortion."

"How did you feel about that?" Benjamin asks.

"I was horribly upset and conflicted."

"Why?"

"I wanted to have the baby."

"Then why didn't you?"

"Gabriel didn't want to have another child," I say.

"And you gave in to his wishes over your own?"

"I wanted to be with Gabriel more than I wanted a child."

"You loved him that much that you would give up having a child for him?" Benjamin asks.

"Yes," I say and bow my head.

Is the jury waiting for the tears? Benjamin's told me they need tears, but I can't cry here, not in front of them. Since Gabriel died, I have not cried in front of anyone except Ham. And that was over a pair of lost gloves.

"Are you all right, Miss Haviland?" Benjamin asks, implying, for the jury that I'm distraught.

"Not really, but I can continue."

Benjamin asks me when I first started noticing changes in Gabriel's behavior and I describe several incidents.

"Now, Miss Haviland, would you tell us when you discovered Mr. Gabriel had Alzheimer's disease?"

New Mexico was hot and dry, warm sun and red clay. Everything on the horizon was long and low. Even the sky seemed wider there. My producer, the crew, and I spent two days filming Poe Linder at his observatory. After listening to Poe talk, I knew how much Gabriel would enjoy meeting him, speaking to him about light and seeing the observatory. I even began to be convinced that here, away from New York and the studio, I could convince Gabriel to stay with my father.

And so I called him.

He arrived late Friday morning and we drove straight from the airport to the crater. Gabriel immediately experienced the magnetic density of the place. "I've never felt like this . . . so awake or alive . . . except when I'm painting," Gabriel said to Poe, who just nodded; he knew. He was well aware of Gabriel's work.

Poe explained how the crater was in line with the supposed mystical alignment of the sun, moon, and earth. "These rooms are aligned on that same axis. All open to the sky. We don't use any electric light, just sunlight and starlight. As an artist, I want to force people to actually see the light as color, as form."

"So there's no fucking barrier between your senses and your surroundings," Gabriel said, staring up into the sky. Then he turned to me. "You remember what I was trying to explain to you about the Impressionists that day near Giverny? This is new. This is what I haven't been able to find."

"Traditional galleries stopped working for me when I realized what a great barrier there was between the art and the viewer," Poe said. "Such a great intrusion of didactic theory you needed a goddamn translator. Here—" he gestured expansively to the desert, "—there's no separation. The art comes in and surrounds you. It's your light, it illuminates itself."

Gabriel was like a parishioner listening to a sermon and I realized what a mistake I'd made. Poe was damning my father's kind of art as useless and old-fashioned.

Poe was exploring the unknown. He was doing what Gabriel longed to do.

After they talked together for more than an hour, Poe instructed us to lie down on the floor and stare up at the infinite blue sky where clouds moved in a convex curve.

We lay there for a long time without talking. I became aware of Gabriel's heartbeat and then mine—in sync.

"Thank you for this," Gabriel said. "It's helped me make up my mind. Art, the way we know it, is dying. I can't do anything more with paint . . . even though painting is all I've ever wanted to do." He sighed deeply and our hearts stopped hitting the same beat at the same moment.

"Why does it have to be so black and white? Can't you let my father sell—"

"Genny, stop."

Silence again. Lonely silence.

"I might need you to help me," Gabriel said after immeasurable time had passed. Something in his voice warned me to stay quiet and wait. "Will you do it? No matter what it is?"

"What do you want me to do?"

"No questions now."

"Genny can you describe Mr. Gabriel's finally telling you about his illness?" Benjamin asks.

On the way back to the hotel, driving along the barren stretch of desert toward the hot, red setting sun, Gabriel suddenly asked me if I believed in suicide.

The question, at first, had no significance. I don't even remember how I answered, but I probably said something like how I thought it was a coward's way out. Then he asked me if I were Marie, wouldn't I rather be dead than to linger, not knowing where or who I was, unable to do anything that gave me pleasure?

"What are we talking about?" I asked.

Nothing. No words. No sound. An astounding silence. The inside of that Jeep filled with the lack of sound.

"I have Alzheimer's disease."

I stopped the Jeep. The sun was slipping below the horizon.

Part of me wasn't surprised. I'd known for a long time that something was wrong. "But you're not old enough," I said, denying it even as I remembered him forgetting words, appointments, where he was— and how he almost killed us in the car in the Hamptons.

"I'm going to forget what I'm trying to say in my paintings. Forget how to say your name. How to cross the street. I am going to forget everything that makes me who I am. I'll become like a baby, unable to do anything for myself. I won't be able to paint."

My body felt light

"Do you understand?" His voice was like a string tethering me to the ground.

"Genny, when the time comes I am going to ask you to help me . . ." There was a long pause. ". . . to die."

Out the window endless space was closing in on me. I shook my head, my hair whipped back and forth.

"Won't it be easier for me to die than disappear in front of your eyes?"

I got out of the car. There were rocks on the ground. Heavy rocks. I picked one up and threw it as far as I could. It skipped along the sand, finally disappearing in the dust it displaced. I threw more rocks. Rocks too heavy for me to lift. I scratched my hands, broke my fingernails, strained my muscles. I didn't care. I couldn't stop. I threw one rock after another, none of them travelling very far.

Gabriel got out of the car and took me in his arms and held me and together we sank down to the floor of the desert where we sat rocking back and forth. I was not thinking of him, but of me without him. Thinking, too, of the baby I could have had.

I had killed the baby for him.

Now he was asking me to kill him.

*   *   *

"When I got back into the car I couldn't drive, so he took the wheel. He wasn't supposed to drive because of the disease, but I didn't care. I half hoped he'd kill both of us," I say and look past Benjamin, over to the jury.

"So Slade Gabriel asked you to help him commit suicide?"

"Yes."

One of the jury members, an older man in the second row, coughs and coughs again and then there is quiet.

"Before your trip, before this conversation, how did Mr. Gabriel react when he had a memory lapse?" Benjamin asks.

"Before New Mexico, he'd panic."

"And after New Mexico?"

"He was calmer. He was relieved that he'd made the decision."

"The decision?" Benjamin asks.

"To kill himself," I say.

I silence the already quiet courtroom. Now these words, like the motive, exist in the room, forms filling space. Yes, I had a motive for murder. But yes, Slade Gabriel also had a reason to commit suicide.

"Genny, what did you do after you and Mr. Gabriel returned from New Mexico?"

"That first week, while my editor worked on the footage we'd shot of Poe's sky paintings, I saw half a dozen doctors and listened to them all tell me the same hopeless facts and figures about Alzheimer's.

"Still doubting them, I spent hours in the library where I read everything I could about the disease, its resistance to any drug therapy and its torturous effacing of a person's self.

"There have been a few articles published about fetal tissue therapy slowing the process but no trials were set up yet. The government is embroiled in the issue of whether it will even allow aborted fetal tissue to be used. I thought of the—I fantasized about getting pregnant again and having another abortion so some doctor could illegally use the embryo to heal Gabriel."

"Did you try and convince Mr. Gabriel to change his mind about the suicide?"

"Constantly. We argued about it every night. He pummeled me with stories about how the illness had affected his friend de Kooning. How when he last saw him in East Hampton, his wife was telling his assistants what colors to premix and put on his palette. They were even deciding when his paintings were finished.

" 'It's not *his* art anymore,' he told me. 'His hands are moving across the canvas by rote—his artistic intellect is gone. These paintings are art only by a fluke of memory and the name of the man holding the paintbrush but they have nothing to do with his passions, his angst. They are nice, light and lyrical shit that any one of his assistants could have done.'

"And then Gabriel told me about the debates going on among critics and curators as to whether this was the work of someone who was just pushing paint around or someone who still knew what he was doing.

"He was upset for de Kooning.

"But he was also horrified at the thought that any of this might ever happen to him or his work."

My voice cracks and I can see approval in Benjamin's eyes. "When did you agree to help him?" he asks.

We were having dinner: I'd made chicken, salad, and bread and had put it all on the table. Then I took a bottle of wine out of the refrigerator and handed it to Gabriel to open. He looked at the corkscrew as if he had never seen anything like it before. There'd been so many of those moments before our trip to New Mexico, but now each one stole a little bit more of my strength and resolve.

When Gabriel spaced-out and disconnected, I struggled to control myself so that I wouldn't upset him when he came out of it, but I wasn't always successful. That night when he reconnected to the moment, he took one look at me and knew what had happened.

"It's time to get ready, Genny. We have to make plans. We have to talk about this," he said.

"No."

"Remember you saved my life once? Please, save it again. Save it from becoming meaningless. From paintings like we saw today." He was imploring me, his eyes locked on mine, pleading. "I need at least forty-five Seconal, but no doctor will prescribe that many pills at once. You'll have to go to different doctors and get separate prescriptions."

Suddenly, I saw myself, as a child, sitting next to Marie, in church, praying, feeling the beads of the rosary slipping between my fingers.

"This is a sin," I whispered to Gabriel.

"I can't do it alone, Genny. I can't go to my doctor. He'd know what I was doing and refuse me and I can't go to a new doctor. What if I get disoriented in the middle of the examination?"

But I couldn't agree to help. Not until Gabriel, desperate, gave me an ultimatum.

"If you help me, I'll renegotiate my contract with your father. Haviland will remain my gallery. If you don't, I'll sign with Ham Lane."

I wondered if the dementia had begun to corrode his brain, or was I the one who had gone mad?

"And how did you get the pills, Genny?"

Smiling, I think of the perverse poetic justice. "I went to my gynecologist, the doctor who had performed my abortion. There were no lines outside his office that day and I didn't bring my father with me. I told Dr. Nash that since the abortion I was having trouble sleeping and that I was considering seeing a therapist. Could he recommend one and, in the meantime, could he give me something to sleep?

"He wrote out the prescription for twenty-eight Seconal. It was too easy. Suddenly I had more than half of what we needed. But I was just going through the motions. I still didn't really believe Gabriel would ever take them."

"But you got the prescription filled?"

"Yes."

"What about the rest of the pills, Genny?" Benjamin asks.

"A few days later I went to my old therapist, Paula Conroy, whom I hadn't seen in several years. I told her about the abortion and that I thought I needed to come back to therapy. We spent a whole session on what I had been doing since she saw me last, but I didn't tell her about Gabriel coming back into my life. Instead, I made up a fictitious lover who had three children, who wasn't sure he could commit to me. She believed all of it, including the lie about my not being able to sleep, and gave me a prescription for twenty-eight Seconal. I had that prescription filled at a drugstore near her office."

"So you admit you got the pills?" Benjamin asks.

"I had the prescriptions filled. I did all those things. It never occurred to me to hide what I was doing. Don't you see? It never occurred to me that anyone would doubt Gabriel wanted to commit suicide."

"Genny, you heard the prosecution's expert witness recite statistics that most men kill themselves with a gun. Why didn't Gabriel use a gun?"

"Calls for conjecture," Linda Zavidow calls out.

Benjamin's eyes light up. Linda has made a very important mistake, by objecting she has given credence to my testimony.

"I'll rephrase. Genny, did Gabriel tell you why he wanted to kill himself with pills?"

"No, but he couldn't have used a gun. He was so concerned with aesthetics—"

"Objection," Linda calls out. Second mistake.

"Sustained."

"All right, Genny, tell us: Was there anything else Gabriel asked you to do?"

"He wanted me to stay with him after he had taken the pills and then to put the . . . the plastic bag around his . . . head . . . and to tie it . . . to make certain he died."

The jury watches me bow my head. Are they looking for tears falling into my lap? Don't they know how much worse it is that I can't cry?

"I'm not sure I understand. Why did Mr. Gabriel need you to do these things? Why did he need you to help him?" Benjamin asks.

"He was petrified that if he was alone he'd fall into a spell, you know, forget what he was doing right in the middle of doing it and take only a few of the pills. He worried the pills might not be enough. He even worried about throwing up the pills and waking up in the psychiatric ward of a hospital. Gabriel didn't want anything to go wrong. He just wanted to die."

"How did Mr. Gabriel finally decide when to end his life?" Benjamin asks softly.

On that last Friday night, I found him standing in front of his canvas, holding his palette, a confused expression on his face. He was lost in that place he went to within the disease.

I walked over to his side and took the palette out of his hand and led him to bed. "You must be tired," I said. He nodded and shut his eyes.

I went back to the studio and washed his brushes for him, swishing the bristles in the turpentine, back and forth.

It had happened: He hadn't known what he was doing with the paint.

When the brushes were cleaned, I wiped them on a soft rag and put them away, then I put away the palette.

I went to look at the canvas.

Crude marks marred the work; he'd begun to destroy the painting with a child's innocent scrawls. Taking a rag, I rubbed at the marks, smeared first one and then another into an indecipherable mass.

"What the fuck are you doing?" Gabriel was standing a few feet away from me.

"I . . ."

How could I tell him what had happened?

"What the fuck are you doing?" He grabbed the rag out of my hand.

"I backed into it, I smeared it, I was just trying to—"

But he knew I was lying. "Genny, why was I in bed? I don't remember going to bed!"

"You were tired. Aren't you tired?"

"No, I was painting and . . ." He stopped. He stared at the scribbles I hadn't completely been able to erase from his painting yet. "Oh my God . . ."

"Seeing those scrawls, knowing that was how he would paint once he disappeared forever into an Alzheimer's fog, was too much for him. That night he told me he was ready and explained what he wanted me to do. He'd planned it all out carefully, to make sure it wouldn't appear I'd been involved. He knew it was a felony in New York State to assist in a suicide."

"Can you tell us his plan, Genny?" Benjamin asks.

"We'd do it Monday, the day before the cleaning lady came, so she'd be the one to find him, not me. He wanted me to give him the pills and put the bag on him, then leave and go to my father's gallery, make sure I was seen there and then drive out to the house on Long Island. He'd said he'd call to rent me a car and make the appointment with the carpenter so there'd be witnesses and proof of where I'd been that day."

"Didn't it worry you that Gabriel was taking such elaborate precautions to give you an alibi?" Benjamin asks.

"Not really. He was just protecting me."

"But it didn't work out that way, did it, Genny?"

"No, I guess he made mistakes."

"What mistakes?"

"He wasn't thinking that anyone would try to *prove* I'd helped him."

"Anything else, Genny?"

"Yes, he never sent the suicide note or he never wrote the note, I don't know."

"You never saw it?" Benjamin asked with astonishment.

"No. He told me he'd written it and was going to mail it to his lawyer on Sunday so he'd get it by Tuesday. But no, I never saw it."

"Genny, do you think you can tell us about the last two days?"

"Gabriel was serene, almost pleased that it was over, thankful he was getting away from the disease. All that was left was for him to finish his last painting. He worked on it for hours with his old energy. As if he was willing the disease to give him a forty-eight-hour respite. "

He painted and I sat there and watched him. Memorizing the way he stood, how he moved, and the way he communed with the paint and the canvas.

He'd stop and we'd eat, or have coffee, or take a walk. Or he'd stop to make love to me.

We were grabbing on to each second, though we did not articulate this. If we were scared—and I was—we did not share that. We did everything in a kind of anesthetized calm.

He painted through the night on Saturday and I fell asleep on the couch watching him. But I never dreamed.

I was half-awake when Gabriel left, as he always did on Sunday mornings, to get the newspaper, orange juice, and fresh bagels. But that morning he was also going to put the note in the mail to his lawyer.

After he'd been gone for more than the usual ten minutes, I panicked. What if he had fallen into an Alzheimer's haze and had gotten lost? What if he had gone into a trance and been in an accident? Should I call the police? The hospitals? Or go out and search for him?

Almost an hour after he left, he came but without the *Times*, the juice, or the bagels and found me in tears.

Neither of us said anything. There was nothing to say anymore. Gabriel just took me in his arms, held me, and let me cry.

That afternoon while he worked on the painting, he played all the music he loved: Nat King Cole, Sinatra, the Rolling Stones, the Beatles, James Taylor. *"Oh, I've seen fire and I've seen rain . . . But I always thought that I'd see you, baby, one more time again . . ."*

"Are you all right, Miss Haviland?" Judge Bailey asks when I fall silent.

"Yes." A lie. But I know what he means; he wants to know if I can continue. I don't want to, but I have to.

"Go on, Genny," Benjamin says, encouraging me. "What happened Monday morning?"

"It was ironic. I threw up twice while Gabriel stood with me in the bathroom and then he gently wiped my face with a washcloth. He told me to take a shower and when I came out I found him sitting in the studio area in front of his last paintings, smiling. I made us both tea and we sat together and sipped the tea in front of his work. A half hour passed and then he asked me for the toast."

"Toast?" Benjamin asks.

"Gabriel had done all this research and knew it was tricky. Eating either too much or too little could make it difficult for Gabriel to keep the pills down. So about nine o'clock I made him toast. Arnold white bread. No butter. No jam. That might cause him to throw up, too. I brought him the toast on a plate and watched him lift the bread to his mouth and chew it. Then I sat down beside him and we held each other. Just held each other. I was scared, trying not to cry, not to panic. I had to keep reminding myself this was what he wanted.

" 'Genny, get the pills,' he said finally and I brought them to him with a glass of water. Opening the vials one by one, I poured the pills into my hand and then into his. He scooped them into his mouth, drank some water, and swallowed.

"But in the last exchange some of the pills fell on the floor and I picked them up but held them back.

" 'Give them to me,' " he said.

" 'No, you can't take them. They're dirty.' "

" 'Oh Genny, it doesn't matter.' "

"He held out his hand and I gave him the last three pills. He popped them, drank the last of the water, and then handed me back the glass.

"It seemed like only minutes before he started getting tired, but I know it was longer. I never took my eyes off him. I actually saw his face muscles relaxing."

"Your Honor?"

I am so far into the past I have to focus to realize it's Linda Zavidow. "I think we've been more than lenient here—"

"Then I don't imagine you'll have any trouble letting her continue. Go on Miss Haviland, Mr. Marks," the judge says gently.

"What happened next, Genny?" Benjamin eases me back to that morning.

"Gabriel whispered to me to get the plastic bag. I went into the kitchen, put the glass in the sink, and brought the bag and the string back to the bed. He asked me to turn the last paintings toward him but by the time I had, his eyes had shut.

"Watching him sleep seemed so natural at first. Then I started to panic. What was happening? What was I allowing to happen? Shouldn't I do something? Stop this? Call 911. For whatever time he had left. That we had left.

"Suddenly his eyes were open and he was watching me as if he could read my mind, as if he knew I had been thinking of rousing him, of calling an ambulance, of letting them take him to the hospital so they could pump out his stomach.

" 'Genny . . . the bag . . .'

"I didn't move. I couldn't. Panic flashed in his eyes, I knew he was afraid I was not going to keep my promise. I was supposed to help him put the bag over his head, and tie it here, but I could not do that. And in the end he did not ask me to. In the end he reached out for them himself and I turned away and left the room.

"Is it so hard to understand? He wanted to die. It was his right wasn't it? To die that way instead of disappearing into a disease. He didn't want to be like de Kooning—not knowing what he was painting. He just wanted to be Gabriel. In charge. In control of his own light.

"Can't you understand that? I did. So I helped him. I did that for Gabriel because it was what he asked me to do."

"Did you always do what he asked you to?"

"I'd never been able to resist him. With no one else was I ever submissive. But from the very beginning, I did what Gabriel asked of me. I always thought it was because it gave me pleasure to pleasure him. That I really was in control and could choose when to give in and when not to. But I didn't really believe that. Deep down I always knew I simply had no power to refuse him anything."

"Mr. Marks, would your client like a few minutes to collect herself?" Judge Bailey says as he takes off his glasses and slowly wipes them again with his large white handkerchief.

Benjamin shakes his head yes.

"No, let me go on . . . get this over with . . . finally."

"All right, Genny, tell us what you did after you left Mr. Gabriel in the bed."

"I ran from there, from the room, from Gabriel . . . sleeping . . . dying . . ."

My palms start to itch and I rub them against my knees.

"You did not help him put the bag over his head or tie it?"

"No—I couldn't—not that."

"So what did you do after you left the room?" Benjamin asks.

"I ran out of the loft and went downstairs. It was still morning. It should have been night. It should have been dark. Then I hailed a cab and gave the driver the address of my father's gallery."

Still scratching my hands, I feel something sticky. Damn, I've opened the scabs and drawn blood. I turn my palms against my black slacks so the jury can't see what I've done.

"Genny, what happened next?" Benjamin prods.

"My father was in a meeting, but he could see me through the glass walls. He waved at me. I waved back and asked his receptionist what time it was. She told me it was eleven. I had to hold on to a chair to keep myself from racing out of there, to keep myself from not going downtown back to the loft and trying to save Gabriel."

"And then?"

"I left the gallery, picked up the rented car, and drove out to Amagansett."

I sat outside beside the small pond at Gabriel's house, the last vestiges of the summer flowers surrounding me. It was early fall and the daylilies were gone but their long green leaves—long like Gabriel's fingers—were bent over in gentle arcs leaning down to the ground. There were rose bushes, too, shriveling roses still on their stems. I picked them off, the petals falling apart in my fingers. And I kept picking them off until I purged the whole bush and had hundreds of dead heads at my feet, in a pile.

"How did you spend the rest of that Monday afternoon at Gabriel's house?" Benjamin steers me on.

"At four o'clock I met with Barry, the carpenter, and then I sat down in the living room with Gabriel's things around me, with his paintings looking down on me. And I waited. I became certain Gabriel was not dead, that he hadn't died—that he was not dead."

I had a fantasy that as soon as I left the loft, Gabriel had changed his mind, deciding he wasn't ready yet. He hadn't put the bag on. Instead he'd picked up the phone and called the police. An ambulance had come. The paramedics had broken down the door, put Gabriel on a stretcher, and taken him, sirens wailing, to the hospital. There they had pumped his stomach. And soon someone would call to tell me he was fine. Soon.

I must have fallen asleep in the living room because that's where I woke up about an hour later.

In my dream a phone was ringing but I couldn't find a phone. The noise was coming from a book lying in a pool of light on a table and when I put my hand out to open the book, I was suffused with a sense of well-being; inside would be all the answers I needed. But when I opened it, I was horrified to find, not words, but drawings. Hundreds of dark drawings I couldn't decipher. It would take so long to learn to read these drawings.

I sat in the living room and went over the dream in my mind, memorizing it, trying to keep it with me so I could keep the feeling of well-being with me.

"Genny, how did you find out that Slade Gabriel had indeed died?" Benjamin asks.

"The phone rang on Tuesday morning. I was almost surprised to hear my cleaning lady's voice, trembling, shrill, and hysterical. 'Mr. Gabriel's dead. He's dead. Here, in the loft. Here. He's dead.' "

"Thank you, Genny. I have no more questions, Your Honor," Benjamin says.

"Your witness, Miss Zavidow." Judge Bailey nods to the assistant D.A., who gets up and walks over to me.

"Miss Haviland, when did Mr. Gabriel first discuss leaving your father's gallery with you?" Linda Zavidow has dressed for her redirect. She is wearing a peach colored wool suit that sets off her skin and light hair. How dark I must seem next to her.

"In mid-March or early April," I answer.

"Did the idea of his leaving disturb you?"

"Yes."

"Were you aware of what kind of financial ramifications his leaving would have for your father's gallery?"

"Yes."

"What would those ramifications be?"

"I object, Your Honor. We have already heard this testimony from other witnesses," Benjamin says.

"Overruled. But let's not dwell on this, Miss Zavidow," Judge Bailey says.

"Miss Haviland, can you tell the court your opinion of what would have happened to your father's gallery if Mr. Gabriel left?"

"It would have been bad for his business. He'd already lost several of his best artists. He needed Gabriel," I say.

"Do you love your father?"

"Yes."

Linda lets that hang on the air for a minute. She nods. "Did you want Mr. Gabriel to leave your father's gallery?"

"Of course not."

"Miss Haviland, did you discuss Mr. Gabriel's suicide plans with anyone?"

"Yes."

"With whom?"

"With Gabriel."

"Other than Mr. Gabriel?" Linda asks.

"No. He asked me to keep it between us."

"But you talked about having an abortion with your friends, with your parents."

"That was a different issue. I had doubts about that."

"But you had no doubts about killing the man you supposedly loved—"

Benjamin is on his feet. "I object, Your Honor."

"Sustained. Miss Zavidow, rephrase," the judge says.

"I withdraw the question, Your Honor. Miss Haviland, why didn't you ask Mr. Gabriel to go to the doctor with you when you had an abortion?"

"I was . . . I was angry at him."

"Angry enough to kill him?"

"Objection!" Benjamin shouts.

"Sustained. Miss Zavidow, this is the last time I will warn you."

"I have no more questions, Your Honor," Linda says.

The judge looks at Benjamin. "Call your next witness."

"I have no more witnesses, Your Honor. The defense rests."

"We'll recess for lunch and hear closing arguments this afternoon," Judge Bailey says.

THIRTY

New York City Criminal Court Building, Room 1317
Thursday, December 10, 1992, 2:00 P.M.

As Linda stands to make her closing argument, I watch the jury follow her every move.

"Cold-blooded murder is not a pretty thought. And it certainly is hard to think of a woman as lovely and successful as Miss Haviland drugging Mr. Gabriel's tea, waiting for him to fall asleep, and then tying a plastic bag over his head. But that is what she did. The evidence proves it. Her fingerprints are on the bottle of pills, on the plastic bag, her hair was twisted in the twine. No evidence links him to these materials. We even have her own admission that she gave Mr. Gabriel—the man she supposedly loved—the pills. Of course she lied about the bag. Why would she stop at the pills? Because that was too painful?

"What a defense! In all my years as a lawyer, I have never heard such a defense.

"Slade Gabriel lived to paint. Can you believe he would be willing to give up painting—even for one day? Yes, he may have had a debilitating disease but we've heard his own doctor's testimony that no one knows too much about Alzheimer's. Slade Gabriel might have lived for years with periods of lucidity. Why should we believe that a man who so loved his life would give up before he had to? Because he told a doctor he'd rather die than not be able to paint? Well, who among us has not said: I'd rather die than lose my husband, my wife, my child, my house, and my job.

"Genny Haviland not only had the means, she had the motive. Gabriel had been Genny's shimmering fantasy. The love of her life. Except that he wasn't a fantasy. He was an egotistical artist, a self-absorbed, selfish man. Imagine Genny's fury when her fantasy lover hurt her by leaving her when she was seventeen. Imagine how her rage grew when twenty years later he came back into her life only to threaten her beloved father's self-esteem and his fortune—a fortune that would, by the way, ultimately belong to her. Imagine how Genny's hatred for Gabriel grew even greater when he insisted she murder their baby. Hatred growing and growing over so many years until it grew so large it motivated Genny Haviland to murder Slade Gabriel."

I swallow the vomit rising in my throat and don't realize Benjamin has gotten up until I see him standing before the jury. For some reason he turns completely around, looks at Linda Zavidow, seems about to say something to the assistant D.A., then changes his mind and faces the jury once more.

"Proof. You must have proof that Genny Haviland murdered Gabriel. Proof of murder. If you have no proof of that, then she is innocent. So what proof have you been presented with? From the doctor's testimony, you know Slade Gabriel was told he had Alzheimer's. You have proof Genny's fingerprints were on the vials of Seconal and the plastic bag. You have proof she was in the loft that morning. And you have Genny Haviland's sworn testimony that she helped her lover commit suicide. But that is not murder. Under no circumstances, ladies and gentlemen, is assisted suicide second-degree murder.

"What has Miss Zavidow asked you to believe? That Genny somehow drugged Gabriel with those pills and then placed a plastic bag over his head for the sake of an art gallery? Ladies and gentlemen, we are talking about Slade Gabriel, the man she had loved since she was seventeen.

"Yes, Gabriel asked Genny Haviland to help him kill himself. For weeks she refused. But then he offered to stay with the Haviland gallery in exchange for Genny's help. He was so desperate he volunteered to compromise his principles in order to achieve his goal. It was only then, when Genny realized how serious Gabriel was about dying, that she agreed. For his sake. Not for her father's—not for the multimillionaire who can live the rest of his life without ever having to work again.

"So what do you think happened that Monday morning? Did Genny Haviland murder her lover or did she help the man she loved end his life the way he wanted, before he would lose his ability to create, before he would become infirm, incontinent, a helpless infant?

"But what are you to make of the fact that no note was ever found? Can you accept that this man committed suicide and left no note? Especially when that note was all there would be to protect the woman he loved from just what is happening here?

"So much has been made over the fact that there was no note. But this man had Alzheimer's disease. You have proof he had become forgetful, proof he was losing his ability to sustain consistent thoughts, and proof for God's sake that he even needed help to kill himself properly. Maybe he wrote the note and instead of mailing it, threw it in a garbage can. Maybe he handed it to a stranger on the street. Maybe in the fog he was living in, he wrote that note and put it somewhere we just haven't searched. Maybe one day someone will examine one of Slade Gabriel's canvases and see the suicide note's message painted under a semitransparent glaze.

"I don't blame you if at this point you're not sure of what really happened. I don't blame you if you're confused, but if you are not sure and are confused then you must acquit Genny Haviland.

"I don't know about you, but if I am ever in Slade Gabriel's position and I ask someone to help me die, I pray to God, that person is as brave as Genny Haviland was. I pray to God someone loves me that much."

THIRTY-ONE

104 Greene Street, Apartment 5
Friday, December 11, 1992, 6:00 A.M.

While the jury deliberated, I cleaned the loft. I put most of Gabriel's paintings away, tried to eat and then go to sleep. I read every newspaper account of the case, all the stories I hadn't read all week, suddenly hungry for information. Ham called, but I couldn't even talk to him—not while I was waiting.

And then at eight o'clock that morning, I took a taxi uptown to Saint Patrick's Cathedral and finally crossed the threshold.

The dull red-orange glow of all the candles twinkling in their glass holders mesmerized me. I went up to the confessional and walked into the darkness and asked the priest on the other side of the grill to bless me for I had sinned, that it had been many years since my last confession.

"Yes, my child?" he encouraged me.

"I am responsible for a man dying. I fornicated without the sanctimony of marriage. I had an abortion. I have lied."

He absolved me, told me what prayers to say and how many times to repeat them, and then it was over. But I didn't feel absolved. I did not think I could remember how to pray.

After my useless confession, I slipped into a pew, knelt down, and, as the mass began, tried to summon the words Marie had taught me so long ago.

Hail, holy Queen Mother of Mercy! Our life, our sweetness, and our hope! To thee we do cry poor banished children of Eve; to thee we do send up our sighs, mourning and weeping in this valley of tears.

They were just words. I was not communing with God. The silence of the church was the same silence I had heard when Gabriel lay dying. Bowing my head, I mouthed more prayers, but I thought about how without turning around, without looking back, I had left Gabriel on our bed. Just walked out and left the loft.

My palms itched and although I tried, I couldn't stop myself from scratching them.

Walking up to the altar for Holy Communion I kept my head down, my hands clasped together feeling the blood sticking. I was going to try the body of Christ, give him a chance to woo me once again. Opening my mouth to the priest, kneeling on the altar, I took the holy wafer into my mouth and let it melt on my tongue.

As I returned to my seat I repeated the appropriate prayers. Once again, all the right words, but none moved me.

Frustrated, angry, betrayed, I left the church, walked out into the weak winter sunlight and headed downtown. At the first red light, I saw a woman gawking at me—at my hands.

I was still holding open the prayer book and didn't know that drops of blood—from the open scabs on my palms—had dripped down, staining the page.

The light turned green but I didn't cross. I wasn't sure I knew where to go. Not home. Not to my parents. I thought about going to see Ham, but instead I turned and walked back to the church.

This time I enter through a side door. There are many niches in the cathedral, small chapels dedicated to different saints. I stop at the one Marie and I had prayed at most often.

The statue of St. Teresa looks down on me from above.

Remembering Marie, I can almost hear her reading me the story about the saint's life. I kneel.

None of the votive candles at the saint's feet are lit.

Reaching into my bag I pull out some bills and push them into the collection box.

I reach for a wooden stick.

You have to light it from an already lit candle—there are no matches in the church—but none of these candles are burning.

Getting up, I walk to the next niche where several votives burn beneath a statue of St. Sebastian. After lighting the stick from one of those flames, I walk back, but too quickly and the fire goes out.

So I go back and relight the stick. More carefully this time, I cup the flame, and slowly walk back to St. Teresa.

Kneeling, I touch the stick to the first wick. It flames and sputters out. I try a different candle. It doesn't stay lit either. I try again. And again. None of the candles stay lit.

Stabbing the burning stick into the sand receptacle, I bow my head. Tears of frustration as hot as flame drip down my cheeks. This time I don't attempt any prayers. I have been defeated. I have lost. Marie. Gabriel. The baby. The trial. My freedom. My hope. My God. There is nothing left.

A breeze blows across my wet skin, cool and soothing. I sense light and open my eyes.

All the candles I'd failed to light are burning brightly. Their flames lick the gold ornaments in the chapel and Gabriel's ring on my hand—making it shine with that light that he tried so very hard to infuse in his painting.

A miracle?

While my head was bowed had someone else been here?

A woman stands at the entrance to the chapel. I want to ask if she

lit the candles? Or if she saw anyone else light them? But while I hesitate she slips back into the sanctuary and is lost in the crowd of peni-
tents and tourists.

Soon after returning home, Benjamin calls and tells me to get
ready. He's picking me up in thirty minutes. The jury has reached a
decision.

"In one day?" I ask him. "What does that mean?"

"No questions, Genny. No guesses, not today," he says.

Everyone is present. We have all stood for the judge who sits down,
takes his glasses off, removes his handkerchief from his pocket and
wipes them clean.

My hands itch but I hold them together tightly and try not to
rub them.

"Have you reached a verdict?" Judge Bailey asks.

"We have, Your Honor," the foreperson, the black woman with the
charm bracelet full of baby shoes, says and hands the bailiff a slip of
paper.

They are all speaking and moving too slowly. I want them to hurry,
to rush, and to finish this finally.

The bailiff gives the piece of paper to the judge who unfolds it,
reads it, refolds it, then hands it back to the bailiff who hands it back
to the foreperson.

"Will the defendant please rise?" Judge Bailey says.

I stand and wait to feel Gabriel rise with me, but he isn't here. He's
not surrounding me, not supporting me. I touch the ring on my middle finger and feel the angel's fat belly, his wings.

"How do you find?"

As she looks at me, the foreperson's eyes fill with tears. I read the
softness as pity and sway. I've lost my center, my balance, but Benjamin props me up.

"We find the defendant, Genny Haviland, not guilty, Your Honor."

Silence. Emptiness. Nothing.

Benjamin and my parents surround me. I know they are there but I cannot focus on them. In a blur, they lead me from the courtroom. Tory reaches out and hugs me by the door. Ham is there and he, too, reaches out for me. They both join us as we all walk through the crowd, past the cameras and the questions and the congratulations and into my parents' waiting car.

My head slumps back against the seat. My father has not taken his eyes off me. My mother is still holding me by the arm. Neither Ham nor Tory is here. We have lost them in the throng.

"Please, can I go home?" is all I can say.

"Of course," my mother answers.

I know they want to take me to their apartment but I have to go home to the loft. Closing my eyes, I feel the bumps in the road as the driver navigates the street.

Finally upstairs, I lie down on our bed and wait, but the relief I expected does not come.

It doesn't matter that the trial is over. Doesn't matter that they have acquitted me. I still know what I have done. The only finite truth is that Gabriel is gone and I have to live with that for the whole of my life.

No, they haven't condemned me to this prison. But I have.

EPILOGUE

Two days after the trial ended, my father had all the paintings picked up by the art transport company and taken to his gallery in preparation for Gabriel's last show. After that I was alone in the loft. Whatever solace the paintings had given me, whatever sustenance, was gone.

The phone rang often during the next weeks but there was nothing anyone said to me, or that I said to anyone, that had any meaning.

Patiently calling every other day or so, Ham didn't give up trying to convince me to come out, to let him take me to dinner, or go to a museum, or just take a walk in the park, but I wasn't ready to see anyone yet. I tried to explain to him that I had delivered my own verdict and it did not match the jury's.

When he argued, I told him I had to get off the phone. I wasn't angry. I just had no energy to debate.

"There would always be people who will never be sure I'm innocent," I told him. "They'll always wonder. And I'm one of them."

And that was the truth. For you see, sitting at the defendant's table, listening to all the evidence, reliving what had happened, I came to accept that indeed I was guilty of murder.

There was a story on the front page of the *New York Times* about my acquittal. I cut it out and taped it to the refrigerator where it hung beside the yellow Post-it notes of Gabriel's that I had never taken down. And I reread the article every morning trying to decide if it belonged in the file that proved there were miracles or the one that proved there weren't.

Through the holidays, I stayed by myself, still refusing to see anyone. Ham had taken his daughter skiing for the week, but he called from Colorado to see how I was.

No different, I said.

I read, I slept, I drank my one glass of wine each night, prepared my simple dinners, and then sat in the dark by myself, smelling the oil paints and turpentine, helplessly remembering. Trying not to.

Yesterday, January 6, Gabriel's posthumous show opened—to rave reviews—but I didn't go. It was Epiphany and I had planned on attending mass. But in the end I didn't go to church either. Instead I just sat—as I had for so many days—and stared at the loft's empty walls and at the drops of wildly colorful paint on the floors, on the tables, on the doorjambs, and cabinets.

The only paintings of Gabriel's that were left.

This morning, my mother called to tell me how well the opening had gone, how many paintings had sold, and to say good-bye. She was going back to Paris for a few weeks. She wanted to see me before she left and asked me to meet her for coffee at a nearby bistro.

I told her to come up to the loft instead.

We didn't speak much about anything that mattered until it was time for her to go.

"I don't think you should stay on here, Genny. There are too many reminders there. It's time to let go."

"I know that. But I can't. I still feel like I'm waiting for something. I thought it was for the verdict. But . . . what am I waiting for?"

She smiled at me. "Such impossible questions. I don't know, sweetheart. Maybe if the answer doesn't come to you soon, you should go look for it."

Putting her arms around me, my mother held me close. A whiff of perfume. Another leave-taking. Once, this was all I'd thought I'd ever had of her.

"Will you come to Paris?" she asked. "I want you to. I miss you when I'm there."

"Yes, maybe. Maybe in a few weeks I will come."

She cupped my face in her hands, and her touch and the light in her eyes was a little like a gift.

It's after eight and I haven't eaten but I'll get something soon. It's so quiet here. I could turn on the stereo. Or the television. But I'm watching the snowflakes coming down and clinging for just a moment to the windows before melting on the warm glass.

At least two inches of powder sits on the sills.

The buzzer rings and I get up. Pressing it, I wait, wondering who it is but not surprised when I hear Ham asking if he can come up.

Standing by the door, holding it open and leaning against it, I watch him get off the elevator carrying a package that—but Ham's not alone.

My father is with him. Despite the storm he's not wearing an overcoat and there is a light dusting of snow on his suit. Something about him seems obscenely wrong. It takes me a minute, and then I realize it is that he was alive.

As soon as he reaches me he puts his arms around me. I don't move, either to hold him or to pull away; this is his embrace not mine. When he lets go, he and Ham follow me inside.

"Do you want something to drink?" I ask, shutting the front door behind me.

My father says he doesn't want me to go to any trouble but Ham says yes, he'd like some wine.

I return from the kitchen with the bottle, glasses, and a corkscrew. Unwrapping the bottle, I let the heavy foil fall on the floor by my chair. Ham bends to retrieve it. I pierce the cork, twist and pull, easing the cork out.

I pour the wine, hand one glass to Ham and then another to my father. Ham holds his up to the loft's wide, empty walls in a silent toast to the one who is missing.

So do I.

So does my father. And then we all drink

"Everyone loves the new paintings, Genny. I was wrong about them and I wanted you to know how sorry I am about that," my father tells me.

I nod and murmur a weak thank you.

"It matters to me that you understand."

"Okay, I understand."

He stares at me intently, trying to pull something from me. I know what it is because this was how I had looked at the priest through the iron grill; my father wants absolution.

I drink more wine.

"Gabriel was my friend, Genny, for so many years," says my father. "I miss him, too."

I have not thought about other people missing Gabriel. I haven't wanted to. The paintings and the drawings have been taken from me, but the missing is something I have been able to keep as my own.

And now my father wants to take this from me, too.

"If he was your friend, then why didn't you understand that he had no choice?" I argue. "Not in his life, not in his death. He just wanted to paint. His want made him devoted, brave, disrespectful of danger. Of you. Of rules. Of risks. Of death. It made me . . . oh Daddy. I killed him . . . ," I blurt out, surprising myself and stunning my father into silence.

"We know you helped him, but it wasn't murder, Genny. It was mercy," Ham answers for both of them.

My father nods.

Is that what they both think or are they really wondering if I really might have killed him?

Would everyone always wonder?

My father goes to the door and returns with the package Ham had been carrying when he arrived.

"This is for you."

Unwrapping the heavy brown paper, I see the edge of a frame and remember the birthday a long time ago when the gift of a painting had made me so very happy.

But this painting is not a Picasso.

A night garden. Blues, purples, and greens; tangled, confused but not lonely because of the figures—abstruse but present. Naked, intertwined, and illuminated by a single shaft of light. In its vortex is a suggestion of wings, stilled just now before ascending and heading home. Or are they swooping down and converging on the lovers? Coming to lift them up?

I search my father's face.

He is not looking at me as if I could have killed Gabriel.

"Thank you," I whisper to him as I reach up to kiss his cheek.

Ham sits beside me on the couch, both of us looking at the painting. My father has left.

"Benjamin Marks didn't know it, but he was right about the note," Ham finally says.

"I don't understand?"

"This is Gabriel's last painting, isn't it?"

I nod.

"It is a message. Not words scratched into the surface of the glaze, but a communication just as real."

I focus on the profuse dark, blooming garden and try to see beneath the surface.

"You told the jury that Gabriel offered you a deal—that if you helped him die he would stay with your father's gallery. Benjamin used that deal to convince the jury you assisted in Gabriel's suicide. Linda tried to use it to suggest a coldhearted murder.

"But you didn't take that deal, Genny. You didn't do either. Not in the end.

"Look at his last garden, at his light. You did what he wanted—for his sake. You know you did. It isn't a question of right or wrong. You had to do what you did because of who he was. Because of who you were with him."

As Ham talks I hear his voice and another—I hear Gabriel's voice rough and rocky, reassuring me, begging me, and giving me permission to help him that last morning, while we lay beside each other on the bed.

"How do I say good-bye to you?" I had asked.

"Another Genny question." He had smiled. "Listen to me, it would be worse to have to say good-bye to me over and over for the next couple of years. To have me be here and not be here. To have me forget who you are."

Gabriel held me to his chest in an embrace so encompassing it fooled me into thinking everything really was going to be all right.

"Once upon a time," he said, "there was a thirty-seven-year-old man who had married and fathered a child but had never let anyone inside of him. Being a painter, he thought, excused him from being a prick. But down deep he was so fucking lonely. You could even see it in his work if you knew where to look.

"There were never people in his paintings—only landscapes—only colors—only escapes.

"And then one day he met this willowy, brown-haired hippie girl who gave herself to him. No demands. No expectations. And he fell for her. For the first time in his life. Christ. It was like feeling rain on your face for the first time, or discovering a new color.

"But he was used to protecting himself. He was used to people flying off in planes and never coming back, so he never told the girl how she had opened up his heart. But she had. And even after he'd met her and lost her, he held on to her.

"He was too screwed-up to tell her. Until it was time for him to go away. And then at the end, at last, he told her how she really had saved his life and given it back to him all at the same time. How much she meant to him and how much he loved her."

He pulled me closer to him. Warm tears—his? mine?—dripped onto my lips and I tasted the salt.

"It will be all right. You will be all right. I promise," he said in that voice I recognized as that of a man trying to protect me.

"Now, Genny, let me go."

"It was awful, Ham—but it *was* what he wanted—to die while he could still paint. Before anyone pitied him. Before he forgot who he was or who I was or where he lived. But damn him, he used me to help him do it."

Now—in front of Gabriel's last painting—Ham takes me in his arms. Now mixed in with the smell of turpentine and oil paints is sunshine and a place where there is blue water and sand.

Holding me and stroking my hair, Ham tells me something that echoes what I had once said to Gabriel a long time ago. "It's not using someone if it's what they want, too."

I close my eyes. "I'll never really know all the answers, will I? But maybe I can learn to stop asking so many questions. . . ."

Ham smiles. It starts in his eyes and travels to his lips. "I don't think you could live without asking questions, Genny."

But for a while, maybe I can.

I am no longer looking at Gabriel's painting, but into Ham's eyes. I lift up my face, lean in, and kiss him.

I kiss Ham.

And of course, he kisses me back.

"Genny, how long has it been since you've taken a walk for no reason? Or gone out for dinner? Since you've tasted your food?" he asks me a little while later and before I can answer he takes my hand and pulls me up.

At the door, Ham grabs his coat off the chair and mine off its hook. Holding it out, he helps me on with it, even buttoning it up for me in a gesture so caring I have to turn away—afraid he will see how grateful I am.

We are in the hall and halfway down in the elevator before I realize that this isn't my coat. It's far too big.

Yes, there on the sleeve is the familiar splatter of red paint drops.

Ham has wrapped me up in Gabriel's coat.

We have reached the front hall.

Shouldn't I say something—stop—go back—get my own coat?

Ham holds the door open for me. I step out and he follows me into a world transformed and silenced by snow. No matter where you look, everything—tree branches, parked cars, sidewalks—is covered and obscured by a thick dusting of white.

"Where are your gloves?" Ham grins. "Did you lose them again?"

Even though it's not my coat, I instinctively put my hands inside the pockets. The right is empty, but there's something in the left one and I pull it out.

In the street lamp's muted light I look down at a sealed and stamped envelope addressed to Gabriel's lawyer in Gabriel's handwriting.

It is the missing note.

Now, after all this time? But why would it be in his winter coat? It was so warm that last Sunday morning in September when Gabriel went out to mail this letter and pick up breakfast. Why would he have worn his winter coat?

I told him what I had observed . . . his sustained reasoning power would eventually be impaired, the doctor had said.

Snowflakes fall on the envelope, the ink begins to run like tears.

"What is it, Genny?"

"I don't have my gloves."

"Are you crying?"

"It's just snow melting."

This time he doesn't have to remind me; I know what to do. The deep breath of wintry air stings but the little bit of pain is bracing. I take another.

The snow swirls around us. Icy sparks alight on my eyelids, catch in my lashes, land on my lips and my cheeks; I feel each one.

Ham encloses one of my hands in his. I slip the other back inside the coat pocket where it rests, touching Gabriel's note. And then we walk away from the loft toward the rest of the night.